THE PLAINS OF
ABRAHAM

THE PLAINS OF
ABRAHAM

a novel

Stephen Parrish

ISBN: 978-1-7344966-9-7

Cover art: "Among the Sierra Nevada, California," oil on canvas, by Albert Bierstadt, 1868.

This is a work of fiction. Character names, locations, and incidents are either the product of the author's imagination or are used fictitiously, and any resemblance to actual persons, living or dead, business establishments, locales, or events is entirely coincidental.

Lascaux Books
www.lascauxbooks.com

For librarians everywhere

Writers and readers come and go, but libraries remain. They house our literature, our science, our very culture. For millennia the greatness of humanity has been documented in words, equations, musical notes, and brush strokes. It has been stored in vast rooms that are appropriately quiet, yet whose tranquility is just as appropriately textured by rustling pages, sibilant whispers, and the occasional reverent hush. When the last human being has expired, libraries will stand as glorious monuments to an extraordinary, if unsuccessful, experiment in civilization.

and for Sarah

And I will make thee exceedingly fruitful,
and I will make nations of thee,
and kings shall come out of thee.

—Genesis 17:6

Part One
Journey into Wilderness

Chapter 1

As I write this, Father Malcolm is building a fire. We found a sheltered spot on the riverbank and I shot a rabbit for dinner. The rabbits in these parts have likely never seen a man before. This one hesitated long enough to give me the once-over, and that was his undoing.

Father Malcolm laughed when he saw how many notebooks I'd wedged into the canoe. Hopefully we stole enough ink for my quill pen. *Verba volant, scripta manent.* I'd drawn myself up to convince the good father of the need for a written record. He's quick to debate and will argue the shape of a cloud if he imagines a more exotic animal drifting across the sky. But he closed his eyes and nodded; something would survive the voyage, even if neither of us did.

We've spent these past seven days out of Kebek paddling upstream on the Laurent River, and my back hurts so much I'm considering asking Father Malcolm if we can stop for a few days to rest. Berries are still available and rabbits are stupid. But he gazes ever westward, and I know he's eager to put distance between us and any martinets that might be on our trail. Leaves are already changing color, swapping their chlorophyll for glorious shades of red that will soon stray to brown. He's afraid we got off to a late start. In this respect we agree. The problem is, we don't know how much farther we have to go. If the legendary lands we seek appear around the next bend we can pat ourselves on the back for having executed a timely get-away. If not, nor around the bends that follow, winter awaits us. And winter is never kind to pilgrims traveling by canoe.

At the moment Malcolm is sitting across from me. The fire is burning, the rabbit is skewered and sizzling just above reach of the flames. Every minute or so Malcolm rotates the skewer and fat dribbles into the fire where it hisses and sputters.

Father Malcolm Marchand is a gaunt man with unkempt black hair that falls over his eyes. He doesn't shave as often as the bishop would like. His gait is lanky, as though he needs all his bones and muscles to propel himself. Sometimes the children laugh as he lopes down the street. Sometimes I laugh too.

He's more afraid of martinets than he is of changing seasons. We're not yet far from the coast, he argues, and if we don't keep moving they'll catch us. Ahead are possibilities, sheathed in myth. Behind is a prison sentence, or worse, for each of us.

All because of a broken radio.

Malcolm taught scripture to the young ones. I, having reached the age of majority, had elected to remain at the school, work as his assistant, and study to become a priest. The priests were the teachers, and the teachers were the bond keeping civilization together.

Proud of this presumably original notion, I shared it with Father Malcolm back when I could still slip into one of the scratched and worn school desks, when I was still a fidgeting runt

2

who habitually avoided eye contact. After pausing to think about it he smiled and said, "So teachers are grout? Is that what you're saying, René Jordan?" I blushed. From then on, when no one else was around, he called me by my new nickname, Grout.

A full year passed, during which I worked as his assistant, before he confided in me, before he shared his great secret: he was hoarding books in the school basement.

At first I was shocked and disoriented. Here was a good and devout Levitican who stood in the pulpit on Sundays, preached the Gospel, and delivered sermons in defense of the laws against unnecessary knowledge and technology. He knew those laws well: technology was dangerous; technology had destroyed the world. The only literature allowed in Kebek schools following the poisoned rains was the Bible, a few related monographs, and some elementary textbooks to teach spelling, arithmetic, and the like. Any new publication required approval of the Council of Bishops, a toilsome procedure. Sometimes books from olden times turned up in attic trunks or on the shelves of dilapidated buildings. If you stumbled across one you were required to surrender it—without opening the cover. Reading it was a sin.

It occurred to me to report Father Malcolm. What he was doing was contrary to the dogma the church had taught me, the dogma *he* had taught me. If his hoard were discovered he'd be defrocked and imprisoned. And if I were discovered with it I'd share his fate.

But as I stood in the basement, poised to take flight, torn between bewitching stacks of bound volumes and all the morality beaten into me, he demonstrated an experiment. On a bench sat two jars. One contained a pale blue liquid, which he said was a copper solution, and the other a clear liquid, which he said was ammonia. He invited me to sniff the ammonia. I did, hesitantly, still ready to make a dash for the judiciary. It was pungent and made my eyes water.

"Now watch," he said.

He poured the ammonia into the copper solution. The mixture turned a deep blue. It was the most intense blue I'd ever seen. More intense than the sky or its reflection in a lake. A colorless liquid, mixed with a pale blue liquid, had produced a deep blue liquid. And yet no divine intervention had apparently taken place. No lightning bolt had struck. No miracle had manifested itself in any discernible way.

It took me a few days to adopt a perspective on what I'd seen. I wasn't about to forego a lifelong belief system and risk my freedom over a parlor trick. But I trusted Malcolm. And I was hungry for what was inside the books. During my next visit to the basement Malcolm placed a few of them into my hands. They were worn and had the heft and feel of forbiddance. I opened them warily.

Puzzling equations. Illustrations. Charts and graphs. Color pictures!

And provocative tales. Of distant lands, of a vast western ocean. Of a legendary civilization called Ellanoy, a pagan culture in the continental interior that resembled Eden, whose citizens practiced unspeakable debauchery.

Father Malcolm showed me where he'd hidden yet more books—behind the Bibles and catechisms, tucked away in cabinets, in coat pockets, even fastened to the undersides of tables and chairs. The basement was a *library*. The word itself wasn't against the law, but nearly so, its utterance tantamount to swearing. There were books about the history of our people. There were stories of love and war and dragons. There were instructions on how to build contraptions, even flying machines.

Flying machines! I was not going to report Father Malcolm to the martinets.

Learning, discovery, invention—the Bible didn't prohibit these, he told me, only the Council of Bishops did. In fact, industry and innovation were encouraged and rewarded in the gospels.

Before long I was spending as much time in the basement as I was in the classroom above. Father Malcolm had somehow come across an old radio and was dissecting it to see how it worked. I speculated on what we might hear when we got it operating again, but he laughed and said we wouldn't hear anything. A radio was a receiver, and to make it operate required a transmitter.

"Then we'll build a transmitter," I said.

He looked at me with a bit of wonder. I think that's when I dropped "Father" and began addressing him merely as Malcolm.

We opened slats in the walls and wedged volumes between the beams. If a book was missing a cover, which was often the case, we rebound it using a bishop-approved binding, typically one to a religious monograph no one wanted to read.

One day when I showed up for work a fresh stack of books was on the table. I asked Malcolm where he got them and he answered, "You don't want to know." In the moments that followed we both sensed the presence of another soul, and we looked up. My younger brother Tomas stood at the bottom of the stairs.

"Teacher sent me for blackboard chalk," Tomas said.

His eyes focused on the table. I tried to position myself between him and the books, but it was too late. His eyes widened in terror. He turned to run.

"Wait!" I shouted.

We showed Tomas the blue solution. He'd always enjoyed tinkering, which was only a mild offense—so long as it didn't result in anything useful. He was captivated by the rich ultramarine hue. Like me, he'd never seen anything of the sort.

We baited him with more curiosities: a magnet falling in slow motion through a copper tube. Water bending in the presence of a hair comb. Powders bursting into rainbows of color when sprinkled into flame.

Before long he was a convert like me. He built a battery out of an armful of potatoes, old galvanized nails, copper pennies, and some wire. It powered a light bulb Malcolm had found while rummaging in a pre-war dump. The three of us sat in the darkness of the basement and watched in amazement as the bulb emitted a soft yellow glow. Our faces were illuminated—without a candle, without the sun, without even scratching a match.

"Given enough potatoes we can power the transmitter," Tomas said.

"That would take a pile of spuds," Malcolm replied.

Tomas had always been a listless and sullen boy. Now he was driven to invent. His eyes, once awash with indifference and resignation, blazed with purpose and ambition.

But then came the day my little brother took some radio parts home to work on—against Father Malcolm's rules. Our sister Danielle found them. Danielle was not a tinkerer. She reported Tomas. I'm sure she wouldn't have, had she grasped the consequences, but she was fourteen, a waif of a girl, perennially barefoot, with a torn dress and a smudged face. She understood to be true only what the council told her was true, therefore was suspicious of anything out of the ordinary, anything that didn't conform to our strict social code.

Danielle led Karl Rasmussen and accompanying martinets into the house and showed them the radio parts in Tomas's room. Pointing indignantly. As a young girl might accuse her older brother of some lesser offence, of having pinched an apple or indulged in tobacco behind the woodshed. When Tomas returned home he was arrested.

Under the law he had an opportunity to repent, as long as he was willing to finger someone else. He refused to speak at all. The light fled his eyes, replaced with the old indifference.

All of Kebek was compelled to witness the execution. Tomas Jordan, tied to a stake in the Place de le Lévitique, was permitted a statement.

He said, "I wanted to build a radio."

The crowd was silent, thinking he would say more. My sister Danielle and I, along with our mother, were bound and gagged, to prevent a disruption. Father Mitchell, who reveled in the task, lowered a torch to the kindling at Tomas's feet.

They say when the fire starts you suffocate before experiencing much pain. Tomas didn't suffocate. He didn't black out. He stared at me helplessly as the flames singed his clothes and ignited his hair. He stared until his eyes melted, until his mouth decomposed into a macabre grimace.

His neck softened in the leaping flames. His face swiveled, scanning the horrified onlookers from empty eye sockets.

Danielle, our mother, and I were forced to watch, but fortunately tears clouded our view. Father Mitchell said a prayer over the crackling embers, beseeching God to bestow gratitude upon Tomas for his delivery to a better place.

The next day the school was raided. But Malcolm and I had been alerted, by Danielle no less, in an act of familial contrition, and we were already gone.

Now I must stop writing, because the rabbit is ready to eat. We've dug a shallow pit for the fire, to hide the light. All we have to drink is river water. But Malcolm blessed it, in cups we carved from a fallen cedar, and he said a prayer over the meal.

"Father in Heaven, thank you for this gift, and for future animals of limited intellectual prowess that Master Jordan might find in the sights of his musket. In the name of the Blessed Virgin Immaculate, may we ever respond humbly and devoutly when you beckon."

"Amen," I said.

Chapter 2

We rose at dawn, broke camp, and set out in the emerging light. Although the current was against us, the water was calm. No wind meant no breakers. For an interminable week we'd been fighting the wind, the breakers, and the rocks.

Always the rocks. To compensate for their frustrating immobility and inevitable erosion they blocked the channels and delighted in pulverizing birchbark. Sometimes the rapids were so populated with boulders we had to walk waist-deep in the river, dragging the canoe behind us, like pulling a sled up a hill.

Our bruised and warped canoe was already ailing when we stole it, but we hadn't been aware of that in the darkness, in our rush to grab and flee. Each new encounter with a rock further battered the hull. Often we stopped to patch a hole with a piece of bark and some spruce gum. A mumbled prayer, the sign of the cross, and we were on our way again.

The Laurent River was wide as a musket shot at its widest points. Small headlands, dense with intrepid hardwoods and giant ferns, jutted into the swiftly moving water. Beyond, where the terrain rose and loomed indulgently over the valley, the hills undulated in mottled greens and browns.

Malcolm took the stern. In a canoe it's the captain's position, where course decisions are made. We knelt rather than sat, to

9

spare our backs some stress. While paddling we only spoke when necessary and usually in single words or short phrases. The only other noises came from paddles chopping water and the honk of mallards overhead as they made their way south.

Malcolm kept grumbling about our late season start. He frowned at maple leaves riotously celebrating the fall and dug his paddle more aggressively into the water. As the day progressed his breathing devolved into soft rhythmic grunts.

It was necessary to pace ourselves. Although the faster we went, the sooner we would reach the fabled kingdom of Ellanoy, the sooner we would also encounter mutants.

They were descended from people exposed to the radiation. Some walked on hooved feet, according to legend. Others had only one eye, centered on their faces, or were headless altogether, with sense organs mounted on their chests. One tribe was ruled by a dog king; its members spoke in a barking dialect. And somewhere out there were people whose legs were reversed at the knee, allowing them to run backwards at high speed. All these and more we learned about in school and sketched uneasily in our notebooks.

The scariest creature inhabiting the interior wasn't humanoid at all. It was the Griffin, with the body of a lion and the head and wings of an eagle. Griffins swooped down and snatched victims up in their beaks, chewing on them even as they returned to their roosts. Some breathed fire.

Malcolm didn't buy any of that. It had been twelve generations since the war, he said. The radiation should have dissipated by now. The myths had been planted in school books, he argued, to frighten would-be explorers and dissuade emigrants.

He pointed at the sky. "See the ducks? They're proof the environment is healthy again. Also the rabbits," he added.

"Stupid rabbits," I corrected him.

My indoctrination had been too comprehensive for me to dismiss mutants and Griffins so readily. Nevertheless the evidence was in Malcolm's favor. We'd paddled past the ancient ruins of Mount Royal and Saint Maurice and encountered nothing but charred skylines and enterprising weeds, storied cities reduced to soot and unearthly silence. If mutants inhabited the rubble we'd probably have encountered them by now.

The canoe leaked, apparently unable to decide whether it wanted to ride above or below the surface. We needed to build a new one and we would have to do so from scratch. It would require stopping for an extended period, which inspired Malcolm to push even harder.

At the outset we paddled night and day, to stay ahead of the posse Malcolm was sure was following us. There'd been no sign yet, but Malcolm remained convinced they were on our tail. "They" would be a search party, a band of ruffians, led by Karl Rasmussen. Karl was not only captain of the martinets, he was the natural choice of leader whenever a posse was mustered. Even coastal cities outside the Montagne Diocese employed him to hunt apostates and other criminals. And when he caught his prey, he built fires at their feet. The burning dated back to when people thought flames purged radiation. Now it was just torture.

We had loaded in a hurry during our escape and made some mistakes. We each grabbed two iron skillets, so now we had four. In truth we only needed one. We had three fishing rods, which was okay, but hadn't thought to pinch any hooks. That was going to be a problem. Fishing was good in the Laurent if you had hooks. Bass, pike, trout, walleye, carp, and other species were plentiful and made tasty meals. If you had hooks. Carp tasted like mud unless you smoked it, after which it tasted like smoked mud. We would have to fashion some hooks out of thorns.

We were smart enough to snatch a few knives, a good machete, and some rope. And of course a Bible. Over Malcolm's questioning frown I also appropriated a flintlock musket in excellent condition. We snitched several bags of dried corn from the community stores and were using it to make sagamité. It was already tiresome. Of all the tasteless mush to cook into tasteless gruel, crushed corn was my least favorite. We seasoned it with animal fat to render it more palatable.

The year had finally grown too late for berries, nevertheless Malcolm insisted we look for things to eat whenever we stopped. It would become a pattern on our voyage: first search the woods unsuccessfully for the easy stuff, which consisted of wild berries, apples, cherries, grapes, nuts, and similar treats. Second, failing to locate any of that, try to shoot a four-legged animal with the musket, an effort that seldom accomplished more than entertain the animal. Third, in desperation, blast at mallards flying overhead and give them a hearty laugh too.

Eventually, resign ourselves to sagamité.

On this day, however, we got lucky and spied a muskrat diving into the water as we returned from foraging to the shoal where we'd parked the canoe.

"Watch and see where he comes up," Malcolm said.

We each went different ways along the bank. The muskrat poked his nose up for air. I dove down to grab him but he slipped away.

Malcolm saw the commotion and shouted, "Back to the first spot! He'll come up again."

And he did. And back and forth we went, until the muskrat tired and remained above the surface longer than usual, to catch its breath. A little too long, as it turned out. Malcolm brained him with the butt of the musket.

"At least the gun is good for something," he said. He stopped and examined his surroundings, contemplating something deep and profound.

"What is it?" I asked.

"Where's the canoe?"

Reflexively I spun around to where it should have been resting. It was absent. I squinted downstream, and there it was, a couple of hundred yards distant, easing its way around a bend, blithely making a getaway.

"Oh goodness," Malcom said.

We took off down the bank, leaving the muskrat in the mud. The current glided eastward, back toward the Sea of Atlantis, carrying the canoe on its back. We ran and stumbled, leapt over rocks and small feeding streams, panting, groaning, cursing, sometimes falling, until we too were around the bend.

Ahead was the canoe, relaxing in the current. We had to get downstream of it before jumping into the river to block its escape. That's when providence brought rapids to our assistance. Or so we thought.

The canoe careened into a weathered boulder, bounced away, and surged forward again, crashing into a sequence of collaborating stone barriers before becoming wedged between two of them. It's trying to commit suicide, I thought. Malcolm and I both dove into the cold water.

As I swam I considered my predicament. Here I was, hundreds of miles from home, in a place I'd never been nor dreamed of being and one perhaps no Coastal had ever seen. Swimming across the Laurent River to retrieve an escaped canoe, even as I was in the process of escaping my native land. I couldn't have orchestrated such circumstances if I tried.

Malcolm reached the stern as I reached the bow. We didn't climb aboard for fear of swamping the craft and ruining our corn. The bottom of the river consisted of silt, and the canoe was full of things that liked to hide in silt when spilled to the bottoms of rivers. So we paddled one-armed to the bank, dragging the canoe behind us.

When I stepped out of the water I could no longer feel my toes. "Let's camp here," I suggested. My hope died when Malcolm looked upstream with that far-away philosophical squint priests tended to affect when they're pondering forms in Plato's Realm.

"We left dinner back there," he said.

"We have sagamité." I was dreaming of a campfire.

"You hate sagamité."

"No, sagamité is good. Sagamité is our friend."

"Rasmussen will gain on us."

"Maybe he'll lose his boat too."

*

Back at the shoal the muskrat was waiting. I'd been hoping a woodland beast would steal him from the bank, but apparently muskrats are just as unappealing to woodland beasts as they are to humans. There was something different about this one; he didn't look like the muskrats back home. His legs were longer and his tail was shorter. I attributed the differences to geographic variation. Malcolm stared at the animal for a long moment and said, "I have a feeling we're going to be seeing stranger things in the days to come."

My legs were numb from the knees down. We built a crude hut by planting poles in the ground and forming a roof with branches and old sheets of bark. Malcolm started a fire with a bow drill.

"Skin the rat," he said.

"Why me? I skinned the rabbit."

"So now you know how to do it."

"We should take turns with stuff like this."

"Who lost the canoe today?"

"I thought we were both at fault."

"Who was last out of the canoe when we stopped, and failed to secure it?"

Hesitating. "I was."

"You see, Grout? That is how one volunteers to clean a rat."

"Tell me, Father Malcolm. How did you get so good at employing false logic to twist arguments in your favor?"

"You have to know these things when you're a priest."

We sat before the fire and ate our meal off slabs of wood, using our fingers. Malcolm spoke of a string of great lakes that awaited us, a watercourse that could be navigated into the interior. But it was only myth; no one had ever made the journey. Also myth was the story of a river that flowed from one of the lakes all the way to the Vermillion Sea. Malcolm's dream was to discover the route, which would grant access to China and the Orient.

He believed in it fervently. When he got excited about a subject he used hand gestures to illustrate the architecture of his thoughts. When he got very excited he paced. Tonight after finishing his meal he circled the fire, spilling a torrent of words, his hands working the air like it was clay.

"China, René. Imagine it: China! It lies somewhere in that direction." Malcolm's outstretched arm pointed due west. As though all we had to do was keep paddling.

He also spoke of Ellanoy, the interior colony of heathens described in several of Malcolm's contraband books. Back in Kebek, even mentioning Ellanoy was a crime. As we conversed we peered beyond the light of the campfire, at the somber stand of trees, afraid a martinet or inquisitor might be listening. Ellanoyans were redeemable, Malcolm argued, and worthy of redemption in the eyes of God. He intended to bring God's word to all the interior heathens he encountered.

My inclination was to believe in Ellanoy, even if I doubted the existence of China and the Vermillion Sea. The authorities wouldn't get so ruffled over pagans and infidels if they were mere fiction.

We were going to need a new canoe to get there. Ours was too battered to continue. And the only option was to build it ourselves, out of birchbark and other raw materials.

That night sharp rocks in the sand kept me up, squirming and shifting. I drifted off and dreamed of exotic spices, great rolling ocean waves, and raven haired women in candlelight, seductively shedding their robes.

And of mutants, the disfigured victims of a long-ago war and their lamentable progeny. Chasing me through the dusky woods. Howling like werewolves. Their cragged shadows overtaking me as I stumbled through the brambles, crying for help.

And Tomas. What was left of him. A rickety skeleton, remnants of flesh dripping from charred bones, shambling into the light of our campfire. As he leaned over me I peered into his eye sockets, into a prophetic expanse, like the dark interior of a crystal ball. His jaw rattled, his exposed teeth clacked a warning: "You too will burn."

Someone was wailing. I bolted upright to the sound of my own mournful voice defiling the nocturnal calm. No Tomas in sight. Nor mutants, nor raven haired maidens. Malcolm lay motionless next to the dying embers. As I lay down again and tried to make myself comfortable I heard him speak:

"He who has God in his heart sleeps restfully on stony ground."

Chapter 3

We moved a mile inland, carrying the canoe between us, upside down and above our heads, like we did on portages. We wanted to be far from the bank of the river in case any pursuers caught up.

First we needed birchbark, and a lot of it. Preferably from trees with great diameter, so we could sew together a seaworthy craft with as few seams as possible. We would need more than one tree. Our travel hut—its surfaces—consisted of bark, but we didn't have confidence in the material. It had been rolled and unrolled daily and was sure to have cracks. We needed fresh bark.

Malcolm sent me off one way and he went off another. We were to return after noon's sun and report on what we'd found.

Birches love light and open space. I took off intending to intersect a meadow somewhere. I found a picturesque creek meandering south toward the river and followed it upstream, as it cut through elephant-eared cottonwoods, until it turned and ran briefly east-west. On the north side of the bank was a grove of birches.

Several looked to be sixty feet tall and at least twenty inches in diameter. They were perfect: straight, healthy, free of knots and low branches. After satisfying myself with my estimates I returned to camp and waited for Malcolm. He came strolling in, smiling.

"Forty high and fifteen across," he said.

"Them's good trees," I said.

"You?"

"Sixty and twenty." I formed my hands as if grasping a trunk.

"No!"

"Yes."

"Show me."

We felled three of them. Two might have been sufficient, but we wanted enough leftover bark for repairs. We made slits down the trunks, cutting all the way through the bark to the hardwood underneath. It was not much different from skinning a muskrat. We used our knives to work the bark off the trunk, then rolled the bark up like stiff blankets.

The trees lay on the ground, naked and pale orange. I felt sorry for them.

Back at camp Malcolm went to work shaping the canoe while I set off again in search of cedars and spruces. We'd make the canoe's wooden parts out of cedar: gunwales, ribs, thwarts, etc. The thin, supple roots of the spruce would serve to lash the canoe together. Its sap would make spruce gum, for gluing seams.

By the time I returned Malcolm had planted stakes in the ground, outlining the bird's-eye shape of the canoe. He had a pot of water boiling and was forming sheets of bark by wetting and bending them. I handed him an armful of wood.

"Good," he said. "Go get some more. And catch us something to eat."

It was only fair. Malcolm had apprenticed as a carpenter before entering the seminary. And he couldn't hit the sky with a gun if he pointed it straight up with both eyes open, so I was the best man to hunt. And gather wood. And do laundry. Still, I couldn't help ribbing him about it.

"How is it you're so well versed in fun activities and so inept at mundane tasks?" I asked.

He looked up from his work and smiled. "Need I say it?"

"Apparently."

"You have to know these things when you're a priest."

"Ah."

*

That night, huddled next to the fire, we gazed at the night sky and talked.

"Do you believe God made the stars?" I asked.

Malcolm rolled over on his side and faced me. "Where is this question coming from?"

"Indulge me."

"Did God make the stars? Yes, God made the stars."

"How do you know?"

"My, but aren't you the inquisitive schoolboy today."

"Well?"

"Because man didn't make them. I know what man is capable of, and star making is not in his repertoire."

"So stuff is made either by God or by man."

"Man may build a house, and a bird may build a house too, but in either case only out of materials made by God."

"So God made the trees."

"He made the seeds from which the trees grow. He is the first, unmoved mover."

"According to Aristotle."

"And Aquinas. Both profoundly wise men."

The fire crackled. Flickering highlights dabbed Malcolm's face. He poked a stick at the coals, pestering them. I waited for him to make eye contact. He kept poking the fire.

"So God set things in motion," I suggested, "and left us to our fate."

"Is that a question? Or a challenge."

"Did God set things in motion and leave us to our fate?"

"He's here. He's all around us."

"Why isn't He on our side? Why doesn't He help us? Why are we on the run?"

Malcolm smiled. "Now I see where all this is coming from. God doesn't take sides."

"Oh. He just sits back and lets evil have its way."

He glared at me. "He gives us free will. We are free to choose between good and evil."

"Then we must be free to choose our own religion."

"Be careful. You're pushing it."

"But why? There are Jewish and Muslim colonies on the coast. God doesn't smite them."

"We're at war with them."

"Cold war. Static war. And what about natural events? Remember when that little boy, what was his name? Got hit by lightning?"

"Wilbur. I conducted his funeral."

"Yes, Wilbur. He chose neither good nor evil. He didn't get the opportunity in his short life to choose much of anything."

"Perhaps he was being punished."

"What could an eight-year-old possibly have done to deserve a terrible swift bolt from the sky?"

Malcolm shrugged. "Wherefore, as by one man sin entered into the world, and death by sin; and so death passed upon all men, for that all have sinned. Romans 5:12."

"So what you're saying is, we're all sinners. Even if we've committed no sin. And whenever something bad happens to us it's punishment. Even if we don't know why."

"I'm saying I don't have all the answers."

We stared at the fire for a several minutes. I said, "I watched my little brother Tomas burn at the stake."

"I know. I did too."

"God could have stopped it."

After a short silence Malcolm pointed up at the sky, where countless twinkling stars bejeweled the night. "God could have withheld the beauty of the cosmos."

"He could have prevented the ugliness of disease."

"He could have denied us the gift of life."

"He could have spared us the pain of death."

"Tell me." He tossed the stick into the fire and sat upright. "Why did you enter the seminary? Why did you want to become a priest?"

"School and seminary are all about learning to read, with a little arithmetic thrown in. The reading is all about the Bible. You and I—and Tomas—learned there is much else to read, much else to learn about."

"So why did you want to become a priest?"

Why indeed. I rolled away from him and stared into the darkness. I'd been taught God was the all-powerful and benevolent creator of the universe. After Tomas's execution I questioned the definition. Could anything be all-powerful? Could something, let alone a universe, be created out of nothing? As for benevolence, there was so much pain and suffering in the world, if there were an all-powerful God, one might consider Him a jerk.

God could not be both omnipotent and benevolent. If He were benevolent, He was clearly impotent. And if He were omnipotent He was surely malevolent. All I had to do was imagine the eyes of my little brother melting in their sockets to conjure a God who didn't care about anything and couldn't do anything about it if He did.

But it isn't enough to merely not believe in a thing. Even atheists have to believe in *something*, have to embrace a non-arbitrary ethical code. Where does the code come from, if not God? I hoped the answers lay ahead. The Leviticans didn't have them; the Ellanoyans, if they really occupied a modern-day Eden, were in possession of wisdom that had thus far eluded me. For Malcolm the quest was proselytism, the procurement of souls for the Levitican Order. For me the quest was nothing less than learning why I had a quest at all.

"So why?" Malcolm pressed. "Why did you want to be a priest?"

My blanket was tight against my neck and my eyes were closed. "I thought they had all the answers."

*

Malcolm spent the next morning finishing the canoe while I broke camp. We left the fire going, so it would serve as long as possible, even up to the hour of departure. The last thing we'd do on our way out would be to hide all evidence of it.

"Let me test the canoe," I insisted.

"Now, just a minute—"

"You got to build it, I get to test it."

He had no counterargument. "All right."

We eased the boat into the water. The first characteristic you want to gauge is whether it will sit upright. This one did, nice and steady.

The next is whether it will remain upright with a twelve-stone man climbing around inside. This one was so steady, you practically had to try to tip it over. Malcolm had made the bottom flatter than the old one. I'd never known a happier canoe in water. But how fast would it go?

"By the way," I called to Malcolm watching from the shore, "before I put this craft to the test, shouldn't we give it a name?"

He shrugged. "You mean like a pet?"

"More like a family member."

"Okay, how about Gaston Chevalier?"

That figured. Saint Chevalier, founder of the Levitican order, was Malcolm's hero.

"No, it has to be a girl's name," I said. "And if you suggest the Blessed Virgin Immaculate I'll capsize her right now."

"I won't sit in the hull of a canoe named after a girl. If you must name the infernal thing, at least give it a boy's name."

"Fine. I'm naming it Wilbur. In memory of Wilbur who was struck by lightning."

"No! Nobody calls their boat *Wilbur*."

"We do!"

Wilbur and I took off downstream, back the way Malcolm and I had come. I knelt halfway between bow and stern and paddled like the devil was after me. Wilbur glided through the water, almost over the water. There was little displacement, although that would change once we loaded up and Malcolm climbed aboard.

No canoe ever traveled a straighter line. I dug deep into the water with my paddle and pulled as hard as I could, switching sides every couple of strokes, building speed. I'd have to grunt my way back upstream, but I was having too much fun to care. Wilbur was flying.

A test of his turning capacity found him responsive. Water gathered in the bilge, which was to be expected of a new boat. We'd spend the next week or so searching for leaks and patching them.

My arms tired and I pulled over to the bank to rest. With Wilbur halfway out of the water I squatted in the gravel, caught my breath, and admired the charm of the country.

We had seats in a cathedral. The straight pines were pillars. The sky, brushed with clouds over a pale cerulean wash, was the vaulted ceiling. I relaxed in the nave, smelling nature's ambrosial scents, eavesdropping on its voices, on echoes murmuring from the dawn of time. At night the moon and planets would shimmer from behind the tree crowns like rays through stained glass, the stars like votive candles.

But here, now, in the daylight, leaves were aflame in orange and red. Deciduous trees were busy shedding their leaves, becoming more naked and vulnerable. Hilltop groves swayed in winds aloft. Outcrops intruded into the scenery, contributing their own textures and low-saturated pigments, arguing that beauty is nothing without contrast.

Moss the color of emeralds. Violets and clover, nature's true jewelry. Reflections on the river, a copy of the forest's dignity and grandeur, broken by eddies and lapping waves into a kaleidoscope of hues, drenched by the sky in indigo and beryl. An artery of fractured elegance, gliding and cascading and burbling its way to the ocean.

Maybe there was a God after all.

My eye caught something far downstream. Tree trunks. Floating toward me, trimmed and sleek. Perhaps felled by loggers and lost in a storm. But how could they be coming toward me, against the current?

It took a few seconds before the reality of the vision registered in my conscious mind. They weren't tree trunks, they were canoes. Three of them. And they were full of men.

Chapter 4

If I could see the men, they could see me. I ran along the bank, dragging the canoe rather than paddling it because I'd be more visible on the water. But I could only run so far before tiring. Still within sight of the men, but far enough away for ambiguity, I put the canoe back into the water. This time the devil *was* after me.

"Go, Wilbur, go." I prayed they hadn't spotted me. But one look ahead, at the smoke puffing from our morning fire, and I realized it didn't matter.

"Malcolm!"

He was still too far away. I paddled hard, my breath coming in short, painful bursts.

"Malcolm! Malcolm!"

He emerged from the trees with an armload of spare bark.

"Malcolm!"

He dropped the bark and ran to meet me. As I landed on the bank I gasped my words. "They're … they're on their way."

"Calm down. Who's on their way?"

"Them." I pointed downstream. He stood up to his full height and shielded his eyes against the sun. Then he closed his eyes and exhaled deeply.

"Help me hide the canoe," he said.

Together we dragged it into the woods and camouflaged it with branches and leaf litter. "The fire," I said.

"There's no time."

We split up, each going in the direction we'd previously taken when searching for birch trees. I had the musket; the only way Malcolm could kill someone with it was if the person snatched the gun from his hands and committed suicide. As I hurried through the woods I kept an eye out for a tree to climb. If the men didn't have dogs, they wouldn't be able to search the trees.

A mature oak appeared, one with a branch within reach. Most of the oak's leaves had fallen. But if I climbed high enough I'd be hard to detect. They'd have to be looking for me, directing their scrutiny to the top of that particular tree.

By now the men had had enough time to reach the camp. There was no missing it—smoke still billowed from the fire. I didn't hear any dogs. So I waited. The question was whether to climb the tree or keep running.

There was also the question of where Malcolm was, how far he had gotten. What he would do, without a weapon, if they caught him.

Men crashed through the woods. The noises were uncomfortably close. I slung the musket over my shoulder and climbed the oak.

They passed my position only fifty yards away, carrying black powder rifles and pistols. One wielded a sword, swinging it back and forth in front of him like a machete. I'd seen his face somewhere before.

Another man spoke, one with a deep, authoritative voice. "Are you sure you saw something?"

The voice was familiar. As its owner turned in my direction, I recognized his face as well. Karl Rasmussen, captain of the martinets. He had a round head, short-cropped hair, a long nose, and a dark beard so thick it made him appear half bear.

"I saw something moving near this spot, I swear it."

"Was it a man?"

"I think so."

"What do you mean, you think so?"

"It was a man."

"Spread out," Rasmussen ordered. "Find him."

"Karl," the man with the sword said, "this is a wild goose chase. We committed to a week, and we're way beyond that."

"The fire is still smoking," Rasmussen said. "They're here. We've caught up to them."

"They saw us coming," one of the men said. "They could be miles away by now."

Another said, "If they keep going they'll be eaten by wild animals anyway."

"Or the radiation will toast them," the swordsman said.

"Stop it." Rasmussen spat tobacco juice on the ground and wiped his mouth with the back of his hand. "Yesterday you all took great sport in describing what you would do to these men when you got your claws into them. Now that we're close you're getting scared and making excuses to quit the search. Man up, spread out, and find them. That is not a request. *Find them.*"

The men fanned out in the woods, trudging half-heartedly through the leaf litter. Rasmussen went due north. I followed his lumbering, well-fed frame with my eyes until it was out of sight. Then I tried to make myself comfortable against the rough bark of the tree.

Hours passed. I dozed. I dreamed of the bed Tomas and I shared under our mother's roof. Downy and safe. It was a time when the world made sense. Because I didn't question authority, not yet. A time when rain was fun, not something that made you cold and soggy. When school was all about performing antics behind the teacher's back and showing off in front of the girls. When my greatest fear was letting people down.

My friend Gideon and I explored the ruins of Old Kebek. Most kids were too scared to enter the city, too scared of being punished by their parents, of "catching radiation" and mutating. My father was dead, my mother was gentle, and girls didn't give me a second glance anyway. Residents of New Kebek could see the glass and steel remnants of the old city from our wooden replacement across the Laurent River. Windswept. Prickly with crumbling bricks, splintered beams, serrated glass. Ragged and haunting. Sometimes we smelled its odors: of death and emptiness and hopelessness.

The kids entered the old city on a dare. Went on treasure hunts, played hide-and-seek. When Gideon and I conducted our rite of passage and canoed nervously across the river we marveled at all the automobiles. There were so many in the streets, and so little room to maneuver, it was hard to imagine any of the drivers getting anywhere. The automobiles sat quietly, what remained of them, and rusted. Dust and ash had accrued and covered everything, the undulating sidewalks too, and had formed drifts, like snow. Before Gideon and I even reached the first broken skyscraper I pulled on his sleeve and said, "Let's get out of here." He didn't argue. The empty windows of the skyscraper were dark and menacing portals, and I didn't want to discover what was on the other side.

My mother tended the fire when my father died. The job fell to her because I wasn't old enough to be the man of the house. The fire kept the house alive, the food sizzling, the tea warm in our hands. I lay in bed, waiting for the dinner bell, enjoying the aromas drifting from the kitchen.

My mother called me Sugar, pronouncing the S like Sh. Once I asked her why. "What is sugar?"

"It's sweet," she said. "Like honey. It's what my mother called me when I was little."

"Can I try some?"

She turned away. "Run along now and do your homework."

She sent Tomas and me out to forage. She kept Danielle in the house, armed with broom and mop. As my little brother and I wandered through the old growth forests beyond the city walls I always kept my eyes open for carrots. I'd heard of carrots so big you could use them as stickball bats. The wild carrots we did find were tiny. Queen Anne's Lace. I could grasp fifty of the roots in my fist.

Once, however, Gideon and I came across an old billboard whose depiction of smiling, carefree children engrossed in the Bible was peeling off. Underneath was a different kind of picture. A woman in a short dress cooking in her shiny kitchen amidst a cornucopia of vegetables.

There was paint on the woman's lips and cheeks. Her dress was above her knees—bare legs went all the way up from her ankles to her thighs. In her petite hand was a carrot as thick as an ax handle.

Gideon and I reported the billboard to the Council and our families were rewarded with extra rations of flour and salt. From then on I always kept my eyes open for the big carrots.

And for contraband. Everyone did. We were always on the lookout for prohibited objects, even if we turned them in right away as required. My great curiosity was for books, but once in a while exotic gadgets such as rusted guns would surface. These were the ones that could be fired again and again without reloading. They were supposed to have been rounded up after the war, so a find was rare. Bullets were unheard of. All modern technology had been outlawed after the war.

We had a pet cat who liked to join me in bed and tuck herself under my arm for warmth, tickling me by pushing her nose into my armpit. I named her Sugar. When I kissed Sugar on the top of her head she licked my arm in return, and I knew she was kissing me back. One day she ate something cats aren't supposed to eat and died on the porch, writhing in agony.

Her death reminded me of my father's. He too convulsed in his bed as the spirits took him. He kept assuring me, "It's okay, it's okay," in labored breaths, his eyes tightly closed, his hands balled into fists.

Prayers for both my father and Sugar did no good. My mother was unable or unwilling to answer why. Had I prayed incorrectly? Had I said the wrong words, made the wrong gestures, bowed my head the wrong way? I'd been sincere in my entreaties, of that I could be sure. I loved my father and I loved Sugar. Both had good, clean souls. I had prayed on my knees. My knees had become appropriately sore; sore enough, I thought, to stroke the ego of a vainglorious supernatural being.

Had God been too busy? Were too many people pestering Him about their trembling fathers and their lurching cats?

"Be grateful to God you had a cat to begin with," my mother said. "And a good man to call your father."

She sang a lullaby to Tomas and me at bedtime before moving on to Danielle's room to do the same. The words were simple and appropriate for children, but the melody was full of flats and sharps. It rolled up and down the scale with both whimsy and confidence:

Sleep, sleep my beloved one
Close your eyes, your day is done
Morning comes, we'll play again,
Cuddle again, be gay again
Fill the day with joy and fun

*

When I woke, the backs of my thighs were numb from constant pressure against the branch. I was lucky I hadn't tumbled out of the tree.

The sun was down and the day had turned to dusk. I heard men shouting to one another from deep in the woods. They sounded miles away. I decided to descend, wanting to find Malcolm. He could be a day's hike away by now, or even dead already, and I'd be taking a great risk by wandering through a mature forest, litter and dead wood crunching beneath my feet, calling out his name. But I couldn't stand the thought of continuing the journey alone.

Which direction to go? It was more likely I'd run into a martinet before I ran into Malcolm.

No one was in sight. I climbed down, lowering myself from branch to branch, my musket slung over my shoulder, and plopped onto the ground.

Twigs snapping. Footsteps. I spun around. Karl Rasmussen was twenty feet away, aiming his musket at me. He'd circled back and been waiting the whole time.

He fired. I fell.

Blood spread on my shirt where it covered my abdomen. At first I didn't feel anything. Like someone else was bleeding, someone else was dying.

Rasmussen busied himself reloading. I rose to my feet again, picked my musket up from the ground where it had fallen, and pointed it at him. By now I could feel the pain and knew exactly where I'd been shot: on my left side, stomach high.

The musket's barrel wouldn't sit still. It undulated and shook in my unsteady arms. I found the trigger. Pulled it.

Nothing happened. Either the powder was damp or it had spilled out of the flash pan when the musket fell.

Rasmussen laughed. The predator. The bearded face, growing ever-hazier. The half bear, half man who had hunted me to satisfy his tyranny and blood thirst. I had passed him on the street as a boy but we'd never made eye contact. Now as he came closer he eyed me like prey. I was the rabbit, the carp, the muskrat. My legs wobbled. My vision blurred.

The birds went silent. Nature anticipated a sacrifice, a contribution of blood to the soil, a removal of one organism to make way for others.

With shaking hand I recocked the hammer of my musket. The puny prey makes a final, desperate, symbolic stand. The book of history, were it comprehensive, would be filled with such heroic if futile acts. After all, the meek shall inherit the Earth. The upstarts shall have their day. The Davids shall slay their Goliaths. The mothers of all the soldiers in all the armies of lost causes shall send their sons off with the same reckless command: *Come home with your shield or upon it.*

Rasmussen aimed at my face.

My fingers groped for the trigger and squeezed. This time smoke belched from the flash pan and the weapon roared.

Rasmussen's face lit up in surprise. His jaw fell open, his eyes widened, and he fell to the ground.

Chapter 5

The deep woods echoed with the muffled shouts of faraway men. In minutes they would converge on my position.

My clothes were sticky with blood. I tore my shirt open and inspected the wound. There was an entry hole on my left side and an exit hole on my back. The ball had gone clean through. I could move and function, so I guessed the ball hadn't hit any internal organs, but it was only a guess. Blood leaked like a crude wooden cask leaked wine. I pressed my torn shirt against my side. But I couldn't cover both holes. If help didn't arrive I'd bleed to death.

There was a crashing in the brush. I looked up. It was the man with the sword. He emerged from the brush and spotted me sitting at the base of the tree.

A greasy-haired hunter. In a flannel shirt. Stumbling upon his prey, finding it helpless. He smiled. His teeth were mossy. But there was something non-predatory about the smile. And something familiar, too.

He crept toward me, looking around, satisfying himself I was alone. I eyed my musket on the ground, within arm's reach, but it would take a minute to reload. The swordsman studied Rasmussen's lifeless form, then turned his attention back to me. He took no action, just stood there, flashing his grimy teeth.

"Well," I said, "aren't you going to kill me?"

The smile vanished from his face. "Kill you? Why would I want to kill you?"

"Isn't that why you're here?"

"Don't you recognize me, René?"

The man before me blurred and blended with a vision from years ago. The resemblance came into focus as the two images merged.

"Oh my God. Gideon?"

"Yeah, it's me." He gestured with his free hand at his own expansive girth. "I've gained a little weight."

He'd just inhabited my dreams. How could that be? But of course: I'd seen him in the pack of martinets and he'd looked familiar. My subconscious mind had been talking to me.

There was no overlooking his sword. He followed my gaze and shrugged, embarrassed.

"Rasmussen tried to kill me," I said.

"Rasmussen lived by the sword, so to speak. Now look at him."

"So what are you here to do?"

"Take you home. We're tasked to instruct you that if you surrender you'll receive a light sentence."

"And if I don't?"

His eyes drifted down. "We've been ordered to bring you and Father Marchand back dead or alive." He pointed at the crumpled corpse nearby. "Karl preferred it one way, I prefer it another."

"So you do intend to kill me."

"Don't make this hard, René. Besides, you don't know what they're saying about you back in Kebek. People understand how upset you must have been about your brother's death."

"My brother's execution," I correct him.

"Very well, execution. I have a message from Father Mitchell. He says he'll allow mitigating circumstances at your trial. You know Father Mitchell; it's a big concession for him."

"Anything from my mother and sister?"

"They were both detained after you escaped. Danielle was released shortly before I departed. She says she wants everything to return to the way it was before all this happened."

"Don't we all. And my mother?"

"She hadn't yet been released by the time I left." He glanced away, into the trees. "But it was about to happen any day, and I'm sure she's out by now. You may not be aware, but something of a movement is underway. The community has divided on the matter of your guilt. Half the town believes you did no wrong."

"Does that half include Father Mitchell, the martinets, and the Council of Bishops?"

He didn't answer.

Rasmussen's lifeless body lay conspicuously nearby. It was the centerpiece of our tableau, yet thus far ignored. I nodded toward it and said, "I killed Karl."

"I'll bury him. No one will know. I'll say I saw him alive after I found you. He must have wandered off somewhere and got eaten by a Griffin."

"Come with us, Gideon."

He smiled and shook his head.

"We're on an adventure. Join us!"

"I'm sure it is an adventure, René, but I have a home to return to. A wife and children."

"Then at least let me go."

He said nothing, just stared at me, fidgeting. Then he noticed the blood on my shirt. "You're wounded."

"Karl shot me."

"Here, let me help you."

He dropped his sword and bent over me. He said, "By the way, have you found any of those big-ass carrots yet?"

There was a rustling sound behind him, followed by a shadow, and a *thunk*. Gideon fell over unconscious. Standing behind him was Malcolm, a log in his hand.

"That wasn't necessary!" I shouted at Malcolm.

"You're welcome. Maybe next time I'll get permission before saving your life."

"He was trying to help me."

"What are you talking about? He's one of them!"

"I was convincing him to come with us."

Malcolm picked up Gideon's sword. He held it away from himself like it was contaminated. "I see they aren't terribly well armed," he said.

Gideon stirred. He shook his head to clear it, then reached for my musket.

Malcolm didn't hesitate. He seemed to act instinctively, thrusting the sword at Gideon's exposed back. The penetration made a sickening noise, sucking and tearing sounds, and brought a shocked grunt from Gideon's throat. The pointed end of the sword protruded from his chest, ripping through skin and shirt.

"No!" I screamed. "No, no, no!"

He clutched at his chest. He scratched and clawed, frantic to undo what had been done. His breathing turned to gurgling as his lungs filled with blood. He looked at me one last time with an expression of confusion. He lay down on his side and closed his eyes.

"Gideon!"

There was nothing I could do. He was unresponsive. Blood flowed from his mouth and he wasn't even coughing.

"He just wanted to help," I said.

Malcolm dropped the sword in disgust. "My God, what have I done?"

"You killed my friend."

He looked at me like he didn't know me, didn't even know himself. Then he said, "Good Lord, have you been shot?"

"I'm afraid so."

"And you think these people are trying to help you…"

There was no point explaining. Gideon lay on the ground, his blood soaking the dirt. Malcolm made me lean against the tree. He patched me up with elderflower he always carried with him. There was no time to search for yarrow or other medicinal herbs. He lifted me to my feet. I was too dizzy to stand, so I sat back down immediately.

More shouts came from the woods. They were west of us and growing nearer.

"We need to go," Malcolm said.

"What about Gideon?"

"We have to leave him." He looked at Rasmussen, lying a few feet away. "My, you've been busy. We'll have to leave both of them. Their friends will give them proper burials."

He slung me over his shoulder and trotted toward the east. A hundred yards away he set me down, crouched next to me, and held his finger to his lips.

We watched from a distance as the other men arrived at the tree and discovered two of their own dead, including their leader. It was clear they were arguing, but we couldn't make out the words. They trudged toward the river in a tight clump, carrying the bodies, scanning the woods around them. When they were out of sight Malcolm inspected my wound.

"It's superficial," he said.

"Doesn't feel superficial."

"Don't be a baby."

"Gideon wanted to take us home."

"I'll do better. I'll take you to paradise."

Light-headed from blood loss, I said, "You can manage that?"

"Of course. All we have to do is go in the opposite direction Gideon wanted to take us."

There was really only one direction we could go. To the east were people very angry at us. To the north, frozen wastelands. To the south, jungles and the abominable creatures inhabiting them. If circumstances favored the west, and thus paradise, so be it.

"Gideon was my friend," I said.

"So am I. Now be quiet."

*

We remained hidden until the next morning. Malcolm crept back to camp to see what was going on. An hour later he returned to where I waited in my makeshift hospital bed.

"They're gone," he said.

"Will they be back?"

"I doubt it. They've lost their resolve. And if they do return, we'll be far away. Rasmussen was their leader. Without him the spirit of the posse is broken."

"What if they went ahead to set a trap for us?"

"Again, I doubt it. We must be near the first Great Lake. No one's ever gone beyond. To Rasmussen's men it might as well be the edge of the Earth."

Malcolm packed me up and carried me back to the old camp. We checked our stores. All the food was gone.

"At least they'll eat well on the way home," he said. "By the way, you never told me: how *does* Wilbur handle?"

"Could be better. Its attributes are limited by the skills of its maker."

"Be polite to your nurse. He's got to do all the paddling now, you know."

"You're right. I'm sorry. Did I ever tell you how nicely shaped your ears are? If I were a girl I'd totally go for you."

"Tease."

My banter was a facade. How could a Levitican priest kill so quickly, so easily? So instinctively? How many more commandments did he intend to disobey? Leviticus 26 had plenty of warnings for such trespassers: *I will punish you seven times more for your sins ... I will send wild beasts among you.*

Chapter 6

It was a week before I could paddle again. Meanwhile Malcolm managed the heavy lifting. The temperature grew warm, a late Indian summer. I reclined in the canoe and watched the landscape sail by. The trees buzzed one another about the coming winter with the nonchalance of a backyard cookout, each one looking to the horizon for signs of approaching snow.

We made hooks out of thorns and hardwood and caught fish. Once in a while I got lucky and shot a rabbit or squirrel with the musket. Dandelions, chickweed, and sorrel served as vegetables. Wild onions if we could find them. Mushrooms if we trusted them.

When I was well enough I climbed trees and scoured nests for eggs. Malcolm always questioned the species.

"How should I know?" I said. "Eggs are eggs. Enjoy them."

"Yes, but what *kind of* bird laid them?"

"A flying bird."

"Aren't birds supposed to lay eggs in the spring?"

"Not these birds."

"We should have brought chickens with us."

"They would have made too much noise as we snuck out in the night. Besides, they'd shit the canoe."

"At least we wouldn't have to eat newfangled eggs."

When it rained we moved the fire indoors, but the smoke struggled to escape the small opening in the top of the hut. We coughed and our eyes stung. At least it kept the mosquitoes at bay, who were fattening up for hibernation. When we slept outside we scattered wet leaves on the fire to repel the beasts. Problem was, the mosquitoes were willing to sit even closer to the fire than we were.

The river narrowed and the current strengthened against us. Sometimes we had to stop and carry the canoe along the bank. We were always watchful in the woods, fearing mutants hiding among the trees.

Headwinds were another hindrance to progress. We stayed close to shore; both wind and current were weaker there. Nevertheless our arms grew weary and as day's end approached we paddled listlessly. The only consolation, if anyone were following, was their muscles were giving out as well.

Evenings we stopped, aching and exhausted, wondering if we'd have the strength to paddle another day. We erected our bark shelter and collapsed into hastily made beds. Mornings we rose before dawn, searched our necks and arms ritually for ticks, lit a fire, and cooked leftovers from the previous evening's meal. If there were any. We packed the canoe and shoved off, willing our sore muscles to face another cycle.

As fish became scarce we saved their bones and ground them up to use as flour.

Nights grew crisp. Paddling kept us warm through what amounted to rigorous exercise. But at night our fingers and toes acted as sentries alerting us to the encroaching cold. We shivered under thin blankets and animal skin quilts, reminiscing about sweltering dusks, even attended as they were by armies of biting insects. The brilliant fall colors had faded to dull, tedious grays. Even the most tenacious of leaves let go and drifted to join their ancestors in the soil.

We made the fire bigger now, no longer fearing a posse, and sat near it longer each evening, soaking in every pulse of heat before retreating inside and wishing each other good night through chattering teeth.

One morning I woke in the early darkness to a scuffling sound outside the shelter. At first I thought the posse had followed us after all, and I readied my musket. Waking Malcolm would have risked creating noise, so I remained still, listening. The scuffling continued, accompanied by angry snorting.

A bear. I cocked the hammer of the musket. If he tore through the bark wall of the hut I'd have but one shot to fend him off. Reloading would task the bear's patience.

We hadn't left anything outside of interest to a bear, so after a few minutes the night was quiet again. I opened the flap a couple of inches and peeked out. Nothing but cold and darkness. I uncocked the musket and went back to sleep.

The rapids got rougher. Each time we hit a rock we winced as though it had struck our own fragile bodies. Every new crack in the bark meant more leakage, more bailing. And a thorough penetration meant stopping for repairs. Wilbur held up admirably. Birchbark no doubt served the birch, but when God made it He had river navigation in mind.

The current was against us. The rocks stood in our way. Even the wind took sides. Somebody didn't want us reaching the first Great Lake. We looked for it, past boulder after boulder, around bend after bend.

Sometimes it seemed like we stood still on the river. I'd check to my right, mark a tall tree, and minutes later it would still be there, a straight shot down the line of my shoulders. Or maybe it was a different tree. Maybe frustration led me to conclude all trees look alike.

Hello again, Tree. Long time, no see, Tree. You haven't aged a bit. We really should stop meeting like this.

We threaded a myriad small islands. Trudged around a sequence of turbulent rapids. Hefted Wilbur over furiously gushing waterfalls. By the time we were ready to concede the Great Lakes were a myth, we were treated to a vast expanse of greenish blue, textured with dark, choppy waves. Water, and yet more water, all the way to a dull, undulating, and mysterious horizon. We'd arrived at the limits of modern human exploration.

Cedars had claimed the shores. Close to the water they gave way to golden marsh grass, which itself gave way to gentle swirls and roils. The land around was craggy with rocks thrusting up from the earth, wearing angry faces. And all of it ceded authority to the flat calmness, the tranquil presence of the lake. Proof that serenity conquers all.

We would keep to the south shore. Because according to legend the north shore harbored Turonado, which still glowed at night from radiation. It had been a large, densely populated city before the poisoned rains. A city of culture and learning. Now it inhabited the nightmares of Kebekian children and served as a handy threat for parents warning them against bad behavior.

In truth Kebek was no better; its surviving citizens lived outside the original city, in a wooden metropolis hastily constructed after the war. We grew up with the historic skyline on the horizon: charred smokestacks like broken masts. Concrete towers gaping penitently at an indifferent sky. Yet as sinister as Kebek was, Turonado housed an evil that Kebek was spared.

An old map Malcolm found and hoarded warned, near its edge, "Beyond this place, there be dragons." It would be a fitting label for our current position. For in all the fireside ghost stories, and in all my childhood nightmares, Turonado was a fortress of mutants.

Chapter 7

Malcolm and I paddled westward, parallel to the southern shore of the lake, keeping a distance of a few hundred feet off shore. The first day was uneventful, and I allowed myself to relax and imagine facing no greater obstacle than sore muscles during the remainder of our journey. I even knocked on wood. Which required little effort since the canoe was made of wood.

The second day was more eventful.

Smell is the first of the senses to detect an approaching storm. The nose captures the moisture, the subtle change in humidity, the microscopic scouts that precede the squall and warn the birds. The birds behave erratically until moments before the rain begins, whereupon they disappear.

The skin registers the sudden temperature drop, the stiffening breeze. The trees begin to speak of it, and no longer in soft whispers.

Halfway through our second day on the lake the sky was torn by lightning. Malcolm turned to me and nodded. His nose was telling him the same tale mine was telling me. We steered toward shore and pushed hard.

But the storm pushed harder. The horizon was bruised and swollen. Clouds that until now had squatted deviously in waiting now darkened and trundled toward our fleeing vessel.

A clap of thunder. More splintered flashes, and almost immediately thereafter an ear-splitting crash. The storm was on us.

"Paddle," Malcolm said.

He didn't have to tell me. I was ploughing the water as if sea monsters were after me. Waves rose, encouraged by the wind, and impeded our progress. They stretched ever higher with clear intent to swamp the boat.

"It feels like we're going backwards," Malcolm said.

"Or else the shore is moving away from us."

"I wouldn't doubt it. Paddle with everything you've got."

"You mean I have to stop lollygagging around?"

We reached the shore with the assistance of a large and accommodating wave that tossed us onto the mud and tried to snatch the canoe away as it receded. Malcom and I each grabbed a thwart and dragged the canoe into the trees.

"Good Wilbur," Malcolm said.

"I thought you didn't like the name."

"I'll forgive him any name as long as he saves our lives."

"How about Sweet Pea?"

"Don't test your luck."

The clouds dumped their cumbersome loads. The forest canopy failed to shield us from the downpour, instead acting as a sponge, collecting rainwater and squeezing it down on our heads. We tipped Wilbur upside down, propped him against a stump, and crouched beneath. A canoe made a good house, even if the rooms were wobbly and narrow. There was no question of erecting our regular shelter; the wind would turn the birchbark slabs into sails and send them flying back to Kebek.

The sounds of the storm beat against the hull. Between wind, rain, and thunder was little room for talk and even less for complicated thought.

"This is icky," I shouted at Malcolm.

"Yep."

"Wouldn't now be a good time for prayer?"

"There's an old saying." A crash of thunder almost drowned out his voice. "Whoever would learn to pray to God must go upon the sea."

Peaking out from under the canoe, I inspected the lake. Roiling waves rose to my standing height. Farther out they appeared even taller. High above, funnel clouds spun in ominous circles, alternating between fast and slow, teasing the lake until they dipped into it, drank its water, and swelled into full-fledged tornadoes, the most chilling and diabolical of natural phenomena.

"Sounds like good advice," I hollered back.

*

The next day the lake permitted us to make good time, as if to apologize for the previous day's storm. The surface was quiet, placid. A sheet of azurite, with scarcely any ripples except those made by our paddles. A mirror image of tranquil clouds.

A current assisted us by running along the shore in our direction. Even the wind gave a gentle, helpful push. We elected to skip lunch and stay on the water, taking advantage of the rare conditions.

The sun lowered and turned the lake's surface into a shimmering plane. A flat, infinite expanse bejeweled with droplets of reflected sunlight. When the sky was nearly dark we stopped and made camp.

Malcolm set up the hut while I fished for dinner. I caught a chinook salmon, easily over thirty pounds. We added some wild carrots we'd been hoarding and some dried berries. It was our best meal in weeks. Afterwards Malcolm wanted to retire early. I stayed up and sat before the fire.

The wine had been intended as a surprise. I'd nicked the bottle from the tabernacle as we were preparing our escape from Kebek. It was sacramental wine, for celebrating the Eucharist; its destiny had been transubstantiation into Christ's blood. If I hadn't nicked it.

My intentions had been honorable. I'd wanted to surprise Malcolm with an unexpected treat. But I never got around to sharing it with him, or even telling him about it. Instead I kept it hidden in the bottom of my bag. Because he would insist it be reserved for performing mass and all I'd ever get was an altar-boy-sip from a makeshift wooden chalice.

After a short walk into the woods, I tested the wine for quality. To ensure it hadn't spoiled. It hadn't. An hour later I tossed the empty bottle into the brush, shuffled back to camp, stumbled into the hut, and collapsed onto my makeshift bed.

Malcolm lifted his head and looked at me. I burped. He lowered his head and went back to sleep. The lecture came the next evening.

We'd developed a routine: one of us would load the canoe while the other took down the hut. We both policed the area, then each of us grabbed one end of the canoe and carried it to the water. It was a routine requiring few words. Nevertheless Malcolm always had something cheerful to say, a bright "Good morning" or "Let's leave paddle prints on the lake."

Not today. We spent the hours pushing against water in silence. That night we heated and ate the rest of the salmon.

Malcolm said wistfully, "I wish we had some wine to go with the meal."

"Go ahead," I said, "get it off your chest."

"Who hath woe?" he quoted. "Who hath sorrow? They that tarry long at the wine. Thine eyes shall behold strange women, and thine heart shall utter perverse things. Proverbs, chapter twenty-three."

"Perhaps you hadn't noticed," I said, "but strange women are a rarity in these parts."

"I'm disappointed in you, René."

"You are? Or the church is."

"Take your pick. We both care about you."

"The church cares about me?"

"God does. With all His heart. He saved you from the storm, didn't He?"

"Why didn't He just prevent the storm to begin with?"

"I'm not getting into that argument again."

We turned in, lying on the shelter floor with our backs to each other. I recalled something Malcolm had asked me earlier in the journey: why I had entered the seminary. I'd given him a flippant response, but now I wondered about the real reason.

It had started when I became an altar boy. Most altar boys who grow up wanting to become priests do so not because of the ideology, rather because of a sense of belonging. It reaches back to their earliest memories. The church is home, often more so than the one they occupy with their biological families. The world outside the church is uncomfortable, unwelcoming, even scary. But the ideology must eventually be embraced, or else inner conflict results. As was happening now in me.

My premises no longer included the notion of a supernatural being. My fundamental metaphysical premise was science; Malcolm himself had instilled it in me. Science explained phenomena. Supernatural beings explained nothing. The reason Moses didn't have a radio wasn't because God hadn't yet decided it was time for portable music, rather because science hadn't yet evolved enough that radios could be invented.

Malcolm's epistemology was predicated on faith. Mine was increasingly predicated on logic. Logic required truth be proven, or at least argued effectively, whether by deduction or induction. Faith required nothing. "God exists because I have faith He exists," and the debate was over. The fallacy was obvious: "The moon consists of green cheese because I have faith it consists of green cheese."

Malcolm believed there were matters one shouldn't question. I was inclined to believe everything was subject to question—and to scrutiny, and doubt. And to demands for empirical evidence. Of course if one believed in a deity one must accept that deity's ethical dictates, no matter how repugnant, no matter how Old Testament. If one believed instead in science, ethical premises were rendered largely arbitrary. Except for those promoting survival—the business in which Malcolm and I were presently engaged.

It was all a question of premises. Malcolm's and mine were steadily diverging.

"Malcolm," I said.

He was obviously awake. When he slept his breathing was labored. Still he waited several long moments before answering.

"What."

"What happened to 'Thou shalt not kill?'"

He rolled over and faced me. I couldn't tell in the dark, but I was sure he was frowning. "What do you mean?"

"You killed Gideon. Without compunction."

The glare in his eyes was almost visible in the darkness. "There was plenty of compunction, believe me."

"And remorse?"

"And remorse."

"Then why did you do it?"

Another long silence. "I valued your life over his."

"And God? Did God have a stake in the matter?"

"If He did He remained blessedly silent about it. Now go to sleep."

His pelts rustled and I knew he was turning away from me again. I also knew that in his own way he had just told me he loved me. *Thou shalt not kill* had been amended to include *unless necessary*. I had a feeling that before the adventure was over, more commandments would undergo a revision.

It had been selfish of me to drink the wine. Malcolm enjoyed a good snort as much as the next guy, and I had deprived him of a rare pleasure on an arduous voyage. I swore to myself I'd make it up to him. We'd reach Ellanoy. And if it was the hedonistic paradise our clandestine library made it out to be, we'd come into enough hooch to send us both staggering into bed after beholding strange women.

Chapter 8

The sun rose lower in the sky with each successive noon, and temperatures eased downward. After several more days of paddling we passed below Turonado, hugging the south shore, on the opposite side of the lake, yet staying far enough from shore to give us a head start over any unseen mutants bent on pursuing us.

Of course no one knew how fast mutants swam or paddled their canoes, or even if they had canoes. Such information was missing from books, both sanctioned and felonious. We only knew through stories that they had a dog's sense of smell and could sniff us out from great distances.

Turonado was a squat silhouette on the horizon, but we could make out its tallest buildings, rectangular prisms poking the sky, their top floors sheared off and ragged. A wound on the landscape. I thought if I tried hard enough I could hear the echoes of tumbling bricks in its empty streets, the hollow whistling of wind through shattered windows. And if I should walk its streets I'd step over weeds and enterprising saplings growing up through pavement, a reclamation in progress, a sober and biding pageant celebrating the ultimate mastery of nature.

In the other direction lay untamed wilderness. I kept my eyes on the tree line, convinced figures lurked in the shadows. Tree trunks took the form of hideously deformed men, branches became their outstretched arms.

Yet nothing happened. We glided past the danger without incident. The Turonado legend was apparently a myth. I was uneasy with such a conclusion, however, because I believed goodness lay ahead and that yin and yang required an integrated balance between good and evil. Save Rasmussen and his posse, thus far we'd experienced a shortage of evil.

The river connecting the first and second Great Lakes was interrupted by an enormous horseshoe-shaped waterfall. The drop was as much as 200 feet and the falls spanned the width of the basin, an astonishing half-mile long brink. Water roared and foamed, flexing brawny muscles in full view of the soft-bodied canoeists confronting it.

The noise alone! The crashing of an immense volume of water, the roiling and churning of the current as it reached the tipping point, anticipating its headlong plunge into soaring foam. The falls were sentient: a singular incidence of the landscape assembling its most impressive assets to fashion a godhead, an allegory of nature's own self-awareness, of its blithe audacity.

The water flowed northward. We paddled southward, until it became evident there was no passage for a canoe, then backtracked to where we could scale the bluffs hemming the falls. As we passed the thundering monster I looked down and imagined trying to navigate it in the future, when we returned to this place traveling the other direction. The plunging water would crush us. There'd be nothing left of man or boat by the time the river finished chewing us up.

We passed into open water and made camp. Malcolm sank to his knees and thanked the Blessed Virgin Immaculate for having spared our lives.

The second Great Lake! No Kebekian had ever seen it. I had wondered myself whether the lakes were only legend, but Malcolm had pointed out that the legend wouldn't be so specific as to list five of them. And to include details we had so far confirmed.

This time we hugged the north shore, to avoid the dead industrial cities to the east and south. The lake stretched to the southwest horizon and beyond, and at first I thought we may have at last encountered the ocean. But the shores remained narrow, as they had in the first lake, the water remained sweet, and nary a seabird came in sight.

At the western end was our next danger point. Chartrain guarded the straights between the second and third lakes.

"We'll navigate those straights when we reach them," Malcolm said. "Right now we're in a race to beat the ice."

What neither of us knew at the time was that we had already lost the race. We had lost the race the moment we set out from Kebek, far too late in the year. It had been folly to think we'd reach Ellanoy before the snow.

To punish us for jinxing the matter, the next morning saw a thin crust of ice on the water's surface. Malcolm tested it with a paddle. It broke easily.

"We'll go as far as we can," he said.

"Our goal ought to be to find the best place to winter over."

"We might make it yet."

"The lake is freezing. We can't finish our journey in a day."

But there was no reasoning with him. We set out and pushed ourselves. Wilbur's bow broke the ice as it went, cutting a narrow channel of water. The inevitable then occurred: a tear in the birchbark fabric. Water spilled in.

We aimed for shore. Malcolm continued paddling while I bailed. Once on shore we turned Wilbur upside down and drained him. Malcolm set about making a patch while I scouted the neighborhood.

The ground was flat, the conifers were dense and would hide us well, and of course there was sufficient wood to burn. As long as we could find enough to eat we could make a go of it. I was ready to try my hand at ice fishing, and I felt that between us we could design and construct an effective animal trap.

"This is as good a place as any to stop," I reported to Malcolm.

"We're moving on."

We didn't get far. Blocks of ice positioned themselves strategically in our way. At points we had to rock the canoe from side to side, to loosen it from persistent chunks. Soon it was evident we could go no farther. If we stayed out much longer an adolescent glacier would grind us to powder like dried corn under a pestle.

"Let's get back to shore while we still can," I said.

Malcolm reluctantly turned the canoe around. Our winter campsite had selected us.

Chapter 9

The snow arrived and buried the forest under a blanket of white down. The landscape turned into a pallid, undulating sea. The lake was a sheet of silver, barren of life and soul and any hint of topography.

The sides of our camp not bounded by lake were walled off with pines, cedars, and firs, their branches laden with snow. Snow drifted down through openings in the canopy, where wind from the lake pushed it here and there to form drifts. We dug trenches through the drifts to make walkways to our shelter. Snow piling up against the hut walls provided insulation from biting gusts.

We were thus compelled to suffer from the smoke of our fire. It bunched up at the roof, attempted half-heartedly to escape through a narrow opening, and stung our eyes on its lazy way out. But the smoke was better than the cold, which strove interminably to penetrate the hut, and when we went outside, got its revenge and worked its way through layers of clothing, through skin and bone.

We'd stomp back inside to recover in the heat of the fire, only to roast by the same fire while turning in our sleep; alternatively presenting our stomachs and our backs, like pigs on a spit, to even the burn.

Malcolm made us both a pair of snowshoes. They were simple flat contraptions resembling the rackets used for certain ball games. He twisted flexible branches into oval frames and lashed their ends together. Then he latticed the frames by cross-stitching thin strips of hide.

The shoes were remarkably effective. You had to lift your foot straight up before taking a step, else you would drag snow as you walked. And you still couldn't move as fast as the animals. But at least you could move. And the animals had less to guffaw about.

We tested the shoes together during an early morning hunt, hiking into the woods, circling, figuring somewhere between us and the lake was an unsuspecting meal. We split far enough apart that no four-legged creature of average agility could get around us with ease, yet not so far apart that any well educated one would venture to escape between us. Our hunting technique was all about matching wits with creatures endowed with significantly smaller cranial capacities. And to my complete surprise, it worked.

We maneuvered toward the lake, making as much noise as we cared to. I had the gun; any potential dinner would have to dart in front of me. Although Malcolm had no gun, the dinner didn't know.

He moved ahead, approaching the lake faster than me. A rabbit, unable or unwilling to venture onto lake ice, crossed in front of me to avoid Malcolm. Had it known Malcolm was unarmed it could have scampered carefree over his toes, even stopping to pee on his leg.

Today's dinner was solid alabaster, a genuine bunny rabbit. I didn't feel sorry for him, since in the absence of snow he would have been gray. Our deception just turned out to be craftier than his.

There was something funny about his eyes. It took me a minute before I realized he was blind. I'd seen cave fish that had what looked like sores instead of eyes, and the resemblance was strong; these were translucent, almost like they were covered with gauze. He couldn't have differentiated between much more than light and dark, maybe the shadow of a predator. I also noticed that his ears were somewhat larger than normal; they'd clearly evolved to compensate. He hadn't seen us coming. But he'd heard us.

His disability didn't affect his flavor. As he seared over the fire, Malcolm thanked God for the gift of food. He also thanked God for the snowshoes that had enabled the hunt. I couldn't help remembering that Malcolm had made the shoes all by himself, but then I remembered too he had used materials created at divine whimsy. So I kept my mouth shut, except to gnaw on tasty bunny meat.

We tried our hand at ice fishing too, and caught a walleye that fed us for days. Walking on the ice was an odd sensation. First because you knew what lurked beneath; only a thin layer of crystalline water separated you from the dismal, frigid depths. Second because the ice made hollow cracking noises that echoed from a great distance.

There was no visible evidence of cracking, just the ominous noise, like a crevasse as long as the lake itself was straining to open, all the while groaning and growling its hunger for human flesh.

The animal trap experiment was less successful. Malcolm and I built it together, bickering like rival siblings over details of its design. When we'd finally compromised on the scientific principles governing its operation we were ready for field trials. The only time it worked was when Malcolm tested it with his foot. It snapped shut on his ankle and sent him hopping away on one leg, cursing the only way a priest is allowed.

"God daahhh! Son of a bi—! Motherfuhhh!"

The trap sits there to this day. Foxes and other mammals bring their children to see it, presenting it to them as an artifact manufactured by creatures endowed with significantly larger cranial capacities.

As winter deepened, our hunts generated less food. We had to venture farther away from camp. The forest creatures had become wise to their human interlopers. Even fish under the ice learned to avoid us. When at one point we had gone two days without eating I realized starvation was a real possibility.

"Where's God now?" I asked Malcolm.

He didn't answer. Instead he laced on his snow shoes and bundled himself up in moose hide. I asked him where he was going.

He picked up the gun. "To get some food."

That cut deep, because I should have been the one hunting, not him. And when I hunted I should have brought home meat. But his "I'll do it myself" attitude annoyed me. Fine, I thought, do it yourself.

He pushed the hide door open and left without saying goodbye. The sound of his footsteps crunching in the snow receded until I was immersed in stillness. Lethargic from hunger, I drifted off to sleep. I didn't wake again until morning.

Malcolm hadn't returned. Which of course meant he'd spent the night outside the shelter. The thought made me cringe: it would have taken too long for him to build a shelter, even a makeshift one, that served any reasonable purpose. He'd therefore spent the night in the snow.

More snow had fallen overnight, and Malcolm's tracks were buried. But I found I could sweep the fresh snow aside and identify the tracks beneath. All that was necessary was to locate subtle hollows, spaced one pace apart, alternating left and right. I bundled myself up, gathered a knife, an ax, and a spare hide, and set out to look for Malcolm. If he was lost, I could become lost too. So I memorized key landscape features along the way. I pretended trees were townspeople from Kebek, and matched characteristics accordingly.

One hickory, rigid and unyielding, vaguely resembled one of my old school teachers. Another, a young maple sapling, reminded me of a girl I once fancied. Yet another tree, a mulberry, was dark and sad and drooping. It was the spitting image of Father Greer, a dark, sad, drooping priest, now retired, waiting for death and sainthood.

Clouds masked the sky, blocking a feeble sun, making the day drab and surreal. After an hour of walking, tracking, and sweeping away drifts to expose footprints, I could no longer distinguish sky from ground. Only the trees, rooted in snow and reaching nakedly for the mist and haze, anchored me in reality. I could see how Malcolm would lose his way in this realm.

His tracks meandered, then faded.

"Father Malcolm! Father Malcolm!" No answer.

If I'd had the musket I could have fired it, and it occurred to me he could do the same. That no shots were fired made me fear the worst. Either he was incapable of firing or he was so far away I couldn't hear it.

It was necessary to think like him. Starting from his last known footprints, which direction would he go? Surely he knew he was in trouble, and the most important task would be to find or create shelter, some way to keep warm.

Running in my snowshoes, kicking my knees high, I made circles with ever-increasing radii, keeping my eyes open for tell-tale depressions in the snow, any sign of his presence or passage.

After a while I gave up. It would be dark soon. I needed to return to camp, otherwise I'd share Malcolm's fate. Already the faraway trees were graying out. Beneath the forest canopy, where it was dusky and gloomy in the best of times, the light was dimming.

"Father Malcolm! Father Malcolm!"

Another half hour passed. It was more than I could afford. Patches of sky visible through the canopy turned from bluish gray to the dull, inky smear of approaching night. A night my scholarly mentor wouldn't survive. And it was my fault. My feet grew numb in the snow, shame turned my stomach, and loneliness enveloped me like a heavy blanket.

"Father Malcolm!"

Reluctantly I turned for home.

A gunshot went off in the distance.

But from which direction, exactly? I ran toward the sound. I ran until I couldn't be sure I hadn't gone too far.

"Father Malcolm!"

The gun fired again. This time it was much closer. I followed the sound until I saw a figure crouched next to a tree.

Father Malcolm.

He'd carved out a cavity in the snow, next to a fir tree, and had lined it with branches. The structure wouldn't have insulated him from above, but at least it blocked the wind. He had survived the night. But he was stiff and only semi-conscious.

"I knew you'd come," he said groggily.

"Wise of you to signal me."

"I only have a little powder left. I frittered the rest away on squirrels."

"Hit anything?"

"Oh yes, a tree or two, and a few innocent snowbanks. The squirrels were much entertained."

"You marksman, you." I wrapped the spare hide around him.

"I tell ya, snowbanks for miles around are quaking in fear."

After gathering deadwood I built a fire at the base of his little snow house. Within minutes the fire was crackling. But the sky was also turning dark. We'd be spending the night in the woods.

"I can't feel my feet," Malcolm said. I removed his boots, slid his feet closer to the fire, and massaged them vigorously.

"Bring anything to eat with you?" he asked.

"What would you like? All selections à la carte."

"Hmm. Steak and potatoes, drenched in gravy."

"What else?"

"Butter. Plain old butter. I'd kill for a taste of butter."

His feet were warming up. "And for dessert?"

"Tart apple pie. Now, off with you, boy, and be hasty about your business."

The fire had enough wood. I went into the forest with my knife, looking for the right kind of tree. It was too late in the evening to hope for anything better. I found a white pine and went to work stripping the outer bark until I reached the soft, white tissue next to the wood. I shaved off a good quantity of the stuff and carried it back to the fire. The light of the flames made the nearby snowbanks glitter orange and blue. I hand-fed Malcolm a piece of my harvest.

"What's that?" he asked.

"The steak."

He chewed on it. "Mmm."

"Here, have some potatoes." I placed more inner-bark in his mouth. "Taste the butter?"

"It's out of this world. And the pie?"

"Coming up." I fed him more. The bark was stringy and chewy, but he savored it like a delicacy.

Yet he still moved and spoke listlessly, like he was semi-conscious. I pressed one of his eyelids wider open. The eye was bloodshot and didn't focus on anything.

"Father Malcolm? Are you okay?"

"Last night I dreamed of snakes."

Snakes appearing in a dream meant imminent death. "I'm sure it was nothing. They were probably friendly snakes."

"The righteous man perishes, and no one takes it to heart."

"You're going to be fine." I bundled him up and made him lie down and close his eyes.

He cried, "Do not take me away, my God, in the midst of my days."

We had enough wood to survive the night. I put more on the fire, then curled up next to him and tried to sleep.

*

Sometime in the night I heard a soft pattering noise, like someone was stomping the ground lightly with one foot. I sat upright. Father Malcolm was prone and inert.

All was quiet for a moment. I peered into the darkness and listened. The sound came again, this time closer. Presently the cause came into view. A deer, confused by the fire and no doubt also by our scent. We were in his territory and he didn't know what to make of us. Except, of course, that we were the ones who didn't belong.

He was right about that. I lifted the musket, swung it around slowly, and aimed. I was careful not to make eye contact with the deer. As if to assist me, he came even closer. Agitated, pawing at the snow-covered ground in confusion, his curiosity and indignation having gotten the better of him. I waited until he was close enough that I couldn't miss if I tried.

He froze, suddenly aware of his folly. I fired. The black powder explosion splintered the night and echoed among the trees.

A small caliber weapon won't always bring down a deer, but it was winter, the deer was emaciated, and the shot was point-blank. This deer didn't put up a struggle. He collapsed cooperatively to his knees and thumped over in the snow.

Malcolm sat up, startled.

"Go back to sleep," I said. "I shot a deer."

"Good," he said. "More steak." He lay back down.

The animal hadn't yet shed his antlers; we'd make use of them. He hadn't eaten much lately, either, and therefore wouldn't feed us for long. I'd gut and skin him in the morning before we made our way back to camp.

Oddly, he only had three legs. The right rear leg was a mere stump. It couldn't have been amputated; he wouldn't have survived the ordeal. He had to have been born that way. Maybe he was an anomaly. Maybe he was something else.

We'd breakfast on deer meat. We'd have to imagine the potatoes and gravy.

*

The next morning, after breaking fast and camp, I lifted Malcolm onto my back.

"You can't possibly carry me the whole way," he said.

"I intend to. All the way home and across the threshold of our honeymoon suite."

67

"You'll poop out on the way."

"Well, if so, I'll just drop you somewhere, and we'll end this courtship before it gets serious."

"I can walk."

"No, you can't. Not at any reasonable speed, anyway. We need to get back home before the riffraff occupy our shelter."

"Riffraff?"

"Trespassers. Squatters."

"Ah. You mean mice."

"Exactly."

"Then what are you waiting for? Giddy up, Grout!"

Halfway there Malcolm asked, "Do you even know where you're going?"

"Of course," I said. "In fact, there's Father Greer, dark, sad, and drooping, as usual. We're right on course."

"Father Greer is out here?"

"In a manner of speaking."

Chapter 10

Winter bore down on us. The sun wasn't aware of our presence, or wasn't concerned. At any rate, it didn't trouble itself to share any warmth. My traditional three shades of sky gray—dark, medium, and light—grew to include nuances like "velvety charcoal gray," and "darkly light with teasing hints of blue," and "brooding gray, aspiring to dark, with shades of faux orange." I would have given anything to see a star at night.

We huddled in our flimsy shelter and choked on the smoke from our fire. "Don't ever let it go out," Malcolm warned repeatedly. No, not me; I was afraid of turning into a human icicle. I was afraid my hands would become so cold I wouldn't be able to start a new fire. Mostly I was afraid of disappointing Malcolm.

We only had to venture out for food and wood. Malcolm recovered from his freeze sickness and could help with the wood, but hunting was on my shoulders alone. Rabbits were hard to find because they had turned white.

Squirrels were a little easier. If I sat on a fallen trunk and waited motionless for a few minutes the squirrels would forget I was there and venture out onto their branches again.

Boom. Dinner.

That is, until the squirrels smartened up. Perhaps they sought advice from their cotton-tailed comrades. I had to travel farther each day for eatables. After a time, eatables were too far away to bring home for dinner. I concluded the squirrels were sharing intelligence with one another as part of a community alert system. The deer population obviously participated in the program, because I never saw one.

"We need a moose," Malcolm said.

"If only one would acquiesce."

After returning home empty-handed a few times in a row I arrived back in camp with an arm load of inner bark shavings. Boiling them made them easier to chew. It didn't make them taste any better, though. We also drank pine needle tea, a welcome if bitter substitute for what we called snowbank tea, cups of snow thawed and boiled and sipped in tedious monotony.

We got so weary of bark, and so hungry, we each ate a piece of squirrel hide. A night of stomach ache and dashes to the outer perimeter of the camp, and we returned, gratefully, to bark.

"Use your imagination," Malcolm said.

My imagination worked overtime: "Roast bark in red wine gravy."

"That's the spirit," he said. "Bark pot pie."

"Bark noodle soup, with crackers."

"Bark stroganoff."

"Bark casserole, topped with goat cheese."

"Bark à l'orange."

Ironically, despite the unpleasantness of eating trees, I found their silhouettes more appealing in winter than in summer. Maybe because their forms were more visible, because amorphous leaf clusters didn't obscure the underlying geometry. The sharply defined trunks and branches stood out against dreary, spiritless skies. And they were dabbed in snow; a landscape painter would have been in his element—as long as he didn't mind eating his subject matter.

We loved the snow when it stayed in the trees. But more snow fell, and at first we got angry about it. Yet more snow fell, and we became philosophical about it. Even more snow, and we laughed about it like deranged kooks.

Presumably Malcolm saw in me what I saw in him: a skeleton of a man. With facial hair sprouting unchecked and eyes that served as windows to encroaching madness.

At night before the fire he spoke glowingly of Ellanoy, the Vermillion Sea, and the Orient, particularly China. Of the legendary river flowing to the Vermillion Sea from one of the Great Lakes, the one that extended south into Ellanoy country. Sailing the sea to China was admittedly a hurdle, but Malcolm was sure we'd encounter people who had mastered it. Perhaps even people who crossed the sea routinely to trade gold and spices.

"Spices," he said, transfixed. He looked down at his plate of bark shavings. "My kingdom for a pinch of salt."

"We'll find salt," I assured him. "We don't have to go all the way to China to find salt."

"The real treasure in the Orient is the infidels. Just think about it: a vast nation of people who know nothing of God. People waiting for a missionary, an emissary of the Lord, to lead them to salvation."

"And the Ellanoyans?" I asked.

"Gravy on the ribs."

Long before either of us was born, an author who went by the name "Shimoda" secretly wrote a book about Ellanoy, the western ocean, the route to China, and other miscellaneous topics like electricity, flight, and even machines that thought for themselves. Shimoda was the source of most of what we knew about these subjects, or wanted to believe, and he was much inclined to validate legends. I made this point to Malcolm.

"Not legends," he said, shaking his head.

"But Shimoda never visited any of those places," I argued.

"Didn't need to. He was recording common knowledge of his time."

Common folklore, I thought. Shimoda's clandestine work spawned a school of thought, a cult underground following, and a new generation of authors, all of whose books were in Malcolm's basement library. Shimoda and his followers were caught and burned, with as many copies of their manuscripts as could be uncovered. A generation of intellectual revolutionaries who dreamed of touring the Ellanoy country, and continuing to the western ocean, had gone up in smoke.

"We're going to find the route to China," Malcolm declared, "and convert the infidels. It's our mission."

"Our new mission?"

"It's the mission of every true Christian, and should have been ours from the first day. When we return home, we'll wipe the coast clean of idolatrous transgressors."

With this he looked at me pointedly. I wanted to say leave the infidels in peace—live and let live—but when Malcolm was in his rapture was not the right time to debate him.

He said his prayers before dinner, thanking God for the bounty "which we are about to receive." He hesitated, however, while scrutinizing the bark mush that filled our wooden bowls.

"Bless us oh Lord," he began.

He paused until he regained control of his voice.

"And these thy gifts."

*

72

Rivulets of water trickled down the slopes. They meandered playfully, but always downward, seeking to join the lake. To fulfill their destiny. Chilled, clean water, deliciously fresh, percolating. Sparkling, dancing water, cascading with purpose and unabashed delight. Meltwater.

Spring.

The lake ice was breaking. The lake itself moaned, reluctant to awaken from its winter hibernation. A fine sheet of vitreous melt covered the surface. We watched its progress like a dramatic play unfolding. We took turns shaving each other. We even heated water for a bath.

The sky tinged with early efforts at turning blue. It speckled with ducks returning home, their cackles and honks waking the land. The forest stirred, its creatures chattering, the annual cycle of death and resurrection taking its turn at youthful exuberance and festivity.

Each day at dawn I rose, walked to the edge of the lake, breathed the sweet aromas of spring, felt it caress my skin. One morning Malcolm inspected the lake and said, "It's time." We bade farewell to the camp and launched the canoe.

Chapter 11

The lake gave refuge to stubborn chunks of ice, but was navigable. It was good to be underway again. I didn't even mind the aching muscles from a full day of paddling.

"Ellanoy dead ahead," Malcolm said.

In truth, Chartrain was dead ahead. And it was rumored to be infested with mutants. But weren't all the dead cities? Turonado was supposed to be crawling with grotesque ogres and freaks, yet we'd encountered no one in its vicinity.

We made steady progress along the south shore of the lake. We still carved our campsites out of snow, for although the ice was melting, snow was still falling.

One evening as I returned from hunting and Malcolm returned from gathering wood, we met at the hut and he said, "There's something you need to see." I followed him into the woods until he stopped and pointed.

A cabin. Made of logs and planks. And a roof of broken pieces of slate. We'd encountered remnant buildings along the waterways, usually scattered piles of rubble or exposed foundations, but an intact structure was rare. Most were destroyed in the aftermath of war in an attempt to erase the past.

"Have you looked inside?" I asked.

He shook his head. "I was waiting for you."

We approached the front quietly and looked through the windows. Inside was dark, but we detected no movement, no signs of occupation. Malcolm tentatively pushed the door open. In the front room was crude wooden furniture, some broken ceramic plates, and a few half-burned candles. On the floor were rugs that crunched and disintegrated beneath our feet.

"Nobody's been here for a while," Malcolm observed.

That didn't make me feel better. There was something about the structure that gave me the jitters. People had occupied this house long ago, maybe generations ago, and their ghosts lingered, invisible yet present. We needed to leave. We needed to get as far away from this place as soon as possible. I told Malcolm so.

He apparently agreed, because all he said was, "Grab the candles."

We found more candles in the two bedrooms, as well as some unidentifiable fabrics. Outside we surveyed the property for tools and other useful artifacts. Once again Malcolm alerted me to something. "Over here," he said.

The remnants of an automobile. And a maple tree growing out of it, having pushed through its rusted roof. If we hadn't known better we might have thought the automobile grew around the tree.

Next to it, prone on his back, was a dead man. His skin was tightly drawn and the color of paste. His eyes were open. Frosted over. Gawking. Lips were splotchy patches of orange and blue. Clothing had rotted away, revealing the rib structure of a hungry man.

"He's been dead a long time," I said.

"All winter."

But there was something else. I knelt down and looked closely. His features were strangely distorted, but not by death or freezing temperatures.

"Was he beaten?" I wondered aloud.

Malcolm shook his head, and he was right: there were no wounds, just exaggeratedly protruding cheekbones, a bulbous nose, an oversized jaw, and a forehead that slanted back at a high angle.

He was a mutant.

We stood up quickly and backed off. We looked around. I clutched the musket with both hands. The woods were peaceful—birds chirped and trees breathed—but the dead thing before us was not of these woods.

"We'd best be moving on," Malcolm said.

That night I was sure I heard noises outside the hut. Mutants creeping about on all fours. Mutants breathing roughly through phlegm-filled nostrils. Mutants going bump in the night. I reproached myself for acting like a child. It's only the wind, I thought hopefully. Wind, branches, owls, mice.

And mutants. I slept fitfully.

We turned north, headed for the third Great Lake, and entered portage country. The waterways connecting the second lake to the third were often too shallow or were impeded by rapids. Sometimes even by what looked like bomb craters.

We carried the canoe and gear from one navigable body of water to the next, making separate trips for each. Wilbur made the trip upside down, with the gunwales resting on our shoulders. It was the most efficient way to go long distances, but it was hard to see where we were stepping because our heads were inside the boat.

If there was enough water in the rapids we dragged Wilbur against the current, sliding him over rocks and around swirling pools of water. If we found a deep, quiet pool we fished it for dinner.

Malcolm kept saying Ellanoy was right around the corner. However the current was still against us; the waters we paddled emptied into the Sea of Atlantis. We were probably less than halfway to Ellanoy—assuming it existed at all. Maybe he was just trying to keep my spirits up.

Chartrain was directly to our west. Remnant buildings poking meekly above the horizon. Skyscraper fragments, hollow and pocked. Tortured stacks of brick and stone. Surely nothing lived there. Chartrain absorbed sound and light, like an infernal gateway. A gray, windswept city, a dead zone, dusty and charred, silent but for the rattling of human bones like wind chimes in the breeze. We hurried to put it behind us.

The river opened wide. Now it was just a matter of paddling to reach the third Great Lake. No more portages. We dipped our paddles into the water, sometimes laughing, sometimes shouting, challenging the river, daring it to present another obstacle.

The place we had feared most was behind us. The city Kebekians spoke of in whispers, followed by the sign of the cross, receded farther into the distance with each cherished stroke. There had been no mutants. The one we thought we'd found had surely been disfigured by the cruelties of natural decay, or else had been born an outlier, a deformity. The whole story had been one to scare children into behaving.

Boogeymen. Monsters under the bed. Purgatory, Hades, Beelzebub.

The ice had melted, the snow had stopped falling, and the days dawned pleasantly again. We were euphoric and made excellent time.

The second day after passing Chartrain we found a riverbank clearing and elected to stop and enjoy a late lunch. The sun was already on its descent, the sky was a glorious vault of lapis and turquoise, and yellow paint glazed the western horizon.

Branches were budding! As we landed and dragged Wilbur onto shore I noticed the tree trunk.

"Malcolm," I said.

But he was already looking at it.

"Maybe the wind took it down," I suggested.

"Unlikely. The wind doesn't cut wood in such neat flat planes."

We stood staring at it, trying to imagine a non-human explanation for a sawn-down tree.

"Let's get back on the water," I said.

Malcolm nodded. We pushed Wilbur into the river and continued our journey upstream.

As I paddled I watched the back of Malcolm's head and neck, the curls in his long dark hair. His arms plunging the paddle into water, pulling back against the river's resistance, lifting and plunging again.

His figure was framed by a pristine landscape of winding waterways, towering pines, and a sky hung with stately clouds so aloof they were unaware of the humdrum world below. A world both blissful and terrifying, depending on whether you were hiding or seeking, chasing or being chased, eating or being eaten.

All the words I knew that described nature came to mind. Pastoral, blissful, idyllic, bucolic. This was God. The good and the ghastly and everything between. This was God, not a sentient entity sitting on a throne, worrying over whether people were praying hard enough, whether their knees were hurting enough. This, the landscape, the sky and clouds, the creatures both audacious and humble, the weeds as well as the flowers, and the humus spicing the soil. This, all of it, was God.

We had gone about a mile when Malcolm turned around, looked past me at the retreating panorama, and said, "Paddle faster."

"Why?"

"They're coming."

Chapter 12

We paddled faster. A couple of hundred yards downstream were two canoes populated with men. Digging their paddles into the water energetically, as though desperate to catch us. As though hunting us.

As though hungry.

We paddled with all the strength we had. Malcolm grunted audibly with each stroke. But we were only two, and our pursuers numbered four in each boat. They were overtaking us.

"Paddle harder," Malcolm said.

"I'm doing the best I can."

As the pursuers drew closer I turned to look at them again. They had exaggerated features and slanted foreheads. Just like the dead guy. I paddled faster than I knew I could. But it wasn't going to be enough. They were gaining on us with each stroke.

Then came the rapids. A spider web for both predator and prey. We had to get out and push the canoe.

"Malcolm," I said, "we need to beach the boat and make for the woods."

"Not yet," he said.

"But they're almost on us."

"Keep pushing."

We kept pushing. The mutants drew closer. I thought maybe Malcolm was looking for an opportunity, the approach of the third Great Lake, or a tributary, or something to climb. Any method of escaping. But the third lake was too far ahead, and the banks of the river were free of both tributaries and slopes.

My arms were getting tired. I looked back again. The mutants were close enough I could see them smiling.

Their teeth were chiseled into points.

"Malcolm," I said.

"Right. Beach it."

We turned toward shore. As soon as the canoe's bow hit the bank we leapt out.

"Don't forget the musket," Malcolm said.

It was in the bilge, buried shortsightedly under slabs of bark. I rummaged around for the ammunition. Malcolm grabbed the ax. We ran into the woods.

"Split up!" Malcolm said. "Make your way to the lake. I'll meet you on the eastern shore."

He disappeared into the brush. I took off in a different direction. Thickets hindered me, in league with the mutants. Maybe the vegetation had mutated too. I ran, stumbled. Brambles got in my way and disoriented me. Thorns tore my face and arms. I paid no attention to the direction I ran, and before long I found myself back at the river, a hundred yards or so north of the point where we'd beached.

Shit! I'd circled around, which didn't make for an impressive escape resume. Wilbur was gone but presumably the mutants were still in the area. I plunged into the woods again and ran even faster than before. This time the trees themselves sought to block my escape. I crashed into them, tripped over their exposed roots, sprawled headlong into the loamy soil.

Too exhausted to continue, I plopped down next to a basswood and caught my breath. The mutants called to each other in the forest. They spoke in horrible shrieks, and if the language was English I didn't recognize the words. Yelps and screeches, punctuated with sharp cries. Sometimes barking sounds. They had learned speech again after the poisoned rains, this time imitating the vocalizations of forest creatures. The vernacular consisted of jungle sounds. Except the voices were throaty, unmistakably human.

Or rather humanoid. I looked around. I was sitting in a pile of old leaves, withered and soggy remnants from the previous fall. They gave me an idea. Ahead was a small creek. I stepped close enough to the water that anyone tracking me would suspect I had entered it. Then I retraced my steps back to the pile of leaves.

The mutants reputedly had a keen sense of smell, much like a hunting dog's. I peed on three trees that formed a triangle encompassing my position, returned to the leaves and buried myself in them. And waited.

Praying. After all, now was not the time to argue with Malcolm. Or with his deity. Now was the time to ask his deity for help.

"Here's your chance," I whispered.

The chance came. Mutants stumbled into the area, sniffing loudly and emitting high-pitched shrieks. From the sound of it all, there were easily half a dozen of them. They stomped around my hiding place; they could detect my presence but couldn't pinpoint it. They followed my scent to the creek.

Minutes passed, maybe years. They returned, more agitated than before. They congregated between the three trees I'd peed next to. After much shriek-arguing they dispersed. Their howls grew fainter the deeper they went into the woods.

Darkness came, turning the forest as still as a graveyard. Not even the crickets ventured to give away their locations. I had no intention of doing so either. The forest protected me; the leaves made a security blanket that hid me from danger.

My body ached from lying motionless for so long. I wiggled my head using infinitely small movements until I could peek out from beneath the cover of leaves and brush. I watched the trees for activity. They were silhouettes against a murky and somber background. One of them was fatter in the lower trunk than it should have been. I focused on the anomaly.

It moved.

A mutant. Sitting next to a tree, facing the lake, occasionally adjusting himself into a more comfortable position. I stuck my tongue out to check for a breeze. A wisp of one glided through the trees from the lake.

In minute increments I crept out of my leaf cover and moved in a wide circle, crouched and tiptoeing, until I was downwind of the mutant. I'd left the musket in the leaves—its discharge would be heard for miles—and instead clutched my knife. I drew close enough to hear the monster breathing. His silhouette now had a head and a torso.

An owl called, and the mutant stirred, cocked his head, listened. I moved closer, holding my breath, planting my feet on the earth with slow, uniform pressure, to avoid snapping twigs and crunching dry brush.

The mutant was directly in front of me, on the other side of the tree. In one continuous motion I reached around the trunk and slashed my knife across his throat.

He leapt to his feet, gurgling. He stumbled around until he spotted me. He raised his face to the night sky and tried to scream for help, or perhaps in rage, but could only make wet, frothy sputtering noises. Blood gushed from his neck.

He lurched at me. I should have taken off after cutting him but was so shocked he didn't die, I'd merely stood watching in stunned disbelief. He grabbed me by the shoulders with ape-like arms and tried to wrestle me down. But he was already weak from the loss of blood. Still, he remained on his feet.

My knife sank into his gut. He winced and tightened his grip on my shoulders, gurgling, blubbering, sloshing blood on me.

The knife went in again. Still he wouldn't go down. He looked me in the eye, almost pleadingly. His features showed clearly in the starlight. The distorted, lumpy growths of flesh. The slanted forehead. The hollow, asymmetrical eye sockets. The sum of his wretched ugliness.

The knife went in again, and again. He staggered and fell.

Crouching over him, I stabbed him some more, the knife going in and out like it was carving a pumpkin.

He lay still. I went to wipe the sweat from my face and realized it was blood. His blood. I'd bathed in it. I retrieved the musket and jogged toward the lake, stumbling, shaking my head like a dog, trying to get the mutant's blood out of my hair.

*

It took me two days to find Malcolm. He had camped on the eastern shore of the third Great Lake, as promised, but had shielded his fire. I didn't see it until I was thirty yards away. I crept up on the camp, assuring myself the fire was his, and that he was alone. I stood upright and walked in.

He was startled at first. Then he rushed to me and gave me a big hug. "Have you eaten?" he asked.

"No. You?"

"Berries, roots. I saved some for you. I see you've still got the gun."

"I'll use it first thing in the morning. Are we safe here?"

"Not as safe as I'd like to be. We should get as far away from them as possible." He looked me over. "Come closer to the fire." We stood next to the fire, and he scrutinized me from head to toe. "Are you injured?" he asked.

"No."

"But you had trouble getting away."

"A little." It was then I noticed the blood on him. His shirt was spattered with stains. "And you?" I asked.

He pointed to the brush behind the camp. Wilbur was there, at home and secure. I breathed a sigh of relief. "Have trouble retrieving it?"

"A little."

"Our tools and provisions? My journal?"

"All intact. Apparently the mutants had no use for them. They left only one guard." He looked down at his shirt, then at mine.

"We'll wash in the morning," I suggested.

"Right. After a hearty breakfast."

As we prepared for bed Malcolm said, "It's good to have you back. I worried I might have to continue the journey alone."

"I prayed," I said. "To your God."

"He came through, apparently."

"So far. Let's see how the rest of the trip goes before we give Him too much credit."

"Don't worry," he said. I could sense him smiling in the dark. "God will answer your prayers. He always does. It's just that sometimes the message needs to be interpreted."

"Right now I'd like to interpret a pheasant sizzling over the fire."

"Pray for pheasant, and pheasant you shall receive."

"The mutants seem well fed."

He settled into his animal skin blanket. "The dead are in good health," he quoted. "But the living fall ill."

Chapter 13

We could determine our latitude, but we could only estimate our longitude. The latitude—angular distance north or south of the equator—only required measuring the angle of a star above the horizon. Since Polaris was almost directly above the north pole, we recorded its altitude to calculate our position. At least that's how it worked in theory.

In practice we used a makeshift astrolabe, a wedge of wood notched every full degree, and sighted along one of its straight edges. It was only accurate to the nearest degree, at best, so our latitude was estimated as well.

Longitude, the angular distance east or west of an arbitrary meridian, required the ability to keep time. Yet we had no clock, nor even an hourglass. So we had to estimate our daily rate of westward travel, the distance we covered paddling or portaging.

Over dinner Malcolm would ask, "How much ground do you think we covered today?"

After mulling it over—all day paddling, no wind in our faces—"Twenty miles," I'd say.

"I think twenty-five." Malcolm would make a note in his log. His estimates were always greater than mine, I believe because he was anxious to reach his destination.

On the third Great Lake we followed the southwest shore as it meandered northwest. We came across a large bay and tried to cross over, to save time, but winds from the west worked hard to impede our progress. Waves several feet high swamped the boat, requiring that we paddle and bail at the same time. We gave up and followed the shore around the bay.

During a rest stop Malcolm stumbled upon some metallic rocks. Most were the size of a pea, but some were as large as a man's fist.

"They're copper," he said. "Pure elemental copper."

"So?"

"So we can make tools out of this stuff."

"Like what?"

"Like knives. Like spear points."

We gathered handfuls of the rocks and put them in the canoe.

As we approached the straits between the third and fourth lakes the current changed direction and flowed westward. It was now helping us rather than hindering us.

The days warmed and we camped under the stars. In the late evenings the big dipper was almost directly overhead. If you extended the arc of its handle about two handle lengths you came across Arcturus, the brightest star in the sky. "Arc to Arcturus," as they say. If you kept arcing another couple of handle lengths you encountered Spica, which sat on the ecliptic. "Spike to Spica."

Lying on his back, staring at the stars, Malcolm said, "I see God."

All I saw were stars.

We were encountering strange flightless birds flocking at the shoreline. They resembled ducks, but with stubby wings and beaks that didn't align properly, the upper and lower halves coming together askew. They hobbled like mad to get away from us, but were nevertheless easy to catch. And they tasted good.

It seemed the deeper we traveled into the continental interior, the more numerous and pronounced the deformities.

Even the trees were affected. What looked like tumors—spiral knots of gnarled wood—had formed on many trunks and branches. The tumors were dense, almost impossible to cut through, but they made for a long, slow-burning fire.

One night we woke to the eeriest sound either of us had ever heard. A wailing, as though the owner of the voice, whether animal or humanoid, were in great agony. The wails varied in pitch, from high piercing cries to low guttural moans. Up and down the scale, rendering every other creature in the woods numb and utterly silent. Including us. It was hard to judge the distance. On one hand the dreadful laments seemed to come from far away, deep in the woods, yet at the same time their source could have been a mere stone's throw from the camp.

The wailing persisted, an hour of the most pitiful crying and howling imaginable, leaving Malcolm and me cringing in our animal hides. Neither of us asked the other what the thing might be. Neither of us was sure he wanted to know.

At the end of the third Great Lake Malcolm declared it was time to turn south. "Shimoda said to do so. The fourth Great Lake extends south, he promised, into Ellanoy country. It's easy sailing from here."

Sailing, yes. Easy, no. The rapids we encountered were muscular and furious. They confronted us in a sequence, one after another, each one louder and more tumultuous than the last, roaring and gushing, tossing Wilbur against boulders the size of small cottages.

We ran them, shot them, performed wild dances with them. They flung us into the air, and as we fell we experienced the sensation of floating, of our hearts rising to our throats. Most of our effort was spent trying to maintain control, to stay inside the canoe, all the while yelling in fright and elation.

The rapids soaked us, drenched us, slapped us with jets of water. Sometimes they turned us around, so that we traveled backwards.

Eventually they delivered us to calm water. The straits opened into the fourth Great Lake, another seemingly infinite basin, lined densely with deciduous and coniferous groves. Malcolm steered Wilbur toward shore, where he knelt and consecrated the ground in the name of the Blessed Virgin Immaculate.

*

The next morning I stepped out of the hut with my fishing gear, hoping to catch something for breakfast. Standing before me on four hoofs, snorting and pawing the ground, rearing up to charge, was the strangest cow I'd ever seen. I stepped back into the hut.

Malcolm rolled over and said, "I thought you were going fishing."

"Fishing…" I said.

He blinked at me. "What's wrong?"

"A cow. With a beard."

"Huh?"

"Outside, I swear it. There's a cow with a beard."

He peeked through the flap. After a moment of gawking at the anomaly he said, "I wonder what he tastes like."

"I have a proposal."

"Do share."

"Let's find out."

We exited the hut, me with the musket, Malcolm with the hatchet, and positioned ourselves on either side of the beast. I didn't know which of us had the better weapon: a lead ball, propelled by gunpowder, that might bounce off the creature's dense hide, or a dull wedge of iron that in order make effective you had to get within the animal's biting range.

The cow's head was enormous. It sported a pair of horns that arced delicately skyward. A large hump made him appear otherworldly. A scruffy mane draped its head. A double chin hung almost to the ground.

It was hard not to laugh; I didn't want to insult and thus possibly anger the apparition. Yet never before had I seen so ridiculous a species.

Malcolm wasn't laughing as he maneuvered himself behind the cow. Maybe because he was hungry. Maybe too because all he had to defend himself was a dull hatchet with a loose handle.

"It might be safer to let him go," I suggested.

"And skip lunch? Not on your life."

"Actually it's *your* life I'm concerned about."

Several more of the beasts were visible down the shore, drinking from the lake. Across the lake, which at this latitude was still narrow, were perhaps dozens more, grazing. Perhaps hundreds.

Pointing at them I said, "There're plenty more where he came from. This guy is just the most curious of the bunch. Or the boldest."

"And therefore the tastiest. You'll see."

"How the hell do you know that?"

"Do I have to keep telling you? You have to know these things when you're a priest."

The cow snorted. He was confused by the pair of two-legged freaks circling him.

"Put him out of his misery," Malcolm said.

Aiming the musket at the beast's heart, I fired.

He jumped in the air a bit, and his eyes widened. At me.

"Oh shit."

"You've pissed him off," Malcolm said. "I suggest you reload without delay."

The ramrod was already out. "Perhaps you could do me a favor."

"Namely?" Malcolm was taking slow, measured steps backwards. The cow pawed at the ground in rage.

"Distract him."

"Ah."

The cow took a step toward me. I fumbled with the powder horn. "I mean it, Malcolm."

Malcolm hopped up and down and waved his arms, making noises like a monkey.

"What the hell are you doing?" I said. "He doesn't know what a monkey is." The cow grunted and took another step toward me. My hands were shaking. I was spilling powder.

"Everyone knows what a monkey is," Malcolm said.

"Be something he wants to eat!"

"Looks to me like he wants to eat *you*."

The cow moved closer, breathing roughly, still pawing the earth. Malcolm danced and waved his arms again, this time croaking like a frog. The cow turned and looked at him like he was an idiot. Apparently he found frogs appetizing, or perhaps idiots, because Malcolm was the two-legged freak he selected.

He lowered his head and charged.

Malcolm raised the hatchet, then thought better of it. No point in antagonizing the animal again. He dropped the hatchet and sprinted toward the trees, yelling "Quack, quack! Ribbit!"

The cow caught up to him, lifted him with its horns, and tossed him like a sack of corn. Malcolm sailed into the brush, limbs flailing, his impertinence hobbled, his predilection for animal mimicry wholly suppressed.

The cow then turned its attention to me.

"Oh darn."

By this time the gun was reloaded. As the brute approached I fired at its head. The shot bounced off, but it stopped him.

"Reload!" came a muffled cry from the bushes.

"Distract him again!" I shouted back.

"What? I can't hear you!"

The cow stomped the ground. I dashed into the hut. The cow followed me and crashed into the bark wall, which hadn't been constructed with requisite foresight. The cow rammed the hut again and again, snorting furiously, its breathing reduced to wheezing, until our shelter consisted of naked poles and shredded tree skins, all in a chaotic pile. And me beneath the pile, hollering "Distract him, dammit!"

Malcolm's voice came from far away: "Here, cow! This way, cow!"

Incredibly, it worked. Maybe the cow didn't like being called a cow. I reloaded once more, and when I caught up to him he was chasing Malcolm around a tree. Malcolm was doing his best to avoid being eaten, by keeping the tree between him and his *mangeur*. Strong fences make good neighbors.

The beast took another musket ball, this time in the gut. That did the trick. He stood looking at me indignantly. I reloaded and fired again, and it hung its hairy head. I shot it yet again and it fell to its side with a ground-shaking thump.

"Stop," Malcolm said, "or he'll be more bullets than meat."

"I'm more worried about ruining the hide."

We waited a while before approaching the dead animal. We were afraid it was playing possum and would spring up suddenly to take a bite. I couldn't get the vision out of my head: of all the ways to die, to pass through the intestinal tract of this aberration of nature, and be dropped to the ground as its poop, had to be the most undignified way to go.

Malcolm's wounds needed tending. I searched the woods for a patch of yarrow and brought a few plants back to the shelter ruins. I picked off some leaves, chewed them up, and spat them out to make a salve. Malcolm had horn scratches and small punctures on his arms and stomach. I applied the salve to his wounds and bound them.

We returned to the cow. I asked Malcolm, "What do you make of this thing?"

He regarded the eccentric creature and said, "God has a sense of humor. I just hope the meat tastes good."

It did. Turns out, God likes a good steak, too.

Chapter 14

We rested a few days while Malcolm's wounds healed. I shot a couple more of the cows. We smoked the meat and preserved the hides to make blankets and robes. We rebuilt the hut. There was now enough wild cow hide to line the inner walls. However, the season was steaming up and the mosquitoes had found us.

"Nature's guardians," Malcolm said.

"Nature's revenge," I corrected him.

The mosquitoes were delighted we had entered their habitat. They buzzed about our heads in their high-pitched whine, singing with joy because here before them, dressed only in rags, with vast swaths of seductively exposed skin, were two succulent meals wandering blithely through the sylvan realm.

The mosquitoes were magnanimous as well as festive: they invited their distant cousins to the potlatch. Thousands of kith and kin, from miles around, all appreciative of a free buffet.

We returned to our journey and the mosquitoes accompanied us. I was sure I recognized some of them, the ones who had evaded my frantic swatting at a previous camp and were back now for seconds and thirds; trailblazers who feasted on us, returned home to clamorous victory parades, and led their compatriots back to share in the debauchery.

Malcolm spent his evening downtime beating copper nuggets into spear points. I'm sure he had cows and mutants in mind, nevertheless the way he clenched the points while rotating his head, trying to locate the source of an infuriating mosquito whine, left no doubt about the true inspiration for his handicraft.

The heat became unbearable. The skin on our faces peeled under the sun. At night the mosquitoes found their way through multiple layers of hides and clothing, so we peeled those away, opting to endure the bites alone rather than bites and suffocation both.

Our arms and legs and faces and necks and ankles and feet were red from slapping and from blood smeared by mosquitoes who gave their lives that their comrades might benefit from flanking maneuvers. We slapped our ears in vain to silence the maddening whine. We blew our noses to expel mercenaries that flew into them.

We built smoky fires, but those only alerted the more distant clans. Like ringing a bell for dinner. We rubbed our skin with various aromatic plants, hoping to disguise ourselves from the contagion, but only succeeded in broadcasting our location.

"Do you smell mint?" one mosquito would say to another.

"Indeed I do."

"It's a Hooman."

"How do you know?"

"Because real mint plants don't run around, stabbing the air with copper points, crying 'Get away from me!'"

Malcolm asked, "Remember when I complained about the snow?"

"Which time?"

"Every time."

"Yes."

"Won't happen again. As God is my witness, I am done bad-mouthing frostbite."

The "bird bugs" arrived next. It seemed the deeper we traveled into the continental interior, the larger the insects. It must have been a law of mutation; some bird bugs were as large as a man's fist. They were slow and stupid, however, and could be batted to the ground in mid-flight. Evenings they kept us awake by crashing witlessly into the cabin's bark walls.

We paddled hard each day, thinking somehow our troubles would end in Ellanoy. As though Shangri-La had no insect population. The eastern shore of the fourth lake was flat but picturesque, adorned with sandy beaches. We camped right on the dunes, dug fire pits in the sand, and roasted great chunks of wild cow. We had thought the mosquitoes were the worst of our problems, until one evening when I felt an itch. I scratched it and felt another.

No-seeum bugs!

Soon I was raking myself all over with my fingernails. Malcolm regarded me as we would a mad man. He asked what was wrong.

"You'll find out in a minute," I said. I ran from the hut and jumped into the lake.

Malcolm shouted, "You're behaving irrationally, René Jordan!"

A minute later he emerged from the hut scratching himself, his fingers trying to reach every spot on his body at once. He writhed and danced like a bewitched shaman conducting a purification ritual. With a cry of surrender he bolted for the lake and plopped in.

Wayward organisms returning to the sea. Ashes to ashes, water to water. We squatted on the sandy bottom with only our heads above the surface.

"Irrationally?" I asked.

"A double minded man," he said, "is unstable in all his ways."

"James, chapter one, verse eight."

"There's hope for you yet."

At the southern tip of the fourth Great Lake we camped for the night at a river inlet. In the morning we reconnoitered and found a path in the woods. Straight and beaten, obviously manmade. It trekked deep into the forest until lost to sight.

"This will lead us to the Ellanoyans," Malcolm said. "We've arrived."

Part Two
The Orchards of Eden

Chapter 15

A breeze descended from the north and brought relief from the heat. The breeze seemed eager to pull us southwards, to assure us we had chosen the right direction. A message floated from tree to tree until it swirled in airy song about our heads: *your destiny lies ahead.*

We hid Wilbur in the bushes, off the path, and packed our belongings for the hike. There was no telling how long it would take to reach Ellanoy country, but Malcolm was sure it wouldn't be far from the lake. The Ellanoyans would want access to the large freshwater reservoir for fishing and travel.

We hiked down the path footloose and chipper. Malcolm even struck up the Lourdes Hymn:

Immaculate Mary,
thy praises we sing,
thou reignst now in Heaven
with Jesus our king.

He nudged me and I joined in:

Ave, ave, ave Maria!
Ave, ave Maria.

We all but skipped down the path. I had never seen Malcolm in such a good mood. He had dreamed all his life of this day. He sniffed the air repeatedly, and when I asked why he said, "Salt water. I'm trying to detect a salt water body. If Ellanoy is around the corner, the ocean can't be much farther away."

"Just think of it," I said, carried away by his exuberance, "we're a stone's throw from Japan!"

In Heaven the blessed
thy glory proclaim,
on Earth we thy children
invoke thy fair name.

"Sing it, brother!" I shouted.

Ave, ave, ave Maria!
Ave, ave Maria.

Malcolm stopped in his tracks, and I almost collided with him from behind. Human figures blocked the path ahead of us.

The figures didn't resemble the Ellanoyans Malcolm had described, the fair-haired and alabaster-skinned Venuses and Adonises who worshipped pagan gods. These figures had severely stooped shoulders and lumps on their faces. They wore skirts made of hides, sported nose rings, and were hairless as mole rats.

More were behind us; we were surrounded. My musket was at the ready, but there were a dozen of them. Malcolm whispered over his shoulder, "Stay calm."

They advanced cautiously. As they drew near I could smell them. The sour smell of men who never bathed. The rancid stench of the not-quite-dead.

The apparent leader stepped up to Malcolm. Like other mutants we'd encountered, his forehead was steeply slanted. Eyebrows sprouted from sharp ridges. A jaw jutted out hideously. A pair of eyes wandered too far apart, suggesting not so much predator as prey.

Up close I could see little tufts of hair growing on the lumps that distorted his face. His bald skin was the color and texture of animal hide, like that of a shaved dog. And the smell.

He looked Malcolm up and down and said, "You're not Ellanoyan."

We both perked up. He spoke English!

"No," Malcolm said. "And I take it neither are you."

The leader chuckled. The chuckle evolved into a laugh. Soon he was bent over, clutching his gut and convulsing in giggles. He straightened up, lifted his face to the sky, and roared in laughter.

The other mutants took the cue. They howled and shrieked and jumped around possessed. The leader caught his breath and pointed at us, giving his men a signal. They took my musket and Malcolm's ax. They emptied our packs on the ground and rummaged through the contents, grumbling in dissatisfaction. They tied our hands behind our backs.

"If you're not Ellanoyans," the leader asked, "what are you?"

"Kebekians," Malcolm answered. "From the Sea of Atlantis, the great ocean bridging our mutual world with the Pillars of Hercules."

The leader's eyebrows raised. "How interesting. I hope you taste better than Ellanoyans. They give me indigestion."

He laughed again. The other mutants joined him and the woods filled with whoops and cackles.

*

They marched us down the path we had already been traveling, poking and prodding constantly with sticks and arrows, taking turns pushing and kicking. They had a funny way of walking; it was a stiff-legged gait, with knees kept straight and rigid.

Often we fell, and a mutant would yank us back up by the hair. If we didn't rise fast enough others would pounce and kick us in anger.

They made us sing as we walked. Malcolm picked up the Lourdes Hymn where we had left off. After a few vicious kicks from the mutants I joined him.

> *We pray for our mother,*
> *the church upon Earth.*

"Sing!"

> *And bless, dearest lady,*
> *the land of our birth.*

"With gusto! Entertain us!"

> *Ave, ave, ave Maria!*
> *Ave, ave Maria.*

Bruised and sore and hardly able to walk, we arrived at their village. Malcolm bled profusely from the nose. We'd done all we could to stay on our feet because falling infuriated them. The deeper we'd gone into the woods, the crazier the mutants had behaved. They'd licked us on the arms and neck and made slurping noises. "Mmm."

The village was double-palisaded, the space between the two spiked walls filled with dried mud. We were dragged through a massive gate that slammed shut behind us.

Hundreds of two-legged frights poured out of cabins three stories high. They surrounded us, elbowing for position. Men, women, and children. Mothers toting suckling infants. The aged, half bent, eyes wide and glistening. All bald, stooped, and lumpy with cancerous growths. Both men and women wore skirts, and both went topless. Malcolm pointedly averted his eyes.

The mutants shoved us toward a row of wooden posts planted in the ground, facing a platform. Already tied to two of the posts were an elderly man and a young woman.

They weren't mutants! Obviously they were fellow prisoners. They had smooth faces and full heads of hair. Rich dark skin. Radiant complexions.

The man was distinguished looking, aristocratic. I would have guessed he was a government official, perhaps a diplomat. The girl was serene, with head held high, and hair spilling across her shoulders in raven black curls. She wore deerskin pants. A female—wearing pants. Neither prisoner displayed emotion.

Mutants lashed me to the post next to the girl. They lashed Malcolm three posts away, on the other side of the aristocratic gentleman. I turned to the girl and asked, "Who are these monsters?"

"They're Garhogs."

"They're not Ellanoyans."

She closed her eyes and shook her head condescendingly. "No, they're not Ellanoyans."

The Garhogs built a fire while whooping and shrieking. Children loped about stiff-legged, chattering, anticipating a show. Dogs roved the camp with barred teeth and pronounced rib cages. Once in a while a Garhog tossed a scrap and the dogs fought for it, growling and snapping viciously among themselves.

"You don't seem afraid," I said to the girl.

"Garhogs consider showing fear and pain to be a weakness. They'll make you suffer more for the display."

"What inspires them to show mercy?"

She made eye contact for the first time. Her eyes were cornflower blue, a pair of pristine mountain lakes.

"The word mercy is not in their vocabulary." She squinted. "Where are you from?"

"Kebek," I answered. "I'm a coastal. And you?"

"I am Adrienne," she said. "Crown Princess of the Kingdom of Ellanoy."

"What are these … Garhogs … going to do to us?"

"First they're going to torture us. Then they're going to kill us. Then they're going to eat us."

Chapter 16

A pair of Garhogs snatched Adrienne's distinguished companion and dragged him up wooden steps to the top of the platform. The structure was built like a low scaffold, ostensibly a temporary affair, except that it was worn and stained: it had obviously been used before. They stripped the gentleman of all clothing and tied him to the solitary post rising from the platform.

He no longer looked distinguished. A round stomach protruded over scrawny genitals. His arms and legs were flabby, their muscles long since atrophied. His knobby knees shook. A beard and a thick mane of gray hair seemed incongruous in the absence of elegant dress.

He stared straight ahead. His expression communicated nothing. For my own part, I was sick with fear. Remembering Adrienne's warning, I struggled not to show it.

Garhogs took the man's fingers into their mouths and worked them around. At first I couldn't tell what they were doing. When one of them spat something out, I realized in horror they were tearing the gentleman's fingernails out with their teeth, jostling one another for the privilege.

They gnawed at his fingertips. Blood trickled down their chins.

"Offer your pain to God!" Malcolm cried out.

A Garhog raced up to Malcolm and slapped him across the face.

Turning to Adrienne I asked, "Is he your father?"

"My manservant."

"We have to do something." I strained against the ropes binding me to the wooden post.

"He's ready to die. So am I. I suggest you prepare yourself as well."

A Garhog with feathers tied to his hair climbed to the platform and motioned for everyone to be silent. It took a minute for the yelps and howls to die down. He bowed his head, and the congregation did likewise.

"Bless us, oh radiant sun, giver of all life, for these thy gifts, which we are about to receive at our humble table. And may we be ever grateful for thy bounty, thy generosity, and thy mercy."

Then he shrieked at the top of his lungs. Hundreds of Garhogs joined him in an earsplitting benediction.

What may well have been the entire community, women and children as well, took turns climbing onto the scaffold to beat the manservant with sticks and thorn branches, competing with one another to deliver the heaviest blows. His head hung low but he didn't cry out. Except for tightly clenched eyes, his countenance was one of peace.

Garhog children worked under the supervision of their parents. They had lumpy little faces like stunted gargoyles, like Hell's cherubs. Moms and dads showed the youngsters where the man's softest parts were, and how to swing up at them from between his legs, to inflict the most pain.

Soon the manservant was red with blood. Still he didn't react. Using clam shells, the Garhogs sawed off his thumbs and fingers and held them aloft like trophies. They thrust sharpened sticks through the stumps and pushed them all the way up to his elbows. They seemed motivated, even inspired, by his courage.

"Remember the nails of the savior!" Malcolm called out. "You share his pain!"

Garhogs beat Malcolm into silence. One held a knife to his throat and warned him not to speak again.

Meanwhile a fire had been prepared at the foot of the platform. Garhogs gathered about it clutching sticks tipped with copper points. They held the points in the fire until they were hot, then took turns climbing the platform to apply the glowing points to the manservant's exposed skin. They touched his arms, legs, torso, face.

His skin sizzled. The sadly familiar smell of roasting flesh made its way to me. He raised his head to the sky. He made no sound, but his eyes mourned, pleaded. Mucous oozed from his nose and tears spilled from his eyes.

"Adrienne," I said.

"Don't speak."

A pair of Garhog children had been toasting fist-sized pebbles in the fire. They brought them up to the platform, pinched between sticks acting as tongs, and as men held the manservant's head back, by pulling on his hair, the children placed the hot rocks in his eye sockets. The old man's eyeballs hissed and sputtered and vaporized into viscous steam.

Finally he cried out in pain. The gallery of mutants whooped and shrieked in approval.

The manservant went mercifully unconscious. The rocks were removed, revealing shallow blackened caverns where his eyes had been.

They cut him down, carried him off the platform, and dropped him to the ground. Women poured vessels of water over his head to revive him. He lifted his head and turned this way and that, trying to take in his surroundings. Searching for light.

"Get up and sing," a Garhog ordered.

The manservant rose unsteadily to his knees and began an uplifting tune.

The sun gave me life,
praise the sun.
The sun gave me life,
call the sun.

"Be quiet," said another Garhog, then pressed a hot copper point to the manservant's chest. He stopped singing.

"I thought I told you to sing," the first Garhog said, and applied his copper point to the manservant's armpit.

He sang.

Only the sun can give life,
only the sun.
Only the sun can take life,
only the sun.

"I told you to shut up," the second Garhog said. He applied his point to the old man's genitals.

The two mutants returned to the fire, to heat up their sticks, and others took their places. Before long there wasn't a patch of skin on the man's body the size of a penny that wasn't charred. His mouth remained closed, but it quivered in agony.

"We're getting too little entertainment from this one," the feathered Garhog said. "Make him scream."

They hoisted the manservant up to a standing position. A Garhog clutched his testicles in his fist, stretched them down, and sawed them off with the edge of a clam shell.

The old man convulsed but did not cry out. Spittle dribbled down his chin. He sang again, in a weak, croaking voice.

Call the sun, call the sun.
Call the beautiful, radiant sun.

"Make him scream."

The same Garhog who had cut off his testicles now stretched the manservant's penis to its maximum extension and sliced it off at the root.

The old man screamed. The assembled crowd cheered like they were celebrating a sports victory.

The manservant was human toast, blackened all over, hair singed off, bleeding from where his genitals used to be. Bleeding from his raw eye sockets, from his nose. Bleeding from his mouth, where he bit himself repeatedly in response to the pain. Bleeding from the ears. A burnt caricature of a man, drenched in red sauce.

He collapsed to the ground. The congregation went wild with joy, many stomping the earth with their bare feet. The miserable victim, limp and barely conscious, was carried to the fire and dropped unceremoniously into it.

He twitched and writhed and instinctively rolled off the coals. Garhogs pushed him back in. He was unable to resist and was roasted alive. A minute or so later he was still. His ordeal was over.

Malcolm's was about to begin.

Chapter 17

The Levitican priest who taught modesty as a virtue and practiced it every day of his life was stripped of all his clothing.
He tried to cover his nakedness with his hands, but the Garhog
women only laughed at his efforts.

He looked so serene on the scaffold. If I didn't know better
I'd have thought he was even smiling. But I knew better. I knew
him well enough to know he was terrified. He was going to meet
God in the face before the day was over, perhaps within the hour.
Meantime he had to endure unspeakable agony to gain admis-
sion. He'd say the price was worth it.

The Garhogs led a small boy to the platform. He was no older
than five. A pair of men held Malcolm's arm, and another one
grabbed his thumb and pried it clear of his hand. A clam shell
was given to the boy and he was ordered to cut the thumb off.

The boy hesitated.

Men made sawing motions with their hands, nodding sagely
at the boy. Still he hesitated. I couldn't hear what he was saying,
but I could see him shaking his head.

A man I guessed was the boy's father climbed the platform
and spoke to him. He got down on one knee and put his arm
around his son's shoulders. The boy lowered his head. He cried.

The father smacked him on the back of the head.

"Cut him!" he ordered.

The crowd took up the chant. "Cut him! Cut him!"

The boy swiped the clam shell against Malcolm's thumb and barely made a scratch. The father took the boy's hand in his own and guided the shell back and forth across the thumb, applying pressure. Malcolm maintained his composure, although his jaw quivered and his eyes moistened.

"Sing, Kebekian."

Let all mortal flesh keep silence,
and with fear and trembling stand.
Ponder nothing earthly minded...

It took the boy and man together ten minutes to saw through Malcolm's thumb. They wrapped the stump in damp leaves and lashed him to the post. Several Garhogs busied themselves re-building the fire, which the body of the manservant had mostly smothered.

For with blessing in His hand,
Christ our God to Earth descending,
comes our homage to demand.

Now a pair of women took their turn. Kneeling before Malcolm, his exposed manhood dangling in their faces, they used clam shells to make cuts in his thighs. I first thought, incredibly, they were carving their names, as boys do in tree trunks. Blood trickled down Malcolm's legs and pooled at his feet.

It soon became clear what they were doing. They pulled strips of flesh they'd sliced from his thighs and handed them to other women, who set them on the fire to roast. They were eating Malcolm alive.

Garhogs clamored around the fire, emitting low hums, anticipating human *hors d'oeuvres*. The first to sample the course was the feathered leader. He lifted a strip of Malcolm's flesh above his face like a spaghetti noodle and dropped it into his mouth.

"You taste good, priest," he said.

The other Garhogs pressed closer to the fire and jostled one another for a share. Meanwhile the two women on the platform were still harvesting raw meat from Malcolm's legs. Below the waist he was solid red, and where skin was missing he resembled an anatomy diagram we had seen in one of his contraband books.

A Garhog brought him water to drink. Malcolm allowed his mouth to be filled, then spat the water in the man's face.

"I baptize thee," Malcolm said, "in the name of the Father, the Son, and the Holy Spirit."

Water was set to boil. When it was ready it was carried in a vessel to the platform and splashed on Malcolm's face.

"In the name of the father," the man who had been spat on said.

He splashed more water on Malcolm's face.

"And the son."

He splashed Malcolm again.

"And the holy spirit."

Malcolm's face was red from the scalding water. He stood gasping, fighting to catch his breath.

"Sing!"

King of kings, yet born of Mary,
as of old on Earth He stood.

Malcolm's voice was still strong, but now tinged with resignation. They untied him from the post and dragged him off the platform. He fell to the ground, but they pulled him to his feet. His expression told me he knew his time had come.

Lord of lords, in human vesture,
in the body and the blood...

They fastened a collar of glowing hot stones around his neck, the stones encircling him and hanging down to his torso. If he leaned forward, to relieve the burning of stones hanging in front of him, the ones behind rested more heavily on his back. Likewise if he leaned back he suffered more in front. And if he maintained an erect posture he was tormented all around at once. It was the most insidious torture ever conceived.

Poor Malcolm jerked and wiggled in a hideous, macabre dance.

"Stop it!" I screamed.

"Shut up, you, or you'll be next," the feathered Garhog said. Then to Malcolm, "Sing, Kebekian!"

As the light ... of light ... descendeth
from the realms ... of endless day.

Malcolm's dance devolved into desperate convulsions, where every movement caused more pain than it relieved, which in turn led to more convulsions, until he was twitching and writhing in what must have been unspeakable agony.

"Sing!"

Comes the powers of Hell! To vanquish!
as the darkness ... clears away

Malcolm collapsed again. They kicked him, but he didn't respond. The crowd converged on him with firebrands and beat him savagely, sparks flying. Still he didn't move. Disappointed, they left him there, collapsed at the base of the scaffold.

It was Adrienne's turn.

Chapter 18

She was still fully dressed, for the sake of modesty, or anticipating some sport with her, or for some other reason, I didn't know. Her skin was the color of umber and her hair was slate-black. In Kebek such complexion would sentence her to slavery, to a life of grueling labor that would fray her femininity and blanch her appeal.

The leader untied her from the post and eyed her head to toe. She met his gaze calmly. Lumps on the Garhog's face, so close to me now, revealed themselves to be iridescent. The skin covering them was transparent, and some of the lumps oozed pus. They weren't growths after all. They were cysts.

He smiled. His teeth were crooked and filed down to points. "Ready for your go?" he asked.

"The question is," Adrienne answered, "are you ready for yours?"

The Garhog's smile dissolved. In one motion he grabbed her tunic and ripped it off, exposing her breasts. She stood proudly, still with a calm expression, still matching the gaze of the Garhog leader. Other mutants circled and packed in behind him. Men and women both reached to touch Adrienne's bare skin.

The leader swung at them and forced them back. He removed a copper dagger from his belt. To Adrienne he said, "Your time has come."

She cocked an ear. Listened to a far-off sound. In the space of seconds the sky darkened noticeably. A breeze rose in the forest canopy, rattling the leaves.

She looked at the Garhog and smiled. "No," she said, "yours has."

The Garhog leader lifted his free hand to slap her.

His body jolted. He froze with his arm raised. He dropped to his knees, his arm still raised, his eyes fluttering. An arrow protruded from his back.

Adrienne took the dagger from his hand and thrust it into his squat neck, beneath his chin, arcing it upwards, into his brain. He toppled to the ground and landed heavily on his face.

Pandemonium. Arrows whizzed across the compound. Garhogs were loud shriekers individually; in a group they were deafening.

The palisades had been breached. Men in leather armor, packing bows and quills, had climbed to the top from the outside and were firing into the crowd. The compound was in chaos.

Adrienne untied me and we ran to Malcolm, who had barely regained consciousness. I removed the stone necklace and swung it at a passing Garhog, knocking him senseless. Arrows whistled everywhere. We supported Malcolm on either side, with his arms draped over our shoulders, and the three of us ran for cover. We found an empty bark cabin and crouched inside. From outside came the cries of men and women in their death throes. Adrienne was tending to Malcolm, so I left to help with the fight.

The Garhogs were scattering. The attackers looked like normal men; I didn't think they'd mistake me for an enemy. I found a club on the ground and joined them in the attack.

We fought the mutants in hand-to-hand combat through their cabins, across their meeting areas and what looked like a playground, to the rear of their compound. Where they crouched in defensive positions, brandishing clubs and spears. Some tried to escape by scaling the palisades, but we brought them down with slingshots and arrows.

One of the attackers, a tall gaunt man with a flowing red beard, ordered his men to line up. They loaded their bows with arrows. They drew their bowstrings.

"Shoot!" the bearded man ordered.

Garhogs stiffened and crumpled to the ground. Those still on their feet waved their clubs and shrieked in fury.

"Shoot!"

More Garhogs fell. While the attackers were reloading a Garhog female rushed the bearded man with a club. I dashed toward them and placed myself between the two. The woman, who wore only a modest wrap around her hips, had arms and thighs rippling with muscles. She appeared as strong as any man I had seen.

She swung her club at the bearded leader, but hit me instead. I went down. She raised her club again. The bearded man drew a sword. The two fought, sword against club, she blocking the sword, he dodging the club.

Arrows launched at the female warrior. They protruded from her shoulder, abdomen, and thigh. She screamed each time she was hit, but continued fighting. More arrows were fired. She screamed more, this time raising her club to the sky in defiance.

The bearded man saw his opportunity and impaled the woman through her gut.

The club fell from her hand. She grunted and looked at the sword with disdain.

He yanked the sword out and stuck it in her again. And again. Her eyes rolled back into her head and she fell.

Now all the Garhogs were scaling the wooden palisades to escape.

"Shoot! Shoot!"

Mutants fell, but others succeeded in crossing to the outside of the compound. We could already hear escapees howling in the woods beyond, no doubt working themselves up to counterattack.

As the battlefield cleared, and humans got busy sending wounded mutants to the afterlife, the bearded man approached and asked my name.

"René Jordan," I said. "Accompanying me is Father Malcolm Marchand. We come from Kebek on the coast of the eastern ocean."

"I am Berthold," the man said, "King of Ellanoy. How beautiful the sun is, now that you are among us."

Chapter 19

Back in the cabin Adrienne was still tending to Malcolm. She had found a top to replace the one torn from her. I was relieved, since her nudity would put Malcolm off. She applied a salve to his wounds.

"Your friend will recover," she assured me.

Malcolm's eyes fluttered open.

"Did you hear?" I asked. "She says you'll recover."

He licked his lips. "God has been good to me this day."

His thighs were stripped of much of their flesh. His torso had broad ring of skin burned black and oozing blood. "God could have been better to you," I said.

"I'm alive. What more could I ask." His voice was feeble.

"So are we, and we were spared being eaten."

"Well, as I've told you, God has a sense of humor. The question of what's for dinner takes on a whole new meaning." He clenched his eyes and breathed in short gasps. But it was consoling to see that he, too, still had a sense of humor.

"You lie still," I said. "Rest quietly. We're going to take care of you." I looked at Adrienne who nodded her agreement. I took her hand and said, "Thank you for doing this."

"No, thank *you*," she said.

"What do you mean?"

"Thank you for coming to us. When we were tied to the poles and I looked into your eyes, I saw mountain lakes. You're a good person, René Jordan. And a good omen."

*

Malcolm was placed on a stretcher and we marched south through the woods. A pair of men also carried the remains of the manservant, bundled in hides. We needed to get away quickly before the Garhogs counterattacked, possibly with help from other Garhog villages.

After a time we came to a stream inlet where the Ellanoyans had hidden their canoes. The vessels launched, and for the first time in our journey Malcolm and I were passengers rather than horsepower.

Malcolm's head lay in my lap. As the flotilla of canoes lined up and glided downstream, Adrienne pointed ahead and swept her arm to take in the land and water and sky before us.

"Ellanoy," she said.

The way she pronounced the word, you'd have thought she was saying "Paradise." Now finally venturing into the country, after reading so much about it, I found myself unable to disagree.

The landscape was breathtaking in its profusion of life. The river—they called it the Markette—was wide with a sandy bottom. It flowed gently westward, the water transparent, crystal blue, reflecting the sky. Oak, walnut, basswood, and the ubiquitous giant ferns lined the banks. Cedars and pines crowned bold sandstone bluffs.

Numerous bird species made a hullabaloo in the trees. They announced their presence and reproductive availability through chirps and songs that fed a collective commotion, a clambake of chatter. All loud and confident, for this was a peaceful land, one in which birds might fly free. Where nature was undisturbed by the hostile intrusion of man.

The birds criss-crossed the river, looking for tasty things to eat, visiting cousins and in-laws. Some had enormous wingspans and all but blocked the sun. Duck-like birds fed near the banks, oblivious to the humans observing them.

We passed islands wrapped in vines. Deer and wild cows drinking from the river. They only lifted their heads, curious but unafraid, as the flotilla drifted by. Now and then we spotted hills and prairies through breaks in the tree line, rich and fertile pastures, stretching as far as the eye could see.

After two days of tranquil canoeing we arrived at the home village of the Ellanoyans, which they called Bounty Rock.

The rock itself was a sandstone butte, more than 100 feet high, overlooking the river. Palisades enclosed the top of the rock, much like they did the Garhog compound, and I assumed their purpose was to keep the beasts out. Riverside the palisades were almost unnecessary; the precipitous drop was defense enough.

Inside the fortress more than a hundred members of the community greeted us. People rushed the gate to welcome Adrienne and the rescue party. They hailed the king as a conquering hero. Malcolm was delivered via stretcher and placed in a cabin, where his care continued.

The Ellanoyans were strikingly attractive. Their skin and hair color varied from intensely dark to markedly light. All were well proportioned, healthy, with good complexion. When they spoke to me they made eye contact; their eyes were bright and alive.

We were herded into a community shelter where a banquet was in the making. I felt a hundred pair of eyes on me. Individuals kept approaching, telling me how good it was that I should visit them. That the sun's beauty was enhanced by my presence.

Everyone took a seat on the ground and a pipe made the rounds. We each took a ceremonial puff. The pipe, which they referred to as a calumet, was carved from a red stone and polished to a high shine. It had been bored to fit a two-foot-long hollow cane and was festooned with bird feathers.

The king rose and thanked the organizers for the banquet. He spoke glowingly of his daughter Adrienne, seated next to him, and expressed his enormous relief she was safe. The audience ahhed their agreement. He ordered a moment of silence for Adrienne's dead manservant, whom he referred to as a lifelong friend.

He singled me out as a new guest, and mentioned Malcolm as well. Two spirits, he said, who had graced the community with their presence.

"And now if the young visitor wouldn't mind saying a few words."

All eyes were on me. I rose and cleared my throat. I wasn't prepared to give a speech, but obviously impromptu public speaking was customary with this bunch, so I got no pity from the spectators. They stared as I stammered. I thanked them for their hospitality, and especially for snatching Malcolm and me from the jaws of death. I briefly described our mission, our desire to know the Ellanoy people. Our commitment to a friendly and prosperous relationship between our two peoples.

They stared. I said, "Never has the sky been so beautiful, nor the sun so bright, as today, in your company." They waited. I continued. "Never has the tobacco tasted so good." I sat down.

Someone whooped, and soon everyone was whooping and cheering.

The king rose again. He raised his hands to settle the crowd. Then he paused, clearly readying himself to express something profound. He spoke:

"Let's eat."

We feasted on wild cow, various waterfowl, and a garden of vegetables, including corn—but thankfully not sagamité. And fish. Fish, fish, and more fish. For dessert we had wild fruits including grapes, plums, apples, mulberries, and chestnuts, as well as others I was unable to name. At the end of the meal I was so full I could hardly rise. Nevertheless it was time to tour the village.

It consisted of three hundred or so sturdy bark cabins, all enclosed within the palisades. Some permanent structures of wood and stone. A couple of them open, spacey, to serve as meeting places. A school, a playground. Grain silos. Flagstone paths lined with flowers. An open market. People came out of their cabins, even the infirm, the children, and touched me lightly on the arm, saying, "The sun is beautiful."

They led me to a small, ramshackle cabin whose bark walls were in disrepair. It was the white elephant of the neighborhood. Regardless, the entourage grew respectfully quiet upon approaching it.

The king called through the closed doorway, "Jonah." Without waiting for a reply he opened the door and we walked in.

Inside sat an old man in tattered clothing. His head was bald, his eyes were watery and jaundiced, and his face was grizzled from infrequent shaving. There was no order to his cabin; books and papers rested wherever carelessness and gravity had delivered them. A lone painting on the wall depicted a solitary iris.

"So you're the Coastal," he said.

"Yes. My traveling companion and I are searching for a passage to the western ocean."

He smiled, a little condescendingly, I thought. "One never goes on a quest for something tangible, and certainly not geographical. Only spiritual."

"If you say so."

His tired eyes looked me over. I felt transparent under his gaze. He passed a calumet and I drew from it, then passed it to the king. We sat quietly for a while, sharing the pipe among us. Finally Jonah said, "We'll talk again."

The king gestured for me to follow him out. Once outside I joked, "That was enlightening."

"He's a wise man. You'll come to know him better."

"Does he aspire to be king?"

The king laughed. "He wouldn't accept the job if you hung him over the edge of a cliff by his ankles and threatened to let go."

They gave me a cabin to sleep in, where I deposited my meager possessions. Before going to bed I wanted to check in on Malcolm. I found Adrienne supervising a young woman who was changing his dressings.

"How is he?" I asked.

"I'm right here," Malcolm said. "You could ask me personally."

"How is he?" I repeated.

"Recovering," Malcolm said.

"Recovering," Adrienne echoed. "Some of his burns will take weeks to fully heal. Maybe months."

"I'll be up and ministering to the heathens," Malcolm said, "before you can say 'Bless me Father, for I have sinned.'"

Adrienne nodded toward her assistant and said, "I'd like to introduce you to Eva. I must return to my regular duties. Eva will take care of Father Malcolm from now on."

The assistant nodded to me in greeting but didn't make eye contact. She fussed with Malcolm's dressings. She either distrusted me or was shy in my presence. Or both.

"We'll leave the two of you alone now," Adrienne said.

The women left the cabin. As soon as they were gone Malcolm asked, "Have you obtained any information about the western passage?"

"I received some cryptic advice from an old sage, otherwise no, nothing useful."

"This river of theirs, it may lead us there."

"Let's get you healthy again first."

Malcolm tried to rise, but flinched in pain and dropped back into his bedding.

"You see?" I said. "We can't trust a paddle to a bedbug like you."

"Got your eye on the princess, do you?" he asked.

"Who, me?"

"I see the way you look at her."

"Fine, I confess. Bless me Father for I have sinned. And how about that nurse of yours? She's a cutie."

"Oh, please. Go now and sin no more."

Adrienne was waiting for me outside. She said, "I'll take you around tomorrow, if you like, and show you Bounty Rock."

Those eyes. Those mountain lakes.

"I'd like that," I said.

Chapter 20

Adrienne showed up at my cabin the next morning with a young man in tow. He was about thirteen, with a smooth face and long blond hair that poured down his shoulders. She introduced him as her brother Eli.

"Eli will be joining us today," she told me.

Great, I thought, a chaperone.

She suggested we start at the children's compound. Like most of the permanent buildings, these were made of wood and stone. Several were built partially underground to keep the occupants cool in summer. Children played on the grounds outside, some pretending to shoot one another with imaginary weapons, taking turns to whoop triumphantly and to crumple and die. Adrienne said they were on recess, but there would certainly be a class in session, and we would sit in on it.

She led us into one of the buildings and knocked on the door of a room. A teacher admitted us, and Adrienne, Eli, and I sat in the back and observed quietly.

The subject was geometry. The teacher had drawn triangles of various shapes and sizes on a slate blackboard. She asked the children to compute the areas of the triangles by taking one-half the base times the height. Almost all of them raised their hands eagerly each time the teacher posed a question.

She wiped the blackboard clean and drew a right triangle. She asked the students to compute the length of an unknown side.

The boys and girls in the room ranged from about eight to twelve years old. Some of the older children raised their hands after a minute of scribbling on their parchments. The younger children squirmed in their desks and put their pencils down to wait for insight. It was a one-room schoolhouse, no different from the one I had attended as a boy. However, I'd been about fifteen before being introduced to Pythagoras.

"Little is known about the man himself," the teacher lectured. "What we know about him was set down centuries after his death. We know he was a mystic; he believed in the transmigration of souls, that all things are numbers, that people are tuned certain ways, like musical instruments."

She spoke without condemnation. My own teacher had spat such words when she lectured us. Pythagoras once stopped a man beating a dog because he recognized a departed friend's voice in the dog's bark. The philosophy was ludicrous, according to my teacher. All things are numbers, indeed!

The Ellanoy teacher continued. "Pythagoras was one of the first philosophers to believe the sun was the center of the solar system."

Blasphemy! We clearly saw the sun move, and felt the Earth sitting still. Or so my teacher had argued. I asked Malcolm about it, when I was in the seminary. He said don't bother with Pythagoras or any of the others. "Aquinas is the only philosopher you need."

"He agreed with Aristotle," I said, "that man is the center of the cosmos."

"And so he is."

Once outside again, I asked Adrienne what the point of the exercise was.

"They need mathematics," she said as she led us toward the main gate. "They need it for planting crops, for building shelters and palisades, even for designing and launching projectiles against attackers."

"Who attacks?"

"The Garhogs, of course. Once in a while, marauders from distant lands."

"Not China, by any chance."

"No, not China."

"How often do the Garhogs attack?"

She turned to Eli and said, "I'm going to let you answer that one."

Eli said, "As often as they perceive an opportunity."

"And there you have it," Adrienne said. "Geometry is one of the tools we use to limit their opportunities."

"How long is the school day?" I asked. "When do the children go home?"

She stopped walking and looked at me. "They don't. They live in the compound."

"They don't live with their parents?"

She looked confused. "You mean with their mothers? The mothers are busy with their own work. The children are raised communally by trained teachers and caregivers."

"What about the fathers?"

"What about them?"

"Don't they have any say in the matter?"

"How would one know for sure who they were?"

Now it was my turn to be confused. "You know who *your* father is."

"Because he is king."

"Otherwise…"

"Otherwise any man in Bounty Rock could be any child's father. Unless for some odd reason a couple elected to mate exclusively."

Best to leave it at that. We crossed the village to the main gate. On the way we passed Ellanoyans hurrying to destinations, many carrying tools and goods. The activity in the fortress resembled the bustle of a small market town. But these people moved with energy and purpose, in contrast to the citizens of Kebek, who shuffled along, never in any hurry to arrive where they were going.

Some of the Ellanoyans were black as obsidian, some the deep rich brown of old copper. Many had light skin as well, ranging from pale amber and sepia to alabaster. Adrienne's skin glowed with hues characteristic of earth pigments, varying from nearly black to low saturation bronze depending on the light. Her brother Eli had light brown skin and blond hair, and neither looked like their father the king, who had pale skin and red hair.

The people dressed simply and unpretentiously in animal skins. I guessed they wore just enough to keep warm, or to accommodate modesty. They wrapped their feet well, to protect them on stony ground, otherwise the dress code was what Kebekians would call liberal—a bad word in Kebekian society, equivalent to "loose."

Adrienne led Eli and me out the main gate, which guards opened by raising the draw bar and pushing the giant wooden door outwards just enough for us to squeeze through. When the door was closed and latched behind us I felt insecure.

Adrienne sensed my discomfort and said, "Don't worry, we have sentries positioned throughout the country. They'll warn us long before we're in danger."

"Then how did the Garhogs catch you?"

"I was on a diplomatic mission. In effect, I wandered out too far."

"Let's not repeat that mistake today, okay?"

Bounty Rock was a 125-foot-high butte overlooking miles of sandstone bluffs carved by the river. Smaller streams feeding the river had hollowed out some eighteen canyons, most of which, Adrienne told me, had their own waterfalls. Beyond the dense forests lining the river were broad rolling plains planted with crops and vineyards. In one direction I saw a herd of wild cows, grazing peacefully. I estimated their number to be in the hundreds.

"They must be easy to hunt," I said.

"They get skittish when hunters fire arrows at them."

"Skittish?" I looked at Eli.

He said, "They gallop away like anything that doesn't want to become food."

In a different direction I watched as what looked like quail rose in a small cloud from tall grasses. "No shortage of food here," I said.

Eli patted his stomach. "Deer and turkey too. I'll take you out, and we'll come back with more than you can eat in a week."

We followed Adrienne into one of the canyons, stepping across moss-bearded stones to enter a horseshoe rock structure bejeweled with a fifty foot waterfall. It was cool and tranquil at the base of the fall. We spread a blanket on the ground and unpacked a knapsack Eli had lugged along.

Obviously there was no such thing as a quick snack in Ellanoy. Meals were rituals, taken slowly and savored. We dined on turkey, unleavened wheat bread, boiled potatoes in sunflower oil, pickled vegetables, and a wine from the nearby hills. For dessert, apples and raspberries.

At the end of the meal Eli wandered off to do some exploring. I asked Adrienne about the passage to the western ocean.

"What you seek is within you," she said.

"Why do I keep getting enigmatic answers to my question?"

"Very well, there is a great river to the west, even greater than ours. No one has ever followed it to its mouth. We call it the Father of Waters. According to legend it empties into the western ocean. But I have my doubts."

"Why?"

"Something so monumental, so near at hand, would surely be more than legend. Also none of our books indicate the river heads anywhere but south."

"Books?" I said.

She smiled. "I'll arrange an introduction."

"Malcolm is hell bent on finding the Vermillion Sea and dining on Chinese food."

"Tell Malcolm it's more likely one of the numerous mutant colonies out there will make him *their* dinner. He's already had a taste of that, so to speak."

"You tell him. He doesn't listen to me." I hesitated, then asked, "What happened to your mother?"

"Garhogs. They've become more aggressive in recent years." She cut herself off and was silent for a moment. "What about your parents? Do they miss you?"

"My father died when I was a boy. My mother scrapes by. I'm sure she misses me. They locked her up briefly when I escaped."

"A hostage?"

"For lack of a better word. I've been made to understand, however, that she was later released. Even Dystopians have a conscience." I struggled not to stare at Adrienne. "What you said about my eyes," I stuttered, "about mountain lakes…"

"Glacial meltwater. Cornflower blue."

"I came up with the same metaphor when I first gazed into your eyes."

She put her hand on my knee. Her touch coursed through my body. "Then it's an omen," she said. After another awkward silence she added, "Is there something you wanted to say to me, René?"

She was offering herself, clearing a path for me to approach her. She belonged to all the world, and as part of the world, was mine for the taking. She was the most intoxicating woman I'd ever met, and like someone who has stumbled upon a treasure, I didn't know what to do with my hands, let alone what words to utter that wouldn't sound inane.

"No," I said. "Thank you for a delicious meal. We should find Eli and head for home."

*

Back at the compound I checked in on Malcolm. He was weak, shivering in pain, and needed help sitting up. Also he was sweating more than usual.

"Does it hurt badly?" I asked.

He closed his eyes and nodded. "For God I would suffer any amount of pain."

"Yeah, well, I think God's received his fair share for a while, don't you?"

He reached for a cup with his mangled hand, winced, and said, "Just this once, I'm not going to argue with you. How was your outing?"

"Nice."

"With the girl."

"Yes, with the girl. But the tour and meal were pleasant as well."

"As was the girl, no doubt."

"Are you trying to communicate something to me, Father Malcolm?"

He relaxed into his bedding, his face screwed up in pain. "I couldn't help noticing the absence of crosses as we entered Bounty Rock."

He looked at me pointedly. I shrugged. "They're not a religious people."

"Exactly. It's a pagan culture."

"As we expected it would be."

"A godless culture."

"A utopia."

Malcolm stiffened. He raised himself up on one elbow. "Be careful how you define your terms."

"Oh, but no definitions have ever been easier," I said. "Just keep in mind the dystopia we came from."

"That's home you're speaking of."

"By comparison, it's beginning to resemble Hell."

He was silent for a long time. Finally he said, "You are dangerously close to crossing a line. I don't know right off hand which one. Maybe impiety. Maybe heresy. In my weakened and relatively helpless state I'm going to overlook it. But I warn you: don't drift too far from your roots. And keep that strumpet at arm's length."

"Strumpet? Did you say *strumpet*?"

"She's exactly the kind of temptress that will lead you to ruin."

Next to him was a bowl of water and a washcloth. I mopped the sweat from his face. He shivered again, and I realized it wasn't from pain. I said, "I'm going to fetch Eva."

"Let the girl rest."

When I returned with Eva, Malcolm's condition had already grown worse. It was clear he had a fever. Although covered with several layers of hide he was shivering out of control. Eva knelt down beside him and placed her hand on his forehead.

"Bleed me," he begged. "Will you, Eva?"

She shook her head.

"René," he said, "you know how to do it."

"I won't permit barbaric medical procedures," Eva said. There was of course the problem of finding a willing surgeon, and she assured us no Ellanoyan was up to the task.

"You do it." Malcolm was looking at me.

"*Nobody* is going to do it," Eva said.

She also refused to have Malcolm sweated, to purge him of evil toxins. Instead she applied a poultice to his burn wounds, made from the bark of the slippery elm, to which she had added lavender and ground moose hoof. I struggled to understand her reasoning. Moose hoof? Bloodletting and sweating were the only ways to purge the body of bad humors. I had even seen head-aches cured by bloodletting. Naturally you must bleed the head.

We were in no position to argue with Eva. Malcolm settled down and waited quietly as she changed his dressings. She had gentle features that at first glance suggested passivity and subservience. But after you watched her treat a patient, and perform with uncompromising authority, and after you'd peered into her eyes, eyes radiating confidence and intelligence like a fire radiates warmth and security, you settled down, like Malcolm did, and waited quietly as she went about her business.

Malcolm observed her for a few minutes before asking, "Are you a God fearing woman, Eva?"

She frowned, apparently perplexed by the question. "I fear nothing," she said, "except perhaps mediocrity."

"Do you believe in a spiritual power higher than yourself?"

"Of course. I believe in nature. I came from the Earth, I will return to the Earth."

"You came from God. You will return to God."

"Call it what you wish." She worked on a dressing. "It's nature that will heal you."

"Nature is the handmaiden of God."

"As you wish."

Adrienne entered the cabin and asked Malcolm how he was doing.

"Fine," he said. "Instructing your young friend on the mysteries of nature."

"Ah." She turned to Eva. "Can I have a word with you?"

The two women stepped outside. Adrienne smiled at me on the way out.

"Therein lies sin," Malcolm explained after the door flap closed behind them.

"Explain."

"It's illegal to fraternize with dark skinned people. You know that."

"Illegal in Kebek. We're not in Kebek anymore."

"Illegal for Kebekians, no matter where they are."

Technically he was correct. In Kebek the dark skinned people, known as sables, were lower caste. They emptied latrines.

Mating with one could result in a prison sentence. When mixed race offspring were produced they were discreetly whisked off to an unnamed place.

"Malcolm, are you unable to appreciate the allure of these people?

"The result of twelve generations of interbreeding. It is illegal for such people to exist."

"Are they not beautiful?"

"That's not the point."

"Then what is the point?"

"What communion hath light and darkness? 2 Corinthians 6:14."

"Right. The Bible is the point. Okay, Solomon loved many strange women. 1 Kings 11:1. Also, Their visage is blacker than a coal. Lamentations 4:8."

"I should not have taught you so well."

"Father Malcolm, I can't believe that after witnessing all this magic you're still trapped in your old prejudices."

"A bird may love a fish—"

"Yeah, yeah, I've heard it before. By the way, maybe you should be lecturing a mirror."

"What do you mean?" He followed my glance toward the door flap, where the two women had gone. He scoffed. "You can't possibly be speaking of Eva and me. She's a child."

"A child in her twenties, who seems devoted to your care."

"She's a nurse. It's her job. Stop smiling."

"As you wish."

Chapter 21

Rising before dawn became a habit. I wanted to see the sun come up.

A wooden staircase ascended to a walkway rimming the top of the palisades. The only intruders upon my privacy were a couple of yawning sentries, their posture confessing a long night of monotonous duty. They ignored me. They wanted to watch the sunrise too.

"Unanchored" best described my feelings. My childhood home, my mother and sister, were behind me. Ahead was mystery and myth, and probably no small amount of adventure. In contrast my present locale was a paradise in the wilderness, a place where one might choose to stay put.

The thought rattled me at first: to remain at Bounty Rock. To court someone like Adrienne. To eat heartily, to sleep in peace. The more time I spent on the walkway, the more I thought about it, the less the idea unnerved me. Yet I could let go neither of what I'd left behind nor of what Malcolm promised lay ahead.

From the walkway I had the highest possible view of the Markette valley. No trees blocked the horizon or the sky above, which grew more saturated with each passing minute I gazed at them. The sun crept over the horizon, first winking at me, then bringing all its light and might to bear and illuminating the world.

Ellanoyans kicked off their morning bustle as soon as the first glow burnished the sky. Citizens hurried to and fro, always carrying something. Always traveling in a straight line, ferrying their goods with an equally linear purpose. They were the happiest people I'd ever met, and the hardest working. You had to wonder about a correlation between the two.

A breeze rose with the sun. It shifted directions on a whim. From the east, then the west, then the east again. It occurred to me that winds by definition were in motion, always journeying from one place to another, with no permanent home. If they ever stopped moving, they died.

*

After a few days of mending, Malcolm felt strong enough to attend a potlatch. The entire community sat in a circle around a colossal bonfire. I carried Malcolm to the event in my arms, with Eva accompanying closely, refusing to leave his side. Adrienne and Eli joined us. Everyone on mats of rushes.

Adrienne's father Berthold, the king, greeted Malcolm and me personally as he entered the clearing. "How beautiful the sun is, now that you are among us." He took his seat on a platform slightly raised above the assembly.

"How does he know how beautiful the sun is?" I asked Adrienne. "It's nighttime."

She answered, "The sun is no less beautiful when you can't see it."

"Well, you have me there."

Food was passed around on rectangular wooden platters. Wild cow, thick grilled steaks. Pheasant and quail. Catfish, walleye, bass. Mounds of vegetables: celery, potatoes, broccoli. Carrots as long as my hand and thick as a cabin pole—Gideon should be here, I thought. Everything drenched in butter. And of course corn on the cob. Red and white wine in squat earthen jugs.

Malcolm's spirits picked up as he ate. He tasted the wine critically and said it would serve well for mass.

"Does it qualify as sacramental wine?" I asked. "Pagans made it, you know."

He took another sip and swished it around in his mouth.

"I'll say a blessing over it," he mused. "You can fix pretty much any deficiency with a blessing." He lifted his cup. "Fill 'er up!"

The dance, we were told, was in our honor. First the singers lined up. They were teenage boys and girls. They lifted their seraphic voices in slow, harmonized chords that sounded like God's own choir. No words, just the sound of human voices. Like wind instruments. The notes rising and falling, and rising each time higher again. Until I thought the song would move the clouds with its grace.

The singers finished, ran off the field, and the drums commenced a beat. Dancers took to the field and arrayed themselves in rows. A lead dancer holding a calumet assumed a position in front of the rest.

It was the largest calumet I had seen to date. The stone bowl was at least a foot long. Bird feathers hung from the bowl and stem like a curtain.

The dancers moved rhythmically to the drums, bending low, stretching back up, raising their arms to the sky. Bending low again. The lead dancer drew smoke from the pipe and blew it out toward the audience. Working his way around, drawing and blowing. Spreading smoke like incense in a religious ceremony.

The Ellanoyans closed their eyes, drew deep breaths, and swayed from side to side in a state of bliss. To my left Adrienne and Eli seemed lost in rapture. To my right, Malcolm sat rigidly on his mat, staring ahead without emotion. Eva watched him with concern.

The second part of the dance consisted of a mock battle between a Garhog and the calumet dancer. A large man had made himself up to resemble a mutant of the north. His face was distorted and lumpy, his cheekbones protruded exaggeratedly, much more so than in a genuine Garhog's face. His nose was the bulbous nose of a clown, and his jaw jutted out ridiculously far. A caricature of a Garhog. But unsettling nonetheless.

He stumbled about, acting dumb and goofy, earning laughter from the audience. The calumet dancer "attacked" the Garhog with his pipe, thrusting it in the mutant's face. The dance proceeded like a story with the accompanying dancers picking up the cadence, playing the roles of Ellanoy and Garhog warriors.

The Garhog recoiled in dread from the calumet, as an evil spirit would from a crucifix, or the Devil from a dash of holy water.

The enemy was thus vanquished. The audience clapped their approval.

In the final part of the dance the audience rose as one and moved in a circle around the bonfire. I remained with Malcolm, sitting on the ground, watching.

Singing a song without words again, one that started low and rose ever higher, the Ellanoyans tapped the earth twice with one foot, resting their weight on it after the second tap. They took a small step forward with the other foot, tapping the earth twice again with that one. The drums alternated between hard and soft beats like a pounding heart.

The pace picked up. People raised their arms to the sky. Stomped the earth with their feet. Turned and twisted in rhapsody.

Malcolm fidgeted uneasily. I asked him how he was doing.

"Take me home," he said.

We maneuvered through dancers writhing in a trance. Eva followed close behind. When we arrived at the cabin I excused Eva and settled Malcolm in for the night. He fell asleep straight away—we shouldn't have subjected him to that much stress—but I stayed up and listened to the muffled noises coming from the potlatch.

Adrienne poked her head in the cabin and asked me to join her outside.

"You left early," she said.

"Malcolm was tired."

"You missed the storytelling."

"I'll catch it next time."

"Will you dance with me next time, too?"

"I don't recall hearing any waltz music, but sure, I'll whisk you into my arms and we'll cut a rug."

We stood in awkward silence for a moment. The moon had risen. It painted her skin with pale yellow light. The dark umber tones and ochre highlights made her seem unreal, an artist's rendition of the ideal, a gilded testament to her loveliness.

She asked, "What are your plans tomorrow? Will I see you?"

"The king has invited Malcolm and me to visit the jail."

"The jail?" She laughed.

"Malcolm likes administering to the infirm and the incarcerated. As far as he can tell, he's the only sick person in Ellanoy."

"If he waits long enough we'll be able to produce another one for him. A Criminal, on the other hand—that might be a little harder to come by."

"What do you mean?"

"You'll see tomorrow."

As I turned to reenter the cabin, Adrienne grabbed my sleeve, spun me back around, raised herself on her toes, and kissed me.

"What else have I missed tonight," I asked, "besides a waltz?"

She kissed me again. Pressing against me, her mouth open slightly, her tongue searching. My hands on the small of her back. Her breasts crushed against my chest.

We went away together. To a place uncluttered by the mundane, the profane. A place populated only by her and me, a few of the gentler stars, a patch of ground to prevent freefall, and once in a while a cricket. No other person. Nothing to spoil the sensation of being alone together.

"Good night," she said. "Have a great day visiting the jail tomorrow."

I breathed slowly and deeply as I watched her disappear into the darkness.

Chapter 22

King Berthold arrived at Malcolm's cabin shortly after dawn. Fortunately Malcolm and I were both early risers, a habit acquired during the long canoe trek. I had risen extra early in my own cabin and enjoyed the rare luxury of a warm bath.

Berthold led us on a short walk across the compound. He stopped near an iron grate in the ground.

"Bounty Rock has only one law," he said, "that no person should do harm to another. Guilt or innocence is decided by a vote of the people."

"Are there no lawyers?" Malcolm asked. "No judges?"

"I am the only judge, and the community comprises a jury."

"How did you become king?"

"I inherited the title. My father was king. And I could lose it too, if I did a bad job."

"How would you be deposed?"

"Simple. No one would listen to me anymore."

"What if you needed to do something unpopular?" I asked. "Like raise taxes. Wouldn't that dampen their enthusiasm for you?"

Berthold looked at me blankly. "Quite a bit, I should say, since the tax rate is presently zero."

"So," Malcolm said, looking around, "where's the jail?"

"You're standing on it."

We glanced down at the iron grating near our feet. Upon closer inspection it turned out there was a room beneath it, about the size one would expect a jail cell to be. I had thought the grating was for drainage.

"You have no prisoners," Malcolm observed.

"Not at the moment."

"When did you last have one?"

The king thought about it. "Four years ago?"

"And what was his crime?"

"As I recall he stole something. That's right, he stole some arrows from someone, I don't remember who, or how many."

"How long was his jail sentence?"

"A day."

"Only one day? Doesn't amount to much punishment."

"It was long enough. A day is all it takes to prepare an execution."

After we had taken leave of the king, Malcolm said, "You still think this is a utopia? Always look beneath the surface. If it sounds too good to be true, it is."

*

After first seeing Malcolm back to his bed, where Eva, waiting anxiously, fussed over him and shooed me out, I stopped by Adrienne's cabin.

"I was hoping you'd come," Adrienne said. "Follow me, there's something I want to show you." She took me to a round building with a conical roof. It looked like a low grain silo. Inside were scrolls, thousands of scrolls.

"Our library," she said proudly.

The scrolls were stacked haphazardly in an elaborate grid of square shelves lining the inner walls of the conical structure. I removed one of them, unrolled it, and read of a battle that took place decades before.

"Flowery language," I noted. "But gorgeous."

"Yes, some of our historians have been, shall we say, ebullient."

There was art in the collection as well. Some of it framed on the walls, most stored flat in cabinet drawers. Watercolors on parchment, painted with natural pigments: ochres, umbers, siennas. Red from cinnabar. An occasional dab of blue, probably from ground lapis. The subjects were landscapes depicting the allure of Ellanoy. Dense forests, endless prairies, majestic skies. Portraits too, of handsome men and angelic women. Figure studies, exquisite, statuesque.

In one section was a modest collection of bound volumes from olden times. I hesitated before reaching for them; in Kebek they were outlawed, considered seditious, and despite my time spent in Malcolm's library I still felt dread and foreboding when in their presence.

"We find them occasionally," Adrienne said. "Abandoned in deteriorated houses, buried in time capsules. Sometimes visitors drop them off. Nobody reads them."

"Why not?"

"Nobody wants to risk being adulterated by their contents."

"Nobody?"

"Well, Jonah reads them. Few others."

We went outside and once again I marveled at the conical building. I asked who built it.

"Everyone built it. The entire community participates in erecting all buildings. Each citizen has a hand in creating each other's home. We make a party of it, turn a job into a game, work into play."

She turned to lead me away but I remained standing.

"Why aren't you married? I asked. It was something I needed to know, and there was no better time to bring it up. No way other than bluntly to ask it.

She turned back around and answered with a wink, "Maybe I'm not done sowing my wild oats."

"Seriously."

"Seriously? Not many Ellanoyans get married. Most prefer open relationships, the freedom to enjoy sex with anyone of their choosing."

She waited for my response. I blushed and looked down at my feet.

"However. Because I'm the king's eldest child, and only daughter, I'm expected to get married and bear heirs to the throne. The heirs must be affirmed, the bloodline must be unambiguous."

She watched me squirming and asked, "Are you okay talking about this?"

"Yes, or rather no. I mean, okay, yes. I guess."

"Until I get married I can enjoy relations with anyone I wish."

She was standing directly in front of me, her face inches away from mine. I was staring at my feet, trying not to appear as agitated as I felt. She lifted my chin with one finger and looked into my eyes.

"Anyone," she said. She held my tortured gaze. "All he need do is ask."

A pair of women walking by rescued me from my dizzy spell. They held hands and greeted us in the traditional Ellanoy manner, noting how beautiful the sun was. Adrienne introduced them to me as Ella and Rachel. When they were gone Adrienne said they, unlike most people, had elected to get married.

"They're very attractive," I said. "Their husbands will be lucky men."

She laughed. "No, I meant they're getting married to each other."

"But…" I thought of Leviticus, but scripture wouldn't mean anything to Adrienne. I thought of what Father Malcolm would say, were he present.

"But what?" Adrienne asked.

"But … but where I come from it's against the law for a man to lie with a man or a woman with a woman."

"Oh. Why?"

"It's considered an abomination."

"I see. Why?"

How to explain to an outsider that an admonition injected into a book thousands of years ago by ignorant and suspicious men resulted in a law today that, if disobeyed, would result in burning at the stake.

"It violates our beliefs," I stammered.

"Oh. Not ours."

On our way back we passed an old woman, hunched over, stumbling along, clutching her abdomen. Accompanying her was a young man, not older than twenty. She held his arm and together they took incremental steps toward the gate.

"Is she okay?" I asked Adrienne. "Shouldn't she be seeing a doctor?"

"It's her time," Adrienne said.

"What do you mean, it's her time?"

"I mean she's dying. We knew this was coming. I didn't know it would be today. That's her grandson with her. He's helping her to the woods."

"To the woods. To die."

"Yes. Where would you have her die?"

"I don't know. Someplace comfortable? Her bed, say."

"She'll be comfortable. She'll be home."

"Will there be a funeral?"

"The grandson will let us know when she's gone. The villagers will follow him to the place where it happened." She scanned my face. "It's a beautiful thing, René. A spiritual ceremony, an elegant way to return home."

"You make it sound like dying is a happy affair."

"Isn't it?"

"No, the end of life is a tragic affair."

"You think death is tragic, even though it's a necessary part of life. Every bit as necessary as birth. It's a return to the Earth. The ceremony is poignant and peaceful. We plant a tree above the grave so the deceased may live on. Relatives visit the tree for years, even generations. The tree may produce other trees. Grafts are made. The deceased lives forever."

She had a point. I thought about it in my cabin, long into the night. Why not mourn birth and celebrate death? After all, given what we must suffer in life, maybe we've got the funeral and the christening party mixed up.

Late in the night I woke to the same cries of pain I'd heard during the journey to Bounty Rock. These cries came from far away, from beyond the Palisades. They sounded like the same voice as before. But would someone—something—have followed us? The howls rose in volume, interrupted by spasms of bottomless weeping. They expressed abject misery, wretched agony. Something indescribably horrible had happened to their author, something only inarticulate wails could convey.

I covered my ears. "Utopia," I whispered into the darkness of my cabin. The wails turned into shrieks, and I buried my head under the hides. "Utopia. Utopia."

Chapter 23

Malcolm didn't feel up to leaving his cabin the next evening so Eva and I walked to dinner together, she only to collect food for her charge. There was something different about her, and it took me a few minutes to figure it out. Her style of dress had changed; she was covering more of herself than before, a practice no doubt intended to appease Malcolm. And her hair was tied back. But it was more than that. She was distracted in a way only someone with something constantly on her mind would be.

Eva was in love. I couldn't help smiling to myself. She was a pretty girl, Malcolm was not immune to pretty girls, and I was curious how this relationship would evolve. At any rate, Malcolm's cabin was the last place I intended to intrude upon that evening.

Eva hurried back to the cabin with a heaping platter of food and a jug of wine.

Dinner was family style. Platters were passed around, and we took what we wanted. I had little appetite. It was a hot muggy night. I drank water copiously.

Adrienne was present, but sitting on the other side of the circle. We made eye contact briefly, nothing more. She spent a disconcerting amount of time talking to another man, a ruggedly handsome, bare-chested fellow who not only made a considerable dent in the food supplies but gobbled up her attention as well. He struck me as the kind of man you'd want on your team if you were cutting down a redwood and you needed someone to drag it home. A lumberjack. Not the kind of person with whom you'd debate the finer points of the Ontological Argument. He laughed generously at Adrienne's remarks, his perfect white teeth gleaming in the firelight.

Without making eye contact with her again, or offering a farewell to anyone, I returned to my cabin where I drank more water. I'd never been so thirsty. It must have been the heat. I left the cabin flap open for circulation and tried to sleep.

Chatter drifted in from the compound. Late revelers socializing after dinner, after dessert, after the older guests had gotten a snoot full and retired to bed. Bursts of laughter. I gave up trying to sleep, got dressed again, and went to join them.

They welcomed me, offered me wine, and resumed their chatter. I couldn't follow the humor. It was about the relative value of crystals, about trading flawed stones for clean ones, substituting quartz for diamond, peridot for emerald. And the stupidity of Garhogs. Belittle your enemy and you fear him less. I kept to myself. A woman with deep set eyes tried to make conversation, but I merely grunted affirmative responses and she gave up.

"Then there was the time Ol' Jaeckle swindled that visitor from the Dirt Scratchers, what was his name?"

"McClure."

"Right, McClure. Dirt Scratchers only have a last name. McClure took three garnets, thinking they were rubies, and Jaeckle walked away with a cartload of beaver pelts, the good stuff, from way up north."

"A high grade garnet is hard to distinguish from a mediocre ruby."

"So tell that to McClure. If you aren't sure of what you're getting, don't get it."

"Even funnier is when Jaeckle himself got swindled. Bought some colorful feathers from a traveler who claimed they were plucked from tropical birds. Tied them to his pipe. First time in the rain, the colors washed off. Turned out they were just common dove feathers."

"Like I said, let the buyer beware."

"Too bad about Ol' Jaeckle. Wandered out one day beyond the sentries, looking for colorful stones."

"The Garhogs probably traded him. He was too old to eat."

"Stringy meat."

"What do you suppose a Garhog would trade him for?"

"Certainly not soap and toothpaste."

My wine glass was empty. I excused myself. As I walked away I noted the silence in my wake and sensed people shrugging and glancing at one another. I stopped by Jonah's cabin and called through the heavy animal hide door flap. He answered "Yes" and I stepped inside.

Jonah was brewing tea. He filled two cups and acted like he'd been expecting me. He said, "So, have you discovered the meaning of life yet?"

"You should be living on a mountaintop. In a cave."

He nodded. "You're no doubt right. But—he gestured at his modest surroundings—this will have to suffice."

We drank tea. He said, "Your timing is good. I'm expecting interesting company."

"Interesting?"

"You'll see. How is your Father Marchand?"

"Father Marchand is healing. Eva is providing good care."

"I'm sure she is."

We sipped tea in silence. Jonah stared at me. After a minute I said, "I should probably go. Check up on Malcolm."

"Sit. Wait. Are you interested in working?"

"You mean a job?"

"Yes, I mean a job. You've visited the library."

"I have."

"You no doubt observed it's lacking a librarian."

"I observed a certain clutter, but I couldn't say whether it resulted from intent or neglect."

"Trust me, it's neglect. We need a librarian."

"To put the collection in order? I'm not familiar enough with it."

"To do whatever librarians do. Well?"

The idea appealed to me immediately. The library had intrigued me during my visit with Adrienne and the offer of a job to examine and sort its holdings didn't require lengthy consideration.

"Um, sure," I said.

"Good. You can start by returning the book I borrowed." He handed me a worn hardcover, clearly one from olden times. The title was *Secular Humanism: Who Needs God?* I tucked it into my bag. God help us all if Malcolm ever saw such a thing.

"I can tell the volume makes you uneasy," Jonah said.

"The very idea is blasphemous. I'm afraid to look inside."

"This God person of yours, he's important to you, is he?"

Jonah was playing with me, but I enjoyed the game too, so I bit. "Yes, critical."

"Where is he, if I may ask?"

"Everywhere. Or so we're taught."

"Ah, already a crack in the armor. Do you see him?"

"No."

"Hear him? Feel him? Sense him in any way?"

Jonah had wasted no time locating the sensitive and tender part of me that struggled hardest in the ecclesiastical world. He leaned back on one elbow. He found a straw on the ground and placed the end of it between his teeth.

"No," I answered.

"Then—you must have known this would follow—how do you know he exists?"

That put me on more comfortable ground. I only had to turn to Aquinas. "Everything has a cause," I said. "Everything changes, and each change—each movement—has a cause. Since the cause-and-effect sequence can't go back infinitely in time, there must have been a first cause, an Unmoved Mover. We call it God."

"How do you know cause-and-effect can't extend infinitely far back in the past?"

"It's an absurd idea."

"Any more absurd than believing in an unmoved mover who existed infinitely far back in the past?"

"It's a premise you either accept or reject."

"Just so. And the premise that everything has a cause: this you both accept and reject, because you posit the first cause does *not* have a cause, the first mover *isn't* moved."

"If Malcolm were here he could explain it better. Everything has to come from something."

"I'll give you that," Jonah said.

A young lady opened the cabin flap and entered unannounced, saving me from ineffectively defending Aquinas's other proofs. She had jet-black hair that hung down to her hips. Jonah introduced her as Olive.

"A relative of yours?" I ventured.

"No, no. My entertainment. Sit back and enjoy."

Olive danced to the sweet notes of her own angelic voice. In Kebek boys and girls were only allowed to perform unprovocative moves while dancing, and were required to hold each other at arm's length. Olive, by contrast, twisted her hips and swayed in a way that inspired a stirring in my loins. If she'd ever kept a man at arm's length it was because he was too far away to reach. And this, after all the talk of God. Could any two subjects be more asymmetric?

"You like?" Jonah asked.

"She knows her trade," I gulped. "How old is she?"

"I don't know. How old are you, Olive?"

"I turn nineteen next month," she said. She positioned herself in front of me and smiled, her eyes crinkling in silent laughter. I had heard of belly dancing and other sinful behavior but had never seen the female body move in such a manner. No wonder it was illegal.

"Care to join us?" Jonah asked.

"Join you?"

He patted the bedding materials next to him.

"Oh," I said. "Thank you, no. I was just—I really should leave."

Before I could escape, Olive held out her hand and said, "One crystal, please. A fine one would be most appreciated."

"A crystal?"

"For the dance."

Making a show of patting my empty pockets, I said, "I'm afraid I don't have any crystals."

"But he has a job," Jonah said. "You're looking at our new librarian."

"Okay. You can pay me next time."

Jonah escorted me out. He said, "About the mountaintop, René, about the cave."

"Yes?"

"The wisdom revealed to you when you climb there is wisdom you brought along, wisdom you carried with you throughout your quest for it."

*

Images of God flickering in and out of existence. Superimposed on moving pictures of a raven haired maiden doing naughty things with her hips. Arousing me more than I was accustomed to being aroused. The hot, muggy air only exacerbating the problem. I knew where I had to go, but I didn't know what the reception would be when I got there.

All was quiet outside Adrienne's cabin. The revelers had retired for the night and the stars overhead shone down on a sleepy village. I knocked. I heard the words, "Come in."

She was alone, sitting on the ground, wearing a poncho that reached past her knees. Which I found odd since the night was so warm.

"I hoped you would come," she said.

"You told me I only had to ask."

"That's right."

"I'm asking."

She stood up. The poncho slipped from her shoulders. She wore nothing underneath.

"Adrienne…"

"Shh." She stepped into my arms. The look in her eyes was one I hadn't seen before. Pleading. She had always come across as fiercely independent. Yet as she pressed herself against me I felt nothing but tenderness and vulnerability. She lay her head on my shoulder and allowed herself to go nearly limp.

The sensation of her touch was reminiscent of accidental contact I'd had with girls at school, when one's elbow bumped against mine or a knee hesitated longer than necessary in a chance graze. Adrienne's arms were bare, and there was nothing accidental about their apprehensive, searching embrace.

She kissed me. The softness, the downy lushness. The incredible sensation of both cool and hot. Her lips parting.

It's not about the stars, like some say. It's about the empty space between them. A universe filled with nothing but you and her. A cosmic purpose so obvious against the backdrop of the vacuum of space, the chasm between chunks of matter, a void through which paltry morsels of energy pass, the occasional speck of dust, and glints illuminating the fragile and tragic meaning of human existence.

"You know what to do," she said.

Charcoal hair splayed across the pillow, like rays of darkness framing her face. Eyes open, vitreous, taking everything in. Ebony-copper-rainbow skin luminous in the candlelight.

The question of universals was thus answered. The circularity of a pair of otherwise dissimilar objects—a merry-go-round and a smoke ring, a beach pebble and a rainbow—was one and the same, a characteristic with its own distinct existence, independent of its mundane earthbound manifestations. Goodness was always present, if often invisible. Love was the deceptively self-evident quality of two halves requiring wholeness to be complete. Aristophanes and the repatriation of souls. My manhood and her womanhood reuniting after an epoch of estrangement, a seemingly interminable sequence of lifetimes filled with longing.

The emptiness of space was merely the fabric connecting the rest, life on Earth a glorious climax to the incidence of raw matter and energy, the sexual experience between two life forms a culmination of their lives, their purpose for living.

And then she was Adrienne again, collapsed on top of me, exhausted.

And then the candlelight flickered again, casting shadows of two people, joined but distinct, on the wooden wall of the cabin.

And then sleep.

Chapter 24

Malcolm recovered mostly from his injuries. He felt useless as a "semiprofessional medical patient," as he put it, so he went to work in the gardens, tending vegetables, despite feeling too weak at times. An hour a day at first. It grew to four hours and to the point where they had to urge him out of the maze of tomato stalks and bean teepees as dusk fell. I wasn't surprised. At home he would have spent all his time nurturing "the bounty of the dirt" if he didn't have to teach in the seminary or conduct mass. He said it made him feel closer to God.

There were always public feasts and we usually attended them together, usually with Adrienne and Eva. It was like double dating, although the comparison would have horrified Malcolm. When there wasn't a public feast there was almost always a private one, a meal served by an individual household, one anybody could attend. Sometimes the private feasts were as populated as the public ones. The food raised and caught by the Ellanoyans was communal, so no hoarding, other than for winter stores, impeded what was already a natural tendency to generosity.

Malcolm sat next to me with Adrienne on my left and Eva on his right. "Every day a holiday," he liked to say, "every meal a banquet." But he was talking about God's good graces rather than pagan epicureanism, the latter of which, in its own way, was manna from Heaven.

The meals concluded with dancing, and once I overcame the discomfort of Malcolm's stern glare, I joined in. At night we slept the sleep of carefree children.

My career began at the library. I was unsure what my duties were, so I asked Jonah. He said he didn't know either. I asked what the previous librarian had done and he answered that I was the first librarian in the history of Bounty Rock, and as far as he knew, in all of Ellanoy.

"You're the beginning of a tradition," he said. "You might want to avoid mucking it up."

It took only a few minutes of orienting myself to discover the problem wasn't one of reorganization. The library had no organization. Books, parchments, maps, even scrolls were jammed wherever they would fit. I decided my job was to sort. Also to attain some mastery of the holdings, ostensibly so I could better serve patrons. But the real reason was that I hungered for the knowledge the library contained.

On the last morning of my first week a pouch appeared on my desk. Upon opening it, out spilled a handful of gleaming crystals. Some transparent, some various shades of violet. One an exquisite ultramarine blue. I'd been paid.

Adrienne and I attended the wedding of Ella and Rachel, as did the rest of the village. Malcolm refused, electing instead to sit in his cabin and sulk. "I will not sanction a heathen ritual," he said.

The heathen ritual was the most charming I'd ever witnessed. The two women wore white deerskin gowns, flowers in their hair, and beaded necklaces that fell to incremental lengths on their torsos. The beads were multi-colored crystals.

A pair of community elders, including Jonah, "gave them away" by escorting them to the center of a nine foot circle of low monoliths, where in the presence of the king they exchanged vows of love and loyalty and a commitment to total responsibility.

Adrienne explained the latter to me. There were no fifty-fifty marriages in Ellanoy. Each party in a formal relationship committed to one hundred percent of the responsibility for the other's happiness. No room for excuses. No comparison of effort. No tit-for-tat. You have one job, and you vow to do it.

Afterwards we congratulated the brides. They each said to me, "How beautiful the sun is, thanks to your presence. I'm so grateful you came."

The two women disappeared, presumably to consummate the marriage. The villagers remained. Adrienne told me a feast was being prepared, but first we had to pay our respects to a tree.

"A tree?"

"Do you remember the old woman you saw being helped by her grandson to the woods to die?"

"Yes." She'd been in pain, and I'd thought she should see a doctor.

"A tree has been planted above her grave. We're going to introduce ourselves."

"You're saying the old woman has reincarnated into a tree."

"As she decays in the soil, and as the tree grows, and she feeds it, what was her becomes the tree."

"But not her identity. Not her consciousness."

Adrienne smiled. "When someone you know well is buried in such a manner, and you recognize the person's traits in the trunk and branches, you'll understand."

The village marched en masse to the site, where in a small clearing a maple sapling poked tentatively out of the ground.

"Why a maple?" I asked.

"It was her choice," Adrienne answered. "You can choose any tree you like, any tree you most identify with."

"I'd choose a giant redwood and look down on you pip-squeaks for a thousand years."

"Shh. My father is about to speak."

King Berthold stood over the sapling and delivered a eulogy. "I knew Ruth as a young woman," he began, "when I was a little boy. Now I have the opportunity to watch her mature and age again."

*

An idyllic summer scrolled by. I spent my days in the library and my nights in Adrienne's arms. We took long walks in the woods, often silently listening to the birds. She knew them all by their songs. We visited villagers in their cabins and exchanged food and gossip. We visited Jonah too, who always had a morsel of wisdom to impart.

"Nothing ever 'happens' to anyone," he once said. "Your actions are your own choosing. Often, however, the consequences of your choices are unpredictable."

One day as we crossed the compound on our way home I remembered a debt I owed. I told Adrienne I had to pay Olive a crystal for a dance she had performed.

She raised her eyebrows.

"No no," I said, "it wasn't for anything like that."

After we'd left Olive's cabin Adrienne said, "I believe you when you say it wasn't for 'that.' 'That' would have cost more than one crystal."

"And how do you know what she charges?" I asked playfully.

"Everyone knows what she charges."

"And her competitors? Do they charge the same?"

"What competitors? She's the only prostitute in Bounty Rock."

"Just her?"

"What would we need another one for?"

"You have me there. She must be busy."

"You might not think so if you knew how much she charges."

Before we parted I asked Adrienne about the Howlers, the cries I'd been hearing in the night, both at Bounty Rock and during our journey. She told me they were called the Sad Ones, and when I asked who they were, she said they were whoever I needed them to be.

Why, I wondered, were Ellanoyans always so cryptic?

She took my hand and explained: the Ellanoyans didn't know who or what they were. No one had ever laid eyes on them. No one had ever even gotten near them. They could only be heard. But everyone seemed to hear something different. Some heard pain, some sorrow. Some even heard hope. It was believed the Sad Ones were trying to communicate something, and it was up to each person to decide what.

"What do you hear?" I asked.

She hesitated, squeezing my hand. "I hear the voice of everyone who has ever lived and not been heard. I listen so they may find peace."

When I had nothing better to do I helped Malcolm in the gardens. We worked side by side uprooting weeds. One morning he was uncharacteristically silent. After an hour of such negative therapy I said:

"Go on, get it off your chest."

"Get what off my chest?"

"You know. My relationship with the king's daughter."

"The strumpet."

"Her name is Adrienne."

"If you're already aware of my disapproval, and you continue your behavior nonetheless, what good would it do for me to lecture you?"

"I think there's a bigger picture."

"Draw it for me, please."

"First, our self-imposed diplomatic mission. Strong bonds with these people are healthy and will serve us in the long run."

"Sexual intercourse being the strongest bond of all." He tossed some weeds into the barrow and planted his spade in the soil. "How did I know this was coming? Of course if the girl were ugly, if she had buck teeth and leprosy, you'd say we need to keep our distance. That diplomacy is all about formality and respect."

"Second—"

"You'd rewrite the manual and make humping the king's offspring a breach of protocol."

"Second, the morals of Bounty Rock are superior to those of Kebek. The people are happier and healthier. The king knows more than the bishop."

"The king should pay better attention to the Bible. Fornicating is a sin. Hebrews 13:4, 'Marriage is honorable in all, and the bed undefiled, but whoremongers and adulterers God will judge.' There are a couple of dozen other references in scripture, if you need more. The free sex practiced in this modern-day Gomorrah is an affront to God."

"And yet Deuteronomy 13:15 tells you what to do when you encounter a modern-day Gomorrah: 'Thou shalt surely smite the inhabitants of that city with the edge of the sword, destroying it utterly.' Aren't you cherry-picking the Bible, Father Marchand?"

"No, I am not. There are other passages—"

"Could it be that you'd go so far as to defy God and spare Bounty Rock merely to protect one of its young, attractive citizens?"

"You are out of line, Master Jordan. I suggest you concentrate on the self-imposed mission you spoke of, rather than Strumpet's britches. The Blessed Virgin Immaculate is watching over our mission. I can feel it. You could feel it too, if you opened yourself up to her. She led us safely here, she'll lead us safely to the western passage and the Vermillion Sea."

He was right. I was out of line. Although I had doubts about the existence of Ellanoy, and it turned out to be real, I had no faith at all we'd find a mythical ocean, a western route to China, or a pot of gold at the end of Malcom's rainbow.

＊

As community librarian I had an opportunity to fill all the time I wished unapologetically reading. I rummaged and skimmed until I found everything the library had to say about Asia and the Vermillion Sea.

Including an old atlas, hiding at the bottom of a stack of other dusty books. I poured over its pages in wonder. Such color, such vivid depictions of geography, of place. Such fine linework and typography.

One two-page spread illustrated North America. The places names were archaic: Quebec, Detroit, Chicago. I traced the Markette River—the Illinois River—to where it emptied into the

Father of Waters, and the latter as it flowed south—not west. The Vermillion Sea, or "Pacific Ocean," was a thousand miles away.

And the journey, if anyone were foolish enough to embark upon it, was brimming with danger. Jonah told me various cannibal species roamed the vast tracts of forest and prairie between Ellanoy communities. Farther west, beyond those communities, were horrors unimaginable. A canoe, he asserted, was a flimsy substitute for palisades.

"What if the atlas is wrong?" I asked Jonah.

He shrugged. "What if the legend is wrong? What if China no longer exists, or never did? When you embark on a journey you accept the destination handed to you."

The library contained scrolls telling the story of the holocaust centuries before, the war that obliterated civilization. I had only been vaguely aware of a major conflict, one described in foggy terms in my school readers. The result of the conflict was a victory of good over evil, of the Leviticans over the infidels and the Great Unwashed. Posters back home illustrated the battles: tall, handsome white men with long golden hair, wielding gleaming swords, smiting the cowering heathens, the darkies, and other trash.

The Ellanoy library told a different story. About bombs of unspeakable destructive power. About entire cities laid to waste in seconds. About mass starvation and desperate, bloody skirmishes for limited resources.

Survivors banded together to protect themselves against swelling confederacies of mutants. They sought answers, first and foremost to the question, How did this happen? According to one Ellanoy writer, some countries had decided they could dictate how other countries behaved. And at the root of it all had been organized religion. Surviving colonies evolved in one of two directions: either they practiced secular humanism, like the Ellanoyans, or they embraced a particular religion and perpetuated a system of self righteousness and intolerance, the exact kind of which that had gotten them into an unholy mess to begin with.

Malcolm would say that without a supreme being dictating law, whether it be our Ten Commandments or someone else's, how would people know right from wrong? My question was, if everyone is dead or mutated in the end, what possible value can those Ten Commandments have?

Jonah listened attentively as I described the geography of the east coast, specifically the religious colonies. I told him the Levitican order overwhelmingly dominated the North, from the temperate latitudes all the way up to where they surrendered jurisdiction to polar bears. A handful of Jewish enclaves neighbored us to the south. Some of these people were true ethnic Jews, some were Christians who when rejecting the Levitican order had sought the roots of their faith. The Leviticans got along with the Jews if the latter kept their distance, and their council. And especially if they kept their emissaries in tow.

Muslims dominated the tropics. The Leviticans and Jews were in a static war with them. I had never met a Muslim, but I'd laid eyes on a few when a deputation came to Kebek to discuss peace. By bouncing up and down on my toes from behind the gathered onlookers I caught a glimpse of the diplomats as they walked tall and proud toward Town Hall. All I could think at the time was, what a funny way to dress. But they were people just like us.

On their way out of town after the meeting they walked neither tall nor proud. I took part in throwing stones at them. I didn't know why we were stoning them, I just followed the lead of others, the rule of the mob. The Muslims crouched, covered their heads, and ran.

Jonah asked me how the gods of the three major religions differed from one another.

"It's interesting," I said. "All three religions venerate more or less the same God, they just differ in how to interpret Him or His prophets."

"These prophets," Jonah said, "they form a liaison between the supernatural and the earthly?"

"More or less, yes."

"So the difference between the three religions—what keeps them apart, and fighting—is the difference between the interpretations of three classes of prophet, interpretations subject to their perceptions and whims?"

"It's actually worse than that. All three religions recognize a single patriarch, Abraham. He was the first monotheist, or at least the first influential one."

"So why the bad blood?"

Good question, I thought. I pictured those poor envoys running out of town in their long robes, only their bloody hands and faces visible through the clothing. They revered the same patriarch, worshipped essentially the same God. We threw rocks at them.

"I guess it's really just because we don't look or talk alike," I said.

Jonah had written several essays housed in the library, including one about choices and consequences. Life always goes our way, he argued, because we have the power of choice. The mistake we make when we conclude life isn't going our way is expecting consequences to submissively align with our goals. I decided to ask him about Malcolm's dilemma, about his struggle to reconcile his spiritual commitments with his earthly needs.

He asked, "Do you remember Olive, who danced for us?"

"Oh yes."

"Of course you do. Tell me, do you consider her profession to be dignified?"

As fond as I was of the attractive young woman, I had to be honest.

"No," I said.

"But why not?"

"She ... sells her body for money."

"And?"

"And ... that's not dignified."

"But my dear René, did she not act in a dignified manner in your presence?"

My eyes were closed. "In my presence, yes, she did."

"Then tell me, where is dignity? In the person, or in the profession?"

"Fair enough. But about Malcolm's dilemma. In the absence of God or of laws handed down by Him, how do we differentiate between right and wrong?"

"Tell me, where is love? In the people, or in their religion?"

Other than historical texts, there were no overtly religious works in the Bounty Rock library. I asked Jonah about it. Even if love and morals and ethics come from our own hearts rather than a higher power, shouldn't they be codified?

"All the religious tomes ever stitched together should bow out and make way for one simple rule," he said. "Do unto others as you would have them do unto you. Kindness is the only religion of any value, with any virtue. If each person consciously practiced kindness, we'd have paradise on Earth."

"And when we die? How does your simple religion prepare you for that?"

"How does your complicated religion prepare you? By promising fairy tales?"

On this subject Jonah's writings had much to say. It was the purpose of living organisms to survive, to reproduce, and to die—the latter to make way for replacements so natural selection and thus evolution could take place. A species couldn't survive, let alone adapt and evolve, if its individual organisms lived forever.

He wrote artfully on the subject of death. He didn't believe anyone truly goes away. If a storm on one side of the globe can't be predicted because a butterfly's wings flap on the other side, surely the words we speak and the steps we take will forever ripple on the Earth.

And if we live on in the hearts of those who knew us, we live on in those who knew them, in turn.

A scroll tucked into one of the pigeonholes purported to outline the entirety of philosophy in two short pages. The scroll was brittle; its edges crumbled to dust at my fingertips. I took great care unrolling it and read the author's name: Clarence of Utica.

"A great philosopher," Jonah declared.

"Not a terribly prolific one," I said.

"One reason he's so great."

Clarence of Utica argued there was one viable premise and one premise alone for each of the three major branches of philosophy. Metaphysics: a dedication to reality. Epistemology: the rules of logic. Ethics: a duty to survive and, if possible, to reproduce.

A being acts in concert with its nature, and its nature dictates that it serve itself. But according to Clarence "self" and "I" are synonymous with "community" and "us," respectively. The duty to survive implicitly acknowledges that "me" is nothing, and not fit for survival, except in the context of "we."

He went further with the bold claim that individual organisms didn't even exist. What separated us wasn't space, rather language and perception. Without labels differentiating one thing from another we wouldn't be able to make the distinction. Even apparent opposites like hot and cold would seem identical.

One Monday morning Jonah visited me at the library to bring my weekly pouch of crystals. He found me sitting in the middle of the floor in a posture of surrender.

"I don't know where to begin," I said.

"It doesn't much matter where you begin, only that you take the first step. The correct path never reveals itself to a stationary traveler."

*

As I passed Ellanoyans on my daily walks I couldn't help marveling at their robust good health. There was no denying they were pagans, and the fact alone would set Malcolm against them. And yet a simple poetry characterized the tenets of their society, the three fundamental themes of nourishment, fertility, and death. Life consisted of choices and consequences. Choices were overwhelmingly in favor of minimalism and asceticism. Necessary themes, in my view, of a utopian society. Such was the extent of their moral code.

And how did the code clash with Christianity? Malcolm would come up with an argument. Something about not accepting the divinity of Christ even if you accepted the spirit of His teachings. You couldn't be a true Christian, no matter how much you loved your neighbor, if you didn't believe in the Trinity. And you couldn't go to Heaven if you weren't a true Christian.

The Ellanoyans didn't want to go to Heaven. They wanted to die in the woods and feed other forms of life.

They lived by hunting, fishing, gathering, and planting. Everywhere I went, people were hustling to some place or another, carrying baskets of food, or lumber for building. Or they lectured clusters of children sitting in the grass on sunny days. Fashioned swords on anvils. Churned great vats of wine must. Food was plentiful and enemies were at bay. No one wanted for anything. Which was to say, the fewer your needs, the greater your wealth. No one was idle except when watching a show, when idleness was recreation, when recreation was participating in the community.

Like most people, I had been raised to want more than I had, and to experience frustration when I couldn't get it. My neighbors had wanted it too. And since there wasn't enough to go around, we learned to compete with one another. If one of us couldn't satisfy his cravings, neither should the other be able to. We were sentenced to unhappiness together.

Is this what Christ wanted for us?

It pained me to acknowledge that priests and bishops devoted themselves to maintaining a state of unhappiness. To them joy was not an acceptable premise. Sin stained every member of the congregation. God wished his children to suffer.

Is this what Christ had in mind for the human race?

The suffering came at the hands of man, and man alone. Ellanoyans were free to choose how to interpret God, even how to define Him, and in which ways to pursue happiness. As long as the pursuit didn't hurt anyone else. In Kebek such talk was blasphemy. The difference, of course, was that in Kebek the priests and bishops strived not to channel souls to Heaven, rather to govern them while they cringed here on Earth.

As I wandered the hills around Bounty Rock I paused to take in the Markette valley, from neat rows of corn, groves of oaks and evergreens, and the infinite amber prairie, to a horizon where muted greens met a dull blue Beyond. Somewhere out there was an enigmatic God.

And that spelled out the essential difference between Kebekian and Ellanoyan religion: in Kebek, God was not the least bit enigmatic.

For some reason the Kebekian God didn't like naked people. The Ellanoyans delighted in their bodies—bodies God himself created. For some reason the Kebekian God didn't like procreation without the sanction of a terrestrial priest adhering to ancient dogma. Ellanoyans were fruitful and multiplied. For some reason the Kebekian God relished suffering if it was in His name. Which wasn't to say Ellanoy was paradise: enemies kept at bay were nevertheless enemies, and they were uncommonly fearsome. But the enemies of the Ellanoyans didn't include the greatest enemy of man, avarice.

No Ellanoyan sought political office or authority. No Ellanoyan sought power over another. In Kebek the priests contrived to become bishops, the bishops to become cardinals, the layman to possess more than his neighbor, the already-well-fed to acquire yet more to eat.

The Ellanoyans had property, but it was of secondary importance. Of primary importance were the relationships with one another. I had not yet met an Ellanoyan unwilling to give away anything he had to someone who needed it more. Although I was a stranger I felt loved and accepted. I delighted in their generosity. And rather than take all I could in response I felt inspired to give at least as much back.

Stopping at Malcolm's cabin one evening after a long walk, I found him resting inside. I said, "Remember when you asked me if I still thought this place was Utopia?"

"Yes. And?"

"More than ever."

Chapter 25

Adrienne's little brother Eli and I spent the day together hunting. He told me the local hunting was good for wild cow, which he called "buffalo," also for deer, ducks, turkeys, pheasants, and even bears, depending on the season. And of course rabbits and squirrels. He liked hunting more than fishing, he said, because he could see his prey.

Today we were going to kill a wild cow. And we were only going to use bows and arrows. The Ellanoyans had no firearms, just projectile points, same as the Garhogs. If either side acquired black powder weapons, the other side would be exterminated.

"Wouldn't that be a good outcome," I asked, "as long as it was in your favor?"

He shook his head. "Then Ellanoy would be in imbalance." He pronounced "Ellanoy" like his fellow citizens did, as though it comprised the universe.

It was an odd attitude to have, not to want your mortal enemies vanquished, but I elected to keep the opinion to myself. Maybe I'd ask Jonah about it. Although I already knew how he'd answer; he'd say something frustratingly cryptic about one's path in life.

We left the gate and marched down the steep slope and through the woods to an open pasture. As we approached a herd of wild cows Eli said, "As soon as you shoot at an animal and determine you've hit him, drop down in the grass. Don't move. One arrow likely won't kill him, it will only make him mad."

"What if he discovers me hiding in the grass?"

"Buffaloes aren't sprinters. They're heavy and their legs are stubby. If one chases you, run. Try to reach a tree." He laughed to himself, and I asked why. He said, "When I was little and learning to hunt, the first lesson I remember was, Cows don't climb trees."

"What happens if one of them catches me?"

"He'll snag you on his horns, toss you in the air, and trample you underfoot. Trust me, you'd rather be up a tree."

"Perhaps we should hunt quail instead."

"Shh. There they are."

Straight ahead was a cluster of hairy beasts, chewing the tall grass. They didn't appear to notice us.

"We make a regular habit of coming in close proximity without attacking," Eli said, "so they don't necessarily see humans as dangers. Would you like to take the first shot?"

"Depends. Where's the nearest tree?"

"Aim for the big ugly one up front, and try to hit him in the chest. We'll eat well tonight."

"I rather doubt I'll hit him at all."

"Go ahead. I've got you covered."

The cow just chewed grass. Killing him wasn't going to feel at all like hunting. I aimed my arrow, approximated a good parabolic arc, pulled the bowstring back, and let fly. The arrow whistled through the intervening space and struck the cow in the head.

The animal jumped in a start. He made a pathetic cry. He looked around for the cause of his pain. I didn't drop into the grass, as instructed. I remained standing, dumbfounded, a human in the crosshairs of a wrathful brute.

The rest of the herd scattered. The wounded member ascertained the source of the arrow and charged.

"Time to find a tree," I said, thinking it would also soon be time to find a toilet.

"I'm right behind you," Eli said.

"What? I thought you were going to cover me!"

"I meant that more or less metaphorically."

We hustled to the nearest tree, a mature oak with low hanging branches. The wild cow gave chase. His angry snorts grew louder as he gained on us.

"You said they weren't sprinters! You called them stubby! Oh, let me guess, another metaphor."

"More like wishful thinking. Hurry!"

We reached the tree three steps ahead of the cow and clambered up like monkeys. The cow stopped at the trunk, sputtering and slobbering. He trotted around the oak twice, looking for us.

Eli broke off a small branch and dropped it on the animal's head.

"Up here, stupid."

The cow looked up but couldn't make us out. As far as he knew we were just a talking tree.

"Finish him," Eli said, "before he loses interest and wanders off."

"Finish him … with what?"

He looked me over. "Where are your bow and arrows?"

"Exactly where I dropped them. Right about the place my sphincter gave out."

Eli sighed, took aim at the cow, and shot him. The cow lurched again, but this time couldn't determine the source of the arrow. He stood his ground and wailed, not unlike a human child. Eli fired several arrows in quick succession, more rapidly than I would have thought physically possible. They all penetrated the cow in the back, behind his neck. The cow went mute and sat down in the shade of the oak.

"Is he dead?" I asked.

"Not quite. We'll wait here a bit and give him time to figure it out." He took out a pipe, loaded it with tobacco, and lighted it. After puffing a few times to get the bowl started he passed it to me. "So," he said, "tell me. How are you and my sister getting along?"

As though we'd just taken a stroll on the prairie, as though we'd not gotten anywhere close to becoming cow poop. "Is that why we're here? Did you contrive to trap me in a tree so you could interrogate me, find out if my intentions are good?"

He smiled. "You give me too much credit."

"Why the question, then?" I knew I sounded defensive, but the truth was merely that I found the subject awkward. You don't talk boy-talk about a girl with the girl's brother.

"Just curious," he said. "We have some time to kill."

"Well, your sister and I seem to be getting along nicely. However, I don't have any knowledge of her past relationships with other men, so I don't know where I stand. Maybe I should be interrogating you."

"Have you had sexual intercourse with her?" he asked.

"Have I ... what?"

"Sex. Copulation. I trust you know what it is."

"I do. But honestly, Eli…"

"Have the two of you done it, or not?"

"We have," I answered meekly.

"You're getting along well, then."

He changed the subject abruptly—and mercifully—to techniques of hunting prey other than wild cow. Deer were more difficult because they were so fast. But their hides were prized. Next time, he said, we'd go after deer. He didn't bother much with rabbits and squirrels; Ellanoyans used traps to catch them. Pheasant hunting was good sport, he felt, because the birds were moving targets, but they were also predictable.

"They don't dart around like deer," he said. "You have to aim very well to hit a deer. To hit a pheasant you only have to understand how a pheasant thinks."

We talked about the economy of Ellanoy. Other than hunting and fishing and farming, Ellanoyans were also committed to a prosperous wine industry. The vines grew on the steep inclines on and around Bounty Rock. Other cultures made wine, Eli explained, but not as well as his countrymen. They traded wine to far-off lands, possibly even as far as the western ocean.

And what about the ocean: did he know where it was?

"Some think the Father of Waters flows into it," he said, "but I don't think so. I think it's much farther west of us. If it were closer we'd have first-hand reports of it. As it is, all we have is legend. If it truly exists, it's far away. And China is even farther."

"According to an atlas I found in the library, the sea is a thousand miles away."

"Sounds about right."

"Father Malcolm intends to search for it."

He studied me for a moment. "Not alone, I hope." He looked down at the cow, slumped over the knuckles of exposed tree roots, arrows protruding from its back like porcupine quills. "I think it's dead enough for us to climb down."

It was. We carved him up for packing back to the village. On the return trip Eli led us on a detour. He wanted to show me something.

We arrived at a stream. He waded into it, prowling along the bottom. The water was pure and clear. I could see the bottom like I was looking through a pane of glass. Eli bent over, reached into the cold water, and pulled something out. It was an abraded crystal, a semi-transparent rock of a pleasant purple color.

"I gather you're earning pay at your library job," he said.

"Yes. I've since become something of a rock hound."

"Those rocks will come in handy. If you need more you can always visit a stream and dig some up. We trade them with other communities that make jewelry out of them. When the traders come with their exotic meats and dried fruits, you'll be glad you waded a stream or two." He handed me the purple stone. "Here, don't spend it all in one place."

"Why isn't this stream crowded with prospectors?" I asked. "If you use crystals for currency you'd think people would seek them out, hoard them, and make themselves wealthy."

"We don't accumulate wealth in Bounty Rock. If you need five crystals, a sixth will do you no good."

"Which explains why Ellanoyans are so generous. You'll probably give most of this wild cow away."

"True," he said, "I'm generous with the meat I bring home. Otherwise it will spoil. I could have all the meat in the world but can only eat my fill. Consider this as well: if I *must* give my meat to you, there is no incentive for either of us to hunt. We carry our own weight as best we can."

As we headed back to the village he said, "You wanted to know earlier why I was curious about your relationship with my sister."

"Yes."

"The man who becomes her husband becomes king."

Chapter 26

Eva was late tending to Malcolm. She'd been called to the cabin of a dying infant. I was with Malcolm when he got the news.

He sat upright. "Fetch my things," he instructed me.

"Malcolm, this isn't a Levitican culture. They don't share our beliefs."

"*Fetch my things.*"

His "things" consisted of a chalice, vestments, a bottle of holy water, a prayer book, some host wafers, and other miscellaneous paraphernalia, all jammed into a beaten-up wooden box. I carried it for him to the infant's home.

Inside the cabin, Eva hovered over the baby while the parents stood by, concern etched on their tired faces. The baby was bundled with only its head exposed. Eyes closed and silent.

Jonah and the king arrived shortly afterwards, the king in his finest beaded deerskins, Jonah in ragged dress that barely served its intended purpose. One look at Jonah's spindly limbs, and you never doubted the earnestness of his fasting.

"How beautiful the sun is," the king greeted us, allowing the rest of the expression to hang unspoken in the tense atmosphere.

"How beautiful the sun," the others repeated.

The king looked at Malcolm and me inquisitively.

"Malcolm wishes to baptize the infant," I explained. Malcolm glanced at me sharply, a reaction to the disdain in my tone. I made no apologies. I felt we were interfering.

"He's a doctor as well as a priest?" the king asked.

"No, just a priest."

Jonah addressed the parents: "It will do the child no harm."

Malcolm glared at Jonah while removing the bottle of holy water from his box. He prayed silently for a minute, opened the bottle, and poured a few drops of water on the little boy's head.

"I baptize you in the name of the Father."

He poured some more water.

"And of the Son."

He poured again.

"And of the Holy Spirit." He recapped the bottle and said, "The child is saved."

"From what?" Jonah asked.

Malcolm ignored him. After blessing the parents he left the cabin. Jonah and I followed him out.

"If you don't mind my asking," Jonah said, "what was the point of that ritual?"

Malcolm was tight-lipped when he answered. "First, to remove original sin."

"What kind of sin, exactly?"

"Adam and Eve, the first man and woman, committed original sin by eating from the tree of knowledge. All people carry the burden of this sin until they're baptized."

"The baby inside—it carries this burden?"

"It did, until I removed it."

"What did the first man and woman eat that caused their descendants such inconvenience?"

Malcolm just shook his head. He rearranged his priestly implements, trying to make them fit into the box. Jonah turned to me.

"Apples," I said.

"Let me get this straight. That baby in there carried the guilt of two mythical people who picked apples from a tree? And you removed the guilt by pouring water on its head?"

"There is no point in continuing this conversation," Malcolm said. "Don't you have a Bible in that library of yours?"

"Ah, the Bible. I'm afraid we don't. It's the one book we don't allow in the library."

"Why in God's name would you disallow a Bible?"

Before Jonah could answer, the father of the infant emerged from his cabin. He said, "My baby is dead."

Malcolm offered his condolences, but a sea change had occurred. The father inched away from Malcolm, suspicion written on his face. As we were taking leave Malcolm said to me, "I think you should refer to me as *Father* Malcolm when in the company of the heathens."

"Yes, Father Malcolm."

"It wouldn't hurt to exhibit respect for my office, either."

"In what way, Father Malcolm?"

"By calling me Monseigneur, for starters, when speaking of me in the third person."

"As you wish, Father Malcolm Monseigneur Marchand."

"I intend to say mass tonight after dinner, and to make a regular habit of it. This place is long overdue for spiritual guidance. You're going to be my altar boy."

"You can say mass all you want, Your Majesty, but you'll need to find another altar boy to assist you."

He did say mass that night, and several Ellanoyans attended out of curiosity. I went to Adrienne's cabin instead, looking forward to an entirely different kind of ritual. A fertility ritual, a deliciously naughty pagan ritual. I opened her cabin flap and entered without announcing myself.

She was inside, but not alone.

It was the rugged, bare-chested man Adrienne had sat with at dinner earlier in the summer. The lumberjack. He was not just bare-chested now. He was bare naked. Kneeling between Adrienne's bare legs.

He didn't notice me, or else didn't care. He thrust his hips and grunted. Adrienne turned to look at me. No more mountain lakes in her eyes, just pity.

She mouthed my name silently, "René."

My knees buckled. I closed the flap and took off in a feeble stride. I didn't know where else to go so I went to the library. I stopped outside the entrance, bent at the waist, and threw up.

*

Deep in the night I awoke to a rumbling noise and the library shaking by its roots. I sat up and tried to orient myself. I'd spent the night among books and scrolls. I hadn't wanted to go home to my cabin, for fear of receiving a visit from Adrienne; apologetic or not, I hadn't trusted myself in her presence.

The rumbling and shaking abated, but returned immediately with greater intensity.

An earthquake. I'd experienced the sensations before, in Kebek. I threw my clothes on and dashed out of the library. The residents of Bounty Rock were spilling out of their cabins and gathering at the central meeting grounds.

The rumbling continued, heightening to a savage roar. Almost to thunder. The Earth bristled, it seemed, with fury.

Stone buildings wobbled. Cabin roofs tilted, first one way, then another. Chimneys swayed like tree branches, the wind mocking the brick and mortar.

The cries of children, their faces wet with tears. Dogs howling in terror.

The bell in the tower rang and rang, yet no one was pulling the rope. The palisade stakes fairly danced in place; a spooky, stiff-legged chorus line. I reached Malcolm's cabin to find Eva helping him evacuate it. He wouldn't leave without his holy implements. The three of us joined the rest of the community at the central grounds.

The earth quivered beneath my feet as I walked. A disorienting oscillation that made me seasick. When I raised my foot to take a step, the soil almost came up to meet it.

At the central grounds were people milling about aimlessly. No one knew what to do, where to go. The rumbling quieted and we held our breath waiting for the next onslaught. Nothing stirred. The air itself suspended movement. The king arrived with Adrienne at his side and commanded attention.

"Is anyone hurt?" he asked.

After some mumbled inquiries it was determined there were no serious casualties. Living in a city made of tree bark had its advantages.

"The earth split open," someone said.

"The hills have been swallowed up," another offered.

"I heard fish screaming from the river."

"God has protected us from harm," Malcolm declared.

The mother of the infant he baptized came forward and shook her fist at him. "How do we know it wasn't your god who did this?"

"Let's get some sleep," the king said, "and we'll go to work on repairs in the morning."

"I don't want to sleep in my cabin," someone said.

"Me neither."

"We can sleep outside tonight," the king said. "The weather is pleasant. Turn a problem into an opportunity. We'll camp under the stars until we're sure it's safe to go back inside."

Adrienne was looking at me over the crowd. When our eyes made contact she nodded. I looked away.

Malcolm took me by the arm. "It was a message from God," he insisted.

"From God?" I was incredulous. "Why would God send such a message?"

"Because you're having intimate relations with that princess."

"Then why doesn't he just pick on me? Why scare the children? What did masonry and rafters do to piss the old fucker off?"

"Watch your mouth."

"Maybe," I said, "he was reacting to you interfering with a native religion."

"Let's do as the king says and get some sleep. You can say penance first thing tomorrow."

We laid bedding next to his cabin, with Eva between us. Her makeshift bed under the stars was measurably closer to Malcolm's than it was to mine.

"Monseigneur," I said.

"What."

"That voyage you want to make, to search for the western passage, the one I didn't want to accompany you on?"

"What about it?"

"I'll accompany you on it."

After a brief silence he asked, "What changed your mind?"

"Nothing in particular. I still think the journey is folly. It just seems like the right time to launch it."

"Fair enough. We'll leave immediately."

Chapter 27

Our plan was on the lips of the entire community, and precisely no one thought it was sound. Eva tried to convince Malcolm the venture was reckless, that he wasn't fit enough. But he pooh-poohed her. Jonah argued we'd wind up on someone's dinner plate.

"Garhogs police the waterways and comb the land," he said, "in search of fools like you. Your smooth skin, free of lumps and pus, makes you a tasty snack."

It was time to share with Malcolm what Eli had said about the western passage. I told him about the atlas I'd found in the library. That it depicted the Father of Waters flowing south, not west. That it depicted the Vermillion Sea much farther away from us than Malcolm supposed. "We should take the atlas with us," I said.

"You can make an atlas depict anything you want," he answered. "The western passage is the main reason we made the trip. To venture out this far, all the way to Ellanoy country, and not finish the job, would be irresponsible if not downright criminal."

He had apparently forgotten that the main reason we'd made the trip was to avoid prosecution, and that we were in fact criminals. Men on a mission turn a deaf ear to rational dissent and inconvenient facts. I wanted to go on the voyage because I wanted to get away from Bounty Rock, from Adrienne. Also I knew Malcolm would take up the mission regardless, and I'd have to look after him. Might as well get it out of the way.

We had to borrow a canoe and beg supplies. The canoe was extra long—it held four paddlers comfortably—but also sleek and fast. For food we packed jerked meat and dried corn for sagamité. We would hunt and fish, and for these we packed our rifle, powder, shot, and fishing tackle. And of course paper, quill, and ink for continuing my narrative.

Adrienne showed up at the launch. I spied her in the crowd, looking at me with pain in her eyes. She lifted her eyebrows as if to say, Can we talk? but I looked away.

King Berthold himself lent us a calumet. "There are Ellanoyans at the mouth of the Markette River. Show them this and you'll pass in safety. Beyond their village are dragons and monsters," he warned. "I implore you to go no further than the mouth."

"Thank you for your concern," Malcolm said, "but our path is set."

"So be it," the king said. "May the sun shine brightly on your path."

As we turned to head to the river I almost collided with Adrienne, who had been standing behind me, waiting for an opportunity.

She slipped me a pouch full of gem crystals. "You'll need these as gifts when you meet new communities. Give them to whomever is in charge."

"Thank you," I mumbled.

"René, the cultures in which you and I were raised…"

"Save your breath."

"If the reason you're making this trip is because of me, please know I'm sorry for having hurt you."

Brushing past her, I went to catch up with Malcolm. She called after me: "Please take care."

Malcolm and I locked arms and marched down the bank to the launch, the population of Bounty Rock following us. We found Eli sitting in the canoe.

"Are you here to say goodbye?" I asked. "Or to give us rowing lessons…"

"I'm coming with you."

"Say what?"

"My addition to the party will double your odds of surviving this foolhardy mission. Besides, with me around you'll have all the wild cow you can eat."

Malcolm and I looked at each other. Malcolm said, "That's an offer we can't easily refuse."

"I'm sold," I said.

Eli regarded the calumet in my hands. "That's the king's pipe," he said.

"Yes, he lent it to us."

"It's a great honor."

"Why?"

"Because it's his."

We set off, with Eli in the bow seat, me at the stern, and Malcolm amidships, an assignment that rewarded him no happiness. Despite missing one of his thumbs he acquitted himself well with the paddle.

The canoe was overladen with supplies. The waterline crept uncomfortably close to the gunwales. The displacement made paddling sluggish, but at least we were off, undertaking an adventure Malcolm had dreamed of his whole life.

We worked our way through the chop as villagers waved goodbye from the bank. Eva stood at water's edge. She didn't wave, she just stared as the boat coasted downstream. I looked for Adrienne but didn't find her.

The vast, fertile Ellanoy country lay before us. Dense greenery. Abundant game: cow, elk, deer, fowl, beavers. Fish in endless abundance. Fruits and nuts for the picking. Urgent skies. Wildflowers subjugating the meadows and riotously advancing up hillsides.

No sign of people. At first we were nervous about this, electing to go ashore only to cook our meals. We slept in the canoe, anchored a safe distance from the bank. After a time, however, we became complacent; sleeping in a canoe gets old quickly, especially when you've sat in one all day. We moved our camp to shore.

The Markette River turned southwest. Riding the current, with three strong and healthy paddlers, we made superb time. A few days of travel and the river turned due south. Knowing we were close to the confluence we paddled all the harder.

Late one Sunday afternoon, when the river had widened and calmed, when birds screeched unintelligible messages and tree crowns waltzed in unison, we ploughed our innocent way down the center of an accelerating current and almost in complete surprise entered the deep, muscular flow of the Father of Waters.

An archipelago of islands peppered the point of confluence. Malcolm suggested we make camp on one of them and say mass. I had never seen him so consumed by purpose. We were at the point of departure for the legendary western ocean, the storied and mythical Vermillion Sea.

The country ahead promised to be as fertile as the one we were leaving behind. So we gorged ourselves that night on smoked meat and our remaining store of berries, and we passed around a flask of good Ellanoy wine.

The alcohol made me light-headed. Paradoxically it also clarified my thoughts. I turned to Eli and asked:

"Your sister sent you to watch out for us, didn't she?"

"Do you want an honest answer?"

"What the hell. Give me a dishonest one. Variety is the spice of life."

"She's mostly worried about Father Malcolm. Your name didn't come up."

Malcolm giggled and hiccupped.

"That's enough hooch for you," I said. "Off to bed."

He stumbled obediently into the hut and passed out as soon as his face collided with the hides. I sat with Eli for a while next to the fire.

"Truth is," he said, "she's quite distraught."

"She has a funny way of showing it."

"You're telling me. When she was little the other kids called her Princess Frosty. But trust me, she's as emotional inside as anyone, maybe more so."

We sat in silence as I resisted the urge to share an observation. Finally I gave in:

"Horny as anyone too."

"When you travel to foreign lands you have to leave your native culture behind, especially your taboos."

"When in Rome."

He stirred the fire and made it glow brighter. "I don't know where Rome is," he said.

"Me either. It's just an expression."

"She's in love with you, René. That man you saw, he's been a companion of hers for years. It doesn't amount to anything."

"Depends on how you measure it."

"Whatever your measuring stick, let go of it. You're in Rome now."

We slept by the fire. I dreamed of Adrienne, holding her in my arms, her warm breath on my neck, her long, slender leg draped over mine. Malcolm no doubt dreamed of explorations to come. What Eli dreamed of, I couldn't guess. What does a young man yearn for when he has everything a young man could want? What does one crave when one lives in Shangri-La?

In the morning I woke to a splashy, multicolored sunrise, radiant sunlight cascading down through a lush, verdant canopy, and a dozen armed men, watching me yawn and gape, their quivers full, their bows taut with arrows aimed at my drowsy, stupefied face.

Chapter 28

The men stood in partially crouched positions, adjusting their aim with short, jerky movements. I resolved to make no sudden gestures, because a drawn bow requires only a casual release of pressure to send an arrow flying with irreversible abandon toward its target.

Eli woke with a nudge. He blinked a few times, then sat up with a start. His hair was disheveled but his eyes comprehended the circumstances instantly.

"Who are you?" one of the men asked. He was a bronzed, meaty specimen with flowing white hair, a man who looked like he could recognize and appreciate a reasonable answer.

"Friends," Malcolm said, emerging from the hut.

"How do we know that?"

Malcolm reached into a leather bag for the king's calumet. As he moved the men drew their arrows tighter.

He hesitated. "May I? We're unarmed."

The leader nodded. Malcolm slowly lifted the calumet out of the bag and said, "How beautiful the sun is, that we are among you."

The dozen men with stretched bows were still for a moment. Then they burst into laughter and lowered their weapons.

"Your heart's in the right place," the leader said, "but you are in no position to be greeting us." He had piercing, intelligent eyes. I liked him, even if he had come within a twitch of killing me.

"That's Berthold's pipe," one of the men said.

The leader leaned forward. "So it is. How did you get it?"

"He gave it to us," Malcolm said.

"Are you sure you didn't kill him for it?"

"Quite sure. I'm a priest, and my companion here is a novice. My other companion is Berthold's son."

The leader examined Berthold's son closely. "I know you," he said. "You're Eli."

Eli searched the older man's face. "Franklin?"

"My God, boy, but how you've grown. Last time I saw you, you were playing with fingers and toes in the dirt."

"Still do sometimes, after a nip or two."

"How's the old man? Is Berthold as Berthold as he used to be?"

"More so. He sends his respects and greetings."

The leader glanced at Malcolm. "You're badly scarred. You've been in battle."

"My encounter with the Garhogs," Malcolm said. "It was King Berthold who saved me."

"And you?" The leader turned to me. Up close his bronze face framed by white hair was not of this world. "What's your excuse?" he said.

By now all weapons had been lowered and the once tense atmosphere was calm and breezy. I said, "I've been known to graciously accept offers of hospitality, especially when food is involved."

He grinned. "Have a reputation for that, do you?"

"I'm legend."

The men helped us hide the canoe. We enjoyed an armed escort to their village, which they called Gryphon. Unlike Bounty Rock it wasn't elevated above the rest of the terrain, nor did it have palisades. Instead it was guarded, incredibly, by a moat. A deeply cut channel, fed by the river, surrounded the village. A drawbridge admitted us to the town square. I asked one of the men what would stop an enemy from cutting off the river and thus drying up the moat.

"Take a look," he said. He pointed at the channel connecting the river and the moat. "Anyone, or any team, trying to block the channel would come well within the range of our arrows. It's easier to attack the village by swimming the moat. And swimming the moat is tantamount to suicide."

"Do the mutants try?"

He nodded. "Oh, yes. The bottom of the moat is strewn with their bones."

Curious villagers engulfed us, many of whom knew Eli and Berthold. There was a stir in the back of the crowd, and the villagers parted to make way for their holy man. He was tall and thin with intelligent, penetrating eyes. The trait seemed endemic to the community. I handed him the pouch of crystals Adrienne had given me.

"From Princess Adrienne of Ellanoy," I announced. "Daughter of Berthold the king."

"How is she?" the wise man asked. "I've not seen her since she was this high." He held his hand level at his waist.

"Grown to a lovely woman," I answered.

"And Berthold? Is he in good health? Good spirits?"

Eli answered. "Excellent health and spirits. Stronger than ever. My father sends his wishes for your own good health and happiness."

"Tell me, why have the three of you come?"

Eli and I turned to Malcolm. This was his show now. Malcolm said, "We seek passage to the Vermillion Sea."

The wise man smiled. "You'll not find it in these parts."

"But the great river, the Father of Waters—"

"No one has ever traveled its entire length. We don't know what there is to find at its mouth, or even where the mouth is, exactly. The farther south you go, the stranger the inhabitants. The mutants get nastier, the non-mutants speak Latin tongues rather than English."

"I speak Latin," Malcolm said.

"Monsters of all size and design roam the interior," one of the villagers added.

"Enormous fish inhabit the river, big enough to swallow a man whole," said another.

"Have you seen these monsters, these fish?" Malcolm asked.

"Not personally, but their existence is common knowledge."

"We're going to have a look for ourselves."

"As you wish," the wise man said.

A meal was prepared for us and all the village showed up. Attendants fed Malcolm, Eli, and me like infants, spooning food into our mouths. We devoured mounds of wild cow meat. When roast dog was offered we refused. When flasks of wine were offered we accepted.

Afterwards we toured the village, stopping briefly at each of over one hundred cabins. The residents bestowed gifts: mostly belts and bracelets made from animal hair. At one point I turned to Malcolm and asked, "What are we going to do with all these belts?" He said, "Look on the positive side. Your pants will never fall down again."

As in Bounty Rock, these people were healthy and attractive, multicolored like the soil from which they sprang. Dry sand to deep loam. Alabaster to ebony and every shade between. Earthy, lush, fertile. Also friendly, industrious, and generous. They put us up for the night in a communal barracks, a kind of hostel for visitors, and left us with plenty of wine, jerky, and tobacco.

It was the first comfortable rest we'd enjoyed on our journey. We drank until our speech slurred. The tobacco smelled funny but tasted sweet. Soon we were giggling over nothing and snacking ravenously on the jerky.

Eli stumbled to the window where he discovered his own reflection in the glass. "Boo," he said. Both he and the reflection fell backwards in mock fright. Malcolm and I laughed until our sides hurt.

"Do it again!" Malcolm said.

Eli snuck up on the window from beneath the pane. He sprang up and stuck out his tongue. So did the reflection. We fell over ourselves laughing.

There was a knock at the door. I shuffled over, giggling, and opened it. Three girls walked in. They had made little effort to clothe themselves.

"The aesthetics are here," Malcolm said.

"Let's just hope they're not ascetics," I said. "Get it?"

"Of course I get it," Malcolm said. "You have to know these things when you're a priest."

Eli looked puzzled. "I don't get it."

The rest of the evening was a blur. The girls smoked some of the tobacco and we smoked more of it, and soon we were out of tobacco, and wine, and jerky snacks. The girls spoke in smooth voices but didn't say anything that made any sense. Likewise Malcolm and Eli spoke, but not intelligibly. I sang a children's song about rosies and posies and falling down. No one listened.

Sleep must have overtaken me, because at some point I opened my eyes to find one of the girls on top of me. Neither of us wore a stitch of clothing. Her skin was supple and smooth and I felt immersed in her like a warm soapy bath. Her moist lips pressed against mine. Her tongue entered my mouth. She squirmed and adjusted herself. She rocked her hips. Tide breakers caressing the sand.

We lay together, the full length of her body resting on mine, her softness blanketing me, her lips pressing wetly against my neck, her fingers toying with my hair. Knees bumping incidentally, toes discovering one another in playful delight.

Her eyes peered into mine. Sapphire crystal caves. Gateways to perpetuity, to a fathomless cerulean world.

She got off and one of the other girls got on. When we were finished the third took her turn. From the gasps and low moans coming from elsewhere in the room, I surmised Eli and Malcolm both were having experiences similar to mine.

*

The next morning Malcolm demanded to be switched.

"It's okay," I said. "There was something in the wine. Or maybe even the tobacco. It wasn't anyone's fault."

He tore his undershirt off, which he had been putting on, and threw it on the floor.

"No, it's not okay," he said. "You'll accompany me into the woods to scourge me with a switch."

"I'll do no such thing."

"You will do it. I command you."

"Scourge *me*, then, for disobedience."

"Very well," he said, "I'll do it myself."

He stormed out of the hostel, leaving his shirt behind. When he returned, his back was bloody from repeated strikes with a switch.

"Let me take care of that," I said.

"No. Leave me alone."

"Eva would scold you if she saw this. She'd scold me for letting it happen."

He climbed into his bedding and lay on his stomach.

"Malcolm, it really is okay. You deserve happiness as much as any man."

"I'm not any man. I'm a priest."

Later he allowed me to apply a salve of Mary's Gold, sunflower oil, and honey to his wounds. He remained on his stomach to let the medicine soak in and do its work.

He said, "You want to know what the worst of it is?"

"Tell me."

"It's not because of what I did, rather because of whom I did it with."

"They were nice girls," I said. "They were just trying to make us happy."

"They weren't Eva."

He was sweating. At first I thought the wounds were to blame, or the guilt, but there was something more.

"Are you ill?" I asked.

He grimaced. "I've been having problems with, shall we say, my bowel movements. It comes and goes."

The next morning the village accompanied us en masse to our canoe to see us off.

"Please keep an eye out for several members of our community," the wise man said, "who have canoed south in search of crystals. All you need do is show them your calumet. They'll recognize it as we did."

Citizens of Gryphon lined up to drop food, candles, and other articles into the canoe. Our supplies thus replenished, we pushed off and were on our way once more.

Chapter 29

The Father of Waters flowed disconcertingly southward. It was a mile wide at its widest, and when tributaries discharged their loads it gorged to distension and its current grew menacingly powerful. We were going to have a much harder time paddling the other way.

At one point the river wound so much, we traveled north for ten miles before the channel narrowed and turned south again. If this was indeed the route to the Vermillion Sea it would have to bend westward before long. Yet through each incremental mile the sun set stubbornly to our right, and with each impatient stroke of the paddle it became more evident the river would spill into a southern rather than western ocean.

We fought to keep the canoe upright in turgid water. By midmorning each day we were drenched in sweat. The mosquitoes tracked us down and reminded themselves how good we tasted. As soon as a few scouts had sampled our blood, word spread throughout the land.

They were miniature lions. And we were foreign cuisine, windfalls paddling blithely into their den. We tried smoking them out of the hut but only managed to broadcast our precise location with towering columns of soot. A beacon, visible and odorous. A lighthouse guiding wayward bugs to the buffet.

"Do you see what I see?" Mosquito A said to his neighbor, Mosquito B.

"Verily, I cannot trust my eyes."

"Trust your nose, then."

"Hmm. Smells too good to be true."

"I'll race you."

The landscape transformed. Prairies no longer receded to the horizon, instead the banks of the river were heavily wooded and the woods ran deep. When we entered them to hunt they never seemed to end.

The daily temperatures crept higher and the air became muggy. Vines climbed the trees and dangled between them like arboreal webs. The leaves on most of the trees grew larger, until an individual leaf could almost serve as a shelter from the rain. I'd read about jungles, and this felt like one: I cocked my ear and imagined colonies of monkeys swinging from branch to branch, squealing in the dense vegetation. The soil turned swampy; our feet made unappetizing sucking noises as we walked. Strange birds flew overhead, which we judged to be tropical. Although having never seen a tropical bird, and none were illustrated in our catechisms, we couldn't be sure.

Clearly the Father of Waters didn't lead to the Vermillion Sea. It emptied into another body of water somewhere south of us. But there was no convincing Malcolm. "It will turn west," he insisted.

"Large, sluggish rivers don't behave that way," I said. "They don't just shift direction like that."

"Remember a while back, when we traveled north for ten miles?"

"Yes," I said, sighing.

"Well, what do you know. A large, sluggish river changed direction."

We sat glowering at each other. I asked Eli his opinion.

"Nothing good lies ahead," he said.

"You see? The locals know better."

"He's never been down this far."

"Nor does he speak Chinese. Come on, Malcolm. It's time to give up."

He said, "Let's make camp, rest up, and get an early start in the morning."

As the sun dropped behind the trees Malcolm and Eli erected the hut while I went in search of firewood. I preferred to trek widely and cover more ground to find pieces of wood ready to burn. Only as a last resort did I use the ax to cut logs. As I wandered I considered a last resort of another kind: a plan to mutiny and turn the canoe back to Bounty Rock.

Subduing Malcolm wouldn't be a problem. Eli and I could manage it together. Eli would have to sign on to the plan, but after his "nothing good lies ahead" statement, I didn't see that as an obstacle. It was just a matter of when. We'd tie Malcolm up, lay him in the bottom of the canoe, and paddle home. I'd sacrifice my friendship with him, but I'd save his life. And my own.

As I turned back to camp with an armful of high-grade dead wood I noticed a flickering coming from deep within the forest. A campfire. I returned to camp and dumped the wood on the ground. "I think I found those Ellanoyans who went south in search of crystals," I told Malcolm and Eli.

"Really, where?"

"About half a mile that way," I pointed. "They're having dinner as we speak."

"Maybe they have something good to eat," Eli said.

"Somebody grab the calumet."

After leading the others to the spot where I'd seen the campfire, Malcolm stared long at it. He said, "Okay, but let's proceed with caution."

"Who else would it be?" I said.

He ignored me and started out in the direction I had pointed. The evening grew darker, and the fire ahead burned larger and brighter as we approached it. The three of us walked, placing our toes down first, to avoid snapping twigs. I preferred to make our presence known, so as not to startle the strangers, which we would do if we emerged silently into the light cast by their fire.

Eli was behind me, and I was directly behind Malcolm, following in his footsteps. We were just at the point where we could hear men speaking when Malcolm turned, grabbed my shoulders, and forced me into a crouched position. Eli immediately crouched as well.

Ahead was a clearing. A man was tied to a stake. He wore an expression of inconsolable anguish. On the ground before him, another man was being devoured by mutants.

The mutants gouged chunks of flesh out of the prone man, who thankfully appeared to be dead, or at least unconscious. They roasted the chunks on pointed sticks over the open fire.

These mutants were even uglier than the Garhogs. Their faces were so distorted, they didn't even look like they *used* to be human. Flattened noses, protruding chins, steeply slanted foreheads. Ears so massive they reminded me of baby elephants. No necks as far as I could see. Comically long arms—except there was nothing funny about them. They numbered perhaps twenty, including women and children. A marauding band of hunters. People hunters.

One of the mutants spoke to the man tied to the stake. "Your friend tastes delicious." Others nodded and laughed, all the while chewing on human flesh, grease dripping from their preposterously jutting chins.

The man at the stake cried out. "Oh sweet mother, please help me."

Malcolm made the sign of the cross. He nudged me. Crouching, we retraced our steps. When we were out of earshot I said, "Shouldn't we do something for him?"

"There are too many mutants," Malcolm said.

"We can't just leave him there. What if it were one of us?"

"It's not one of us. He's in God's hands now."

"You mean, if he's killed, if he doesn't miraculously escape on his own, it's God's plan he be killed and eaten, and digested, and crapped onto the ground by knuckle draggers?"

"Yes, that's exactly what I mean."

"What if God's plan to save him was to send us to his aid?"

"No more of this talk. We're going back to camp."

"Maybe I'll just have to do this on my own."

"Keep talking like that, and we'll cold-cock you and throw you into the bottom of the canoe."

"These are your people," I said to Eli. "Don't you want to help them?"

"They're beyond help. We're outnumbered. Get a hold of yourself, René."

*

We built no fire that night. We couldn't risk it being seen. We had no appetite anyway.

"I'm reconsidering our situation," Malcolm said. "This waterway isn't a passage to the western ocean after all. It's pointless to continue."

Interesting, I thought. All it took to loosen a stubborn resolve was the imminent threat of torture and agony and horribleness. There's nothing like the idea of becoming mutant poop to reverse one's irreversible plans.

He continued. "One of the major tributaries emptying into the river from the west may yet provide a route. We'll explore those tributaries in the future. For now, we should return to Bounty Rock."

No argument from me. I missed Adrienne. I suggested to Malcolm that he must miss Eva, but he turned away and said nothing. At first I was surprised he had changed his mind so abruptly, and was giving up on his mission. Unless it wasn't his real mission. Unless his real mission was on Bounty Rock. Unless, coincidentally, so was the love of his life.

Later, while lying beneath the stars, Malcolm said, "If this is China, I don't care for the food."

Eli and I let out a chuckle. Malcolm himself joined in. Soon the three of us were laughing our fool heads off. The tension of the day caught up and we let loose. No wine, no jerky snacks, no funny tobacco, but we laughed and laughed.

Chapter 30

When we returned home we were greeted like wayward sons. Once safely inside the Bounty Rock palisades, word went around and people streamed out of their cabins. Naturally there had to be a feast.

"Why all the fuss?" I asked the king.

"We're frankly surprised you're still alive." He observed me looking around and said, "Adrienne isn't here. She's on a diplomatic mission to a nearby colony and won't be back for a few days. We'll send word for her."

He received the bad news about Gryphon's overdue citizens stoically. He listened to the details, then walked away. I felt awful for not having tried to save the remaining survivor. But Malcolm and Eli had been right. We would have merely added ourselves to the number of victims, and the king would have never known what happened to anyone in either party.

That night I slept in Adrienne's cabin. I stayed up late, making notes in my journal by candlelight. It was fortunate she was out of town. I didn't know what to say to her. I was angry with her and I missed her, two contradictory feelings that nevertheless resided side-by-side in my heart. I wanted to hold her in my arms and push her away at the same time.

The next morning I rose early and went to Malcolm's cabin. The journey had been arduous—my muscles still ached—and I wanted to see how he felt. As I was arriving, Eva was furtively departing. She saw me coming, saw that I saw her, and our eyes locked. I nodded a quiet good morning. She nodded back and hurried away. Malcolm was getting dressed as I entered the cabin. He was startled to see me.

"What are you doing here?" he asked.

"Since when do I need a reason to come here? Or is it only when you have something to hide…"

"I've got nothing to hide."

He continued dressing. In local garb: deerskin, moccasins, a cloak to shield himself against the morning chill. Not his usual black robe, the uniform of a Levitican priest.

"I saw Eva outside," I said. "I just want to say—"

"Save it."

"You're not going to scourge yourself again, are you?"

"No. There isn't any punishment on this Earth that could serve justice for what I've done, for what I'm doing."

"Malcolm, listen."

"You don't understand, because you're still a novice."

It was best to change the subject. "How do you feel? How are your … bowel movements?"

"They're fine."

"Are you sure?"

"It's nothing. It's temporary."

But his face said something different. "What are you not telling me?"

He hesitated, then said, "Blood. It comes and goes. It's nothing for you to worry about."

We walked to the gardens, where he went straight to work yanking weeds. I worked next to him for a while and tried to make conversation, but he only grunted one-word responses to my questions and remarks. He wasn't going to open up about anything substantial. So I gave up and went to the library, figuring it was probably as neglected as the gardens.

And it was. All was quiet. Exactly as I'd left it. No one had visited the place in my absence. I sat in a chair and listened to the hollow silence. At least Malcolm had weeds to pull.

Why do we hold against others the thoughts, words, and actions we ourselves are guilty of? Why are we quick to assign blame and slow to accept responsibility? Is it merely a defense strategy? A product of natural selection that implicitly rewards individuals who dodge castigation? I didn't think so. You can get away with vice for a short time. In the long run the people who stand against it, who practice virtue and prove the ultimate product of evolution is character, will reap the effort and moral growth of their ancestors.

You can't hide from integrity.

The door opened. Adrienne stepped in.

Nothing beautiful is more beautiful than when you see it again, after a long time away. Her copper skin, her bare arms and shoulders, lustrous in the dim light. The light dancing in her hair as she stood in the doorway.

Her face, the strength and pride and symmetry. Her eyes, portals to boundless wisdom, to the almanac of the universe. Plato's Realm. God's workbench. Fields of radiant lavender. Moody, unsettled nights. Beauty is all about truth, and truth is all about contrast, and contrast is all about the delightful and the unexpected.

"I came as soon as I heard," she said.

She remained in the doorway. I didn't answer, I just stood up from my chair. I wanted her to come to me, to complete the trip. She did, and at first we touched each other with our fingertips. Making sure of our mutual corporeal reality. Or maybe to prove to ourselves we weren't dreaming. She pressed close and we held each other, first in a hug, then in the passion of melding. For life is all about love, and love is all about harmony, and harmony is all about unconditional acceptance.

"I hurt you, René. I know that now. I knew it the moment you saw me with another man. I ask you to understand. It was a difference in our respective cultures, rather than a lack of love for you. I ask you to forgive me for being inconsiderate of your feelings. I ask you to take me back. I promise never to hurt you again."

Tears filled her eyes. "I beg you, René. I love you."

"I love you too."

"Don't leave me again."

"I won't."

We kissed. The contact of her lips with mine was more than sensual, more than a pleasant experience. A circuit connected. Every off-kilter atom in the universe falling into place. I looked around the room. At the dusty floor, the wicker chairs. "We have to go someplace," I said.

"I know just the place."

"First I have to make a confession."

She put a hand over my mouth. "Please don't. It's not necessary."

"I have to, honestly. It's necessary."

"No. Whatever it was, I hope it made you happy."

She led me to a quiet clearing in the woods. A modest grove with branches arching in the upper canopy, forming a natural cathedral. The clothes melted from our bodies. I lay on my back in the soft grass and pine needles. She lay on top of me, her hair spilling to either side of my face. Her wonderful silken skin. Her spreading legs. Neither of us spoke again. Nor did the universe intrude or make a sound, other than the murmurs and whispers of nature's approval as two lovers became one.

Following our lovemaking I couldn't shake a small feeling of dread. Because whereas I would have happily spent my life on Bounty Rock, among the Ellanoyans, I didn't know how my mentor and traveling companion would fare, whether he could ever fit in.

Adrienne sensed something was wrong. "What is it?"

"Malcolm."

"He'll find his way. Just as you will."

"My mother used to sing me a lullaby," I said. "It was simple to the point of frivolity, but it always made me feel better. It gave me hope."

"Sing it for me."

"No, I'd rather not."

"I'll tickle you until you do."

"Okay, I give up." I sang:

Sleep, sleep my beloved one
Close your eyes, your day is done
Morning comes, we'll play again,
Cuddle again, be gay again
Fill the day with joy and fun

"And is your hope restored?" Adrienne asked.

"My way is clear."

She lay her head on my chest and said, "You won't ever leave Bounty Rock." It sounded like a declaration, a command. But it was a question. A wish offered up for concurrence or dispute.

After a long silence I answered, "Not without you."

She tightened her embrace and exhaled soft noises of security and contentment.

"Will you marry me?" I asked.

"Yes."

"Really?"

"Yes."

"Tomorrow?"

"Yes."

Chapter 31

When I asked Malcolm to perform the ceremony he agreed, having finally resigned himself to my relationship with "the strumpet." He prattled on about preparations until I interrupted and said the ceremony would be in the Ellanoy tradition.

After a pause he clarified, "You mean in the pagan tradition."

"Well, yes."

"You're asking me to perform a pagan ceremony."

"More to the point, I'm asking you to marry us."

After another pause he said, "Okay."

The ceremony required two witnesses. Adrienne chose Eli and I chose Jonah. We didn't lack for witnesses, however, since the entire village turned out for the event.

The members of the wedding party assembled within a nine foot circle of short monoliths, the same place Ella and Rachel had wed. King Berthold, his flowing beard in braids for the occasion, escorted Adrienne to the center of the circle, where he symbolically gave her away. The village members gathered outside the circle.

My ceremonial garb used to belong to the king. Deerskin shirt and pants, dyed red. A green cloak embroidered with scenes from nature. As Eli helped me on with the robe, I questioned a depiction of a kitten in the embroidery.

"It's supposed to be a lion," he said.

"Oh. Not a terribly frightening lion."

"The person who did the embroidery might possibly have never seen one."

Adrienne also wore red, long sleeves, an ankle-length dress, and a green elbow-length cape. Which was also embroidered, with flowers rather than kittens. Eli explained the sleeves and the length of the dress were to symbolize a covering of the bride, who was not to be uncovered until the wedding night.

"It's a little late for that," I said. "Don't you think?"

"A common dilemma in these parts, believe me."

Candles were placed and lighted at the major compass points of the circle. Malcolm, who had sought guidance on how to conduct the ceremony, rang a bell. Adrienne and I walked the perimeter of the circle four times, to symbolize the four elements: earth, air, fire, and water. We faced each other, holding hands. Jonah draped a short rope across our clasped hands.

Malcolm said, "Do you, René, take Adrienne to be your wife? To love her all the days you spend on this Earth, and for all time in the hereafter?"

"I do."

"Do you, Adrienne, take René to be your husband? To love him all the days you spend on this Earth, and for all time in the hereafter?"

"I do."

Jonah removed the rope. Malcolm handed me a chalice of wine. I took a sip from it, gave it to Adrienne, who did the same. Malcolm rang the bell again and said, "I now pronounce you husband and wife."

We kissed. And we were alone in the nine foot circle. She and I and the electricity binding us. Until our lips parted, and people were among us once more, and a breeze, one now familiar and welcome, carried sanction from the woods and prairies.

King Berthold shook my hand and congratulated me. "How beautiful the sun is," he said, "now that you are part of our family."

As we left the circle I made a remark to Adrienne about the brevity of the ceremony. She said, "It's because people want to get to the food." Indeed a sumptuous banquet followed, during which neither Adrienne nor I were permitted to lift a finger to serve ourselves. Villagers took turns spooning food into our mouths and lifting chalices for us to drink from.

One of the sentries called down from the walkway at the top of the palisades. No one could understand him, so the king ordered silence. The sentry called down again:

"Runner approaching!"

The gate opened and a man stumbled into the compound, out of breath. "Garhogs," he said. "On their way."

We sat in stunned silence as the runner caught his breath. "How many?" Berthold asked.

"An army. They'll be here in minutes."

The guests buzzed in confusion. Berthold raised his arms high to command attention. "Garhogs—sound the alarm!"

Somewhere a horn blew. People scattered to pre-assigned posts. Adrienne said she had duties to attend to. That I should look out for Malcolm. She took off. I searched the crowd and found Malcolm searching for me.

"This is a madhouse," he said.

"Where's Eva?"

"She had to run. Everyone but us has assigned tasks when something like this happens."

"She'll be fine," I said.

He looked at me and nodded. "Thanks. So will Adrienne."

"I'm headed for the cabin to get the musket. Do you need anything?"

"A weapon of some kind."

"All these people have are bows and arrows."

"Then I'll be needing a bow. And some arrows."

"You've never shot one before."

"No, but I have the one essential qualification to learn quickly."

"And that is?"

He raised his hand to show the thumb was missing. "I know what the Garhogs can do to me."

Malcolm found a bow and quiver, and I retrieved the musket. We assembled with the other men in the central square, where children were moving banquet tables out of the way and packing up the food. King Berthold handed out assignments. The best marksmen would man the palisades, the elderly and infirm would wait in reserve, and the strongest fighters would leave Bounty Rock and bring the attack directly to the Garhogs.

"What?" I said. "You're sending men … out there?"

"The more Garhogs we can kill in the open, the fewer can attack the wall."

"Send me too. I can kill many with my musket."

"And if you're captured, so is your musket. No, you'll man the wall. And you," he said to Malcolm, "will wait in reserve."

From my position in the narrow walkway at the top of the palisades I watched as a squad of Ellanoy warriors spilled out the gate below and double-timed into the woods. Eli was among them. My heart went to my throat. What would Adrienne think? It was a suicide mission. Then again, she'd say it was his duty and she was proud he was doing it.

In the compound behind us, women were fashioning arrows. I looked for Adrienne but couldn't find her in the crowd.

The men with me on the wall peered expectantly into the woods. The air grew still. The women ceased chattering. Even the birds disappeared from the scene. They knew what was coming.

One of the men near me said, "There."

In the direction he was pointing were no Garhogs, instead a strange motion deep in the trees. A rustling of vegetation. Like a giant was approaching, the forest was clearing a path for him, the brush was trying to get out of his way.

A Garhog emerged from the thicket, his shoulders stooped, his hairless head glistening in the sun. I could almost smell him. He raised his lumpy face to us and grinned. In his hands was a calumet.

"He comes in peace," I said to the man next to me.

"Look at the feathers decorating the pipe."

They were dyed red. The Garhog raised the pipe above his head.

"Red feathers signify war," the man said.

More Garhogs appeared, crowding behind their leader. Soon there were dozens of them. They milled about in the tall grass, drinking out of flasks.

"They're getting themselves drunk," my companion said, "to build courage. They've probably been drinking all morning."

One of the Garhogs threw down his flask, yelped, and took off toward the compound. The others followed, barking and howling. A hundred grotesque creatures, armed with bows and spears, loped toward us.

"What about our advance unit?" I asked. "How could they have survived such a force?"

"If I were them I'd be up a tree right now, waiting for a signal."

The front of the compound was the only side where the palisades had a walkway. The other side, the semicircular rear of the compound, overlooked the limestone cliff and the long drop to the river. Only a few men guarded it, from towers rising above the massive wooden stakes. Garhogs would have to scale the cliff to mount an attack on the village. On our side all they faced was a sloping field between the woods and the palisades, cleared of trees and just steep enough to slow a man down. Whether it would slow a Garhog down remained to be seen.

They whooped and shrieked and raced in their stiff-legged way toward our defenses. As more of them swarmed up the slope, yet more spilled out of the woods and into the clearing. Some were hauling ladders in two-man teams. The earlier stillness was shattered by the deafening torment of monsters howling at the top of their expansive lungs.

The king, positioned at the center of the palisade wall, raised his right arm.

The men drew their bows. I aimed my musket at the hoard and followed one of the monsters in my sights. The Garhogs were within twenty yards of the gate.

The king dropped his arm. "Shoot!"

My finger pulled the trigger. The hammer struck the frizzen. Sparks ignited the powder in the pan. A lead ball was on its way.

The Garhog I aimed for staggered and fell.

At the same time several dozen arrows flew into the charging mutants. Here and there figures stopped abruptly and either sank to their knees or collapsed when their legs crumpled beneath them. I reloaded.

The Garhog leader halted the charge. He raised his arm in a signal. The mutants drew their bows. The leader's arm dropped, and a hundred arrows floated toward us like a surreal storm.

We ducked behind the heavy wooden spikes. Some of the arrows lodged in the wood, others whooshed overhead, into the compound. One pierced the head of an Ellanoyan fighter whose curiosity had gotten the better of him. He fell backwards and writhed on the planks, an arrow protruding from his eye socket.

The Garhogs resumed their charge. They were almost at the gate.

We fired again, this time with better effect, and more of them fell. Still they came on. When they reached the wall they raised their ladders and clambered up.

"Climbers!" the king yelled up and down the line. "Aim for the climbers!"

We picked them off, but still they came. When one fell another took his place. The Garhogs who weren't climbing were firing flaming arrows. The arrows landed in the compound where women quickly put them out.

Adrienne wasn't visible in the melee. I knew Malcolm was safe somewhere in the rear, waiting with the rest of the reserves. I wondered what Eli was doing, what must be going through his mind. If in fact he was still alive.

Loading and firing, loading and firing, I cursed myself each time I missed, thanked God each time a goon took a ball in the head or chest and plunged gracelessly, his oafish figure hitting the ground with a thud.

Still they came. Their flaming arrows found a few cabins that consequently went up in smoke. They also found communal wooden buildings. Women raced to the fires with buckets of water.

A new presence beside me. It was Malcolm.

"What are you doing up here?"

"I couldn't stand waiting back there, doing nothing."

"You have a job, and an important one. The reserves are the last line of defense."

"René, I had to join the fight."

Down the line, most of the men were still firing. A few lay dead on the walkway. The king hadn't yet called for reserves. Yet the Garhogs were climbing ever higher on the ladders. And for each one that fell, another was on his heels.

"Shoot some arrows," I told Malcolm.

He looked uncertainly at his bow.

"Dammit, Malcolm, God wants you to kill mutants!"

He drew his bow, aimed down at a cluster of beasts, and released. One sat down heavily with an arrow protruding from his gut.

"I got him!" Malcolm shouted.

"How does it feel?"

"Not bad. Not bad at all."

"Here's a tip: the more you kill, the better it feels. Think of it like knocking down bowling pins."

He fired again. "I got another one! God must be pleased."

"Great. Please Him even more. Make Him wet His pants in joy."

The Garhogs came closer to the top of the palisade stakes. Meanwhile several more Ellanoyans had fallen. Flaming arrows struck the building housing children. Women hurrying to put out the fire shouted they were running out of water.

"Lower buckets to the river," the king yelled impatiently.

"Garhogs are on the river, cutting our lines!"

The king called over to me, "René, can you use your musket to clear vermin from the river?"

"I thought you'd never ask." I took the stairs down from the palisade walkway and ran across the compound to the other side, then climbed up one of the towers to peer over the rear wall. A pair of canoes, filled with mutants, floated on the river. They didn't bother trying to scale the rock face. They knew they'd be picked off easily. But they were in a splendid position to deny access to water.

Ellanoy sharpshooters attempted to hit them, but the Garhogs protected themselves from arrows by holding bark slabs over their heads. When an arrow planted itself in the wood, or sliced fruitlessly into the water next to their canoes, the Garhogs laughed.

"They won't be laughing for long," I said. I fired at one of the canoes, which immediately sprang a leak. The Garhogs scrambled to plug it. I reloaded and fired again.

Before long the canoe was a sieve filled with frantic mutants who, it turned out, couldn't swim.

"Educate the bastards," a female fighter next to me said.

One of the bastards was floundering in the river. I fired at him. He went limp with his face down in the water and drifted downstream with the current.

"There's one ogre who won't be tucking his children in tonight," the fighter said.

The other canoe had already turned back to shore, the mutant occupants paddling madly. I shot at it anyway, but it was out of range.

The women lowered their buckets to the water.

"Call me if you need me again," I said, and rushed back to the front wall. There the Garhogs had reached the top of the wooden stakes and a few had climbed over. Ellanoy archers were fighting hand-to-hand.

"Malcolm!" I shouted.

"Over here."

He was shooting almost point-blank at monsters ascending the wall. He couldn't get all of them, however, and one was winding up to swing a machete. I fired, and the beast's brains came out of his head.

Then I noticed the arrow protruding from Malcolm's shoulder. And another one protruding from his calf.

"Malcolm, you're wounded."

"God has been good to me this day."

A horn blew. I looked through the tangled combatants and saw King Berthold blowing it. His garments were spattered with blood. He blew the horn again and again. Loudly into the frenzied midday heat.

"What does that mean?" I asked an archer fighting next to me.

"It means all is about to be lost. Don't hold back. Give everything you've got."

The reserves swarmed across the compound and climbed up to the walkway. They were rested, impatient, bloodthirsty. We battled side-by-side to retain command of the walkway. We fought with a ferocity that can only be galvanized by knowing you occupy a final protective line. If they get past you, they get your loved ones, they get your children.

The slow sizzle and bang of my musket. Eye-stinging smoke from black powder. The disheartening stench of burning cabins. The whistle of arrows. Guttural grunts in response to impalement. The chop of hatchets into wood, through fingers gripping wood. Screams of falling mutants, of men with multiple wounds, fighting like animals.

Another horn sounded. This one from some distance away, from inside the woods. Moments later Ellanoyans who had been hiding there emerged from the tree line and attacked the Garhogs from behind.

Mutants climbing the ladders glanced down, startled, then up again, unable to decide what to do. Arrows flew at them from behind, striking them in the back, knocking them off the ladders. Now the enemy was on the defensive.

"Oil!" the king commanded. His face was slick with blood. Combined with his naturally red hair and braided beard, he looked terrifying in the midday sun.

Men hefted buckets of oil, lighted them like great oil lamps, and emptied them down on the panicking Garhogs. Flaming figures scattered in all directions, some crashing into one another, sparks leaping from their torched heads.

The squad from the woods reached the palisades and a fierce battle raged between them and the remaining attackers. Some of the enemy fought to the death. Most ran for the woods, shrieking in shame and fury. The Ellanoy force pursued them.

Men guarding the gate from the inside shouted up to the walkway. "Berthold! Berthold!" I leaned over the wall and looked down. Remaining Garhogs, now isolated, had surrounded an Ellanoyan and backed him up to the gate.

It was Eli.

"Come with me," I said to Malcolm. He had snapped off the arrows penetrating his shoulder and calf, but was bleeding and could only limp along. At the moment I couldn't afford him any comfort.

We climbed down to the gate. I ordered the sentry to open it.

"I can't. Garhogs are out there."

"Our people are out there too," I said. "Open it!"

He shook his head. "I have my orders."

Pushing him out of the way, I unlatched and opened the gate.

Eli fell into my arms. He carried no weapon. Before us were three desperate mutants who had nothing to lose.

"Give Eli your bow and arrows," I shouted to Malcolm.

We spilled as a group into the compound. The sentry who had refused to open the gate ran. I shot one of the monsters. Eli impaled another with an arrow. The third tackled Malcolm to the ground and was strangling him when Eli and I dragged him off. Other fighters arrived and helped us subdue him.

"Tie the fucker up," I said. "And close the gate." To Malcolm I said, "Sorry for my language, Father."

"I forgive you, my son." Then to the others, "Do as René says. Tie the fucker up."

The battle was winding down. I wondered why our warriors weren't celebrating. When I saw a few of them carrying a bloody body down from the walkway I understood why.

It was King Berthold. An arrow jutted from his chest. His arms hung limply and his eyes stared vacantly at the sky.

Chapter 32

Those of us who weren't hurt in the fighting, or weren't hurt seriously, tended to the wounded. Arrowheads were buried in Malcolm's shoulder and calf. Eva had begun searching for him as soon as the battle ended; she found us at the makeshift outdoor hospital, a patch of grass in the central meeting area where wounded and dying men were laid out and being triaged. Less than a stone's throw away, where I'd enjoyed fine food, wine, and dancing at my own wedding, some of the residents of Bounty Rock hastily erected a platform and planted a stake in the ground behind it. For victory speeches? I wondered. Eulogies?

The reason for the stake became clear when the captured Garhog was wrestled onto the platform and tied to it. And appallingly clear when a pair of Ellanoyans built a fire a short distance in front of it.

Adrienne showed up and went to work nursing the wounded. I asked her how she was doing.

"Fine," she said. "Busy at the moment."

"I'm sorry about your father."

"Let's make sure we don't lose any more."

Malcolm stood up on wobbly legs, pointed at the platform, and demanded to know what the plan was.

"Lie back down," Adrienne said. "You'll only worsen the bleeding."

"Are they going to torture that creature?"

"You're an outsider. This is not your business."

"Of course it's my business," Malcolm said. "Garhogs are men. They must be treated like men."

"Sit down and be quiet."

Adrienne had never spoken to anyone that way in my presence. She saw me staring at her and said, "Tell me how you'd feel if they killed *your* father."

"I wouldn't feel differently than I do now."

The Garhog shouted from his elevated pulpit: "I am Stout, conqueror of Kormoran and Whispertal. How beautiful the sun is, on this, the day I will die."

Men wielding copper knives mounted the platform and sawed on the mutant's fingers. After a minute one of the men lifted a long bloody finger in the air and exclaimed, "Number one!" Some of the onlookers clapped their approval.

The Garhog showed no sign of pain. Instead he sang a high-pitched song consisting of chirps and howls as well as words. It was his death song.

Malcolm made a fist. "This must be stopped."

Jonah was nearby and overhead. He came over and said, "Must it?"

Another of the Ellanoyans on the platform called down, "Number two!" The swelling crowd broke out in applause. Malcolm tried to plough through the crowd, but Jonah and others restrained him.

"Keep up that behavior, keep trying to interfere," Jonah said, "and we'll strap you to your hospital bed."

"You'll do no such thing," I told him.

228

He bowed slightly and said, "Yes, my king."

My king? But of course. I had married Berthold's daughter that morning. And Berthold had died that afternoon.

"Number three!"

The Garhog interrupted his song long enough to ape his tormentors. "Number three!" he mocked. "Make it four!"

One of the cutters raised a curling appendage for all to see. "Four it is!"

Malcolm turned to me. "You have the authority to stop this."

"So it would appear."

"Then stop it. Otherwise you condone it. And you, too, are a barbarian."

"If I'm a barbarian, so are you: Then shalt thou bring forth that man or that woman, which have committed that wicked thing, unto thy gates, and shalt stone them with stones, till they die. Deuteronomy 17:5."

"You're cherry picking again."

"That man and his friends killed Berthold, Malcolm." I gestured toward the dead Ellanoyans on the ground, their faces covered with hides. "And a dozen other people."

One of the Ellanoyan tormentors ordered the Garhog to quit singing, but the mutant ignored him. The man found a wooden bat and clubbed the victim's arms with increasingly hard blows until his bones cracked.

Still the Garhog sang.

I'm grateful to my Lord the Sun
for all the Ellanoyans
I've have had the pleasure
to kill, to kill, to kill.

He cast a defiant gaze on the assembled crowd.

And to my fellow warriors,
who fought with me so bravely
and who will eagerly avenge
my death, my death, my death.

A woman mounted the platform and cut the Garhog's scalp from his head, by inserting a knife beneath the skin and working her way around, making in-and-out sawing motions. Blood streamed down the monster's face and soaked his shirt. Others tore his clothes from him. He stood naked, drenched in blood.

"Stop this madness," Malcolm cried to my face.

"Let it proceed," Adrienne snapped at me in response. "Number five!"

They cut off his nose. They cut off his ears and shoved them into his mouth. He continued singing, his voice muffled.

By this time the fire was blazing. They pressed firebrands to his naked flesh. His skin secreted a greasy ooze, like fat sizzling on skewered meat. He didn't flinch. His song rose in volume.

They cut strips of flesh from his torso and thighs and cooked them over the fire. "You taste good, Stout." The Garhog sang even louder.

"It's time to shut this fucker up," someone suggested.

They clubbed him in the face. They broke his jaw and shattered his teeth. His song ceased and he fell unconscious. They threw a bucket of water in his face to revive him. They lined up to mount the platform with firebrands. They found unburned patches of skin and scorched them. They held a flame under his dangling penis and ignited it like a wick.

The Garhog was blackened and smoking and delirious.

"Let's save some for tomorrow," a man suggested.

There followed general agreement. The torturers retired for the night. The Garhog was left tied to his stake, at the mercy of mosquitoes and other flying insects drawn by the scent of blood. Malcolm climbed the platform under the watch of several Ellanoy men. He sprinkled water on the Garhog's face.

"I baptize you, Stout, in the name of the Father, and of the Son, and of the Holy Spirit. Your suffering will soon be over. Without the grace of Holy Baptism your suffering would continue for all eternity. I have extinguished the fires of Hell."

The Garhog spat at him.

*

Adrienne and I spent a restless night together in the new cabin we shared. I lay facing away from her, ignoring her attempts at affection.

"They do it to us," she assured me.

"And to justify doing it, right now someone in Garhog Land is saying, 'They do it to us.' Have the two populations ever made an effort to know and understand each other?"

She pulled on my shoulder until I rolled over and faced her.

"Point du Sable," she said, "home of the Garhogs, was once a lakeside metropolis containing millions of people. It's now a skeleton of a city. Hollow, sooty buildings. Picked clean by an uncivilized population of mutants. Various tribes that banded together not for survival, not for self defense, rather for the sake of overpowering the unaffected human population. They love the taste of garlic, which in their language is 'chicagoua.' Hence their name, Shikaakwa, which is what they call themselves. We know them, René. We know them all too well."

A question had been bothering me during my entire stay. "Ellanoyans have the intelligence and technology to employ sophisticated weapons. Yet you only use bows and arrows and other archaic implements. Why? You're capable of annihilating your enemies and creating a Paradise on Earth."

She answered my question with a question. "What is your definition of Paradise?"

After thinking about it I said, "I could list attributes. One of them would be a scarcity of Garhogs."

"Are you so sure?"

"Yes, I'm absolutely sure."

"Then how would you know you're in Paradise?"

"I would observe the lack of evil."

"But then how would you recognize good? Your definition of Paradise involves the absence of something, without which you wouldn't know how well off you are. You wouldn't know you're in Paradise."

According to her argument, there was no meaningful difference between the Ellanoyans and the Garhogs, between Bounty Rock and Kebek. Between Utopia and Dystopia. All societies ultimately have the same underbelly, and their citizens believe God or Nature is on their side. Like it or not, any realistic concept of Utopia must include suffering and ruthless justice, if for no other reason than to provide the necessary contrast.

"I can conceive of great evil," I said. "Dragons breathing fire on our village, torching babies. The dragons needn't manifest themselves tangibly for me to know they're bad. I didn't know Garhogs existed before I arrived here, yet I knew eating people was wrong."

"Wrong in your view. Besides, if we wiped the landscape of these mutants, other mutants, or something else equally evil, would take their place."

"That's cynical and fatalistic."

Minutes passed, and I thought she'd fallen asleep. I was drifting off fitfully myself when I heard her say, "I suppose it is."

*

In the morning the torture resumed. Fresh wounds were inflicted over old ones, the latter now putrid and breeding worms. I found Malcolm in the crowd, heavily bandaged but mobile. His face was twisted in anguish. Jonah the sage stood next to him, watching the torture stoically.

"Convince them to let the Garhog kill himself," I suggested.

"He would not avail himself of the opportunity," Jonah said. "It would be an act of cowardice."

"For ye are bought with a price," Malcolm recited, "therefore glorify God in your body, and in your spirit, which are God's. 1 Corinthians 6:20. If he kills himself, if he hastens his death, he won't enter Heaven."

"I think he's already disqualified himself," I said. "One more sin isn't going to tip the scale."

"One more sin is nevertheless one more sin."

Jonah said, "Let me see if I understand your religion. You believe a man nailed to a wooden cross rose from the dead."

"Yes," Malcolm answered.

"And he is now an invisible sky wizard."

"He is the Son of God."

"Very well, the son of the invisible sky wizard. This wizard and his son, they control your destiny?"

Malcolm closed his eyes. "There is no point explaining to someone who is not receptive to the explanation." He turned to me and said, "Help me stop this barbarian ritual."

"Are you sure that's what you want?" I said. "Have you considered this may be the same Garhog who tortured you?"

"Because all Garhogs look alike?"

"Well, they do."

"Not to each other, they don't."

By this time men, women, and even children were crowding the platform, each armed with a firebrand, a sharp object, or a club. They took turns mounting the platform to burn, impale, or beat the mutant. When the firebrands lost their heat the tormentors hopped down from the platform and returned them to the fire.

They wedged firebrands between the mutant's back and the stake to which he was tied, to make sure his entire body was covered with burns. His blood had dried on his skin and darkened overnight. Other than preserving the general form of a man, he was an amorphous lump of blackened, greasy smudge.

They applied firebrands to his encrusted wounds, opening them up to deliver exquisitely painful burns deep in his flesh and muscle. They pressed glowing coals to his eyes to blind him. His eyeballs sizzled and gelatinous liquid squirted out from behind the coals.

They inserted a freshly heated firebrand into his anus. He fainted. They threw water on him. He came to, turning his head this way and that, his lifeless eye sockets like caverns in his skull.

Malcolm wept for the Garhog. Adrienne stood by me, holding my arm, to steady me. Or perhaps to prevent me from interfering. I felt pity for the poor monster despite everything. But I was not going to lift a finger to help him. The woman I loved, as well as the entire village of Bounty Rock, would be against me.

They tied cords around his chest and torso and set them on fire. His toasted flesh hissed. He was burned so badly now, smoke rose lazily from his body and dissipated in the breeze.

"Mercy!" Malcolm cried out. "Will no one have mercy on this creature?"

"You do not kill men where you come from?" Jonah asked.

"We kill men, but we are not so cruel."

"You do not burn men?"

"Yes, but only for heinous crimes. Specifically for crimes against God."

"Crimes against the invisible sky wizard," Jonah said. "I submit to you, this Garhog has committed crimes that would be considered heinous in any jurisdiction."

"Cut him free," I said. I'd had enough.

"Cut him free," Jonah called to the platform.

They cut the Garhog free. He ran, blindly, and tumbled off the end of the platform. The crowd laughed. He stood up again and ran in circles, shrieking in anger or agony, unable to form words because his jaw was broken and his tongue was severed.

"Kill him," I said. "Put an end to this."

The Ellanoyans armed themselves with blazing firebrands and encircled the Garhog. Everywhere the creature turned he met a burning stick. He howled and shifted directions, only to be burned again.

By now he was unrecognizable as a man. A blackened, smoldering hunk of oozing, hissing meat. With a charred head whose skin had mostly melted off, leaving a thinly dressed skull and rows of broken teeth.

One of the Ellanoyans clubbed him. He fell. He scrambled to rise, but was clubbed again. He tried to crawl.

The mob fell upon him and cut off his hands and feet. They lifted and carried him to the fire, where they laid him on the low remnant flames. His blood dripped into the glowing embers, sputtered and popped, and filled the air with the scent of death.

Incredibly the monster rolled out of the fire and dragged himself toward his tormentors on his elbows and knees. They speared him as they would a wounded bear.

Still he crawled toward them, blubbering in pain and rage. They clubbed him in unrestrained fury. They beat and kicked and punctured him until he lost his strength and will, flopped to the ground on his chest, and was inert.

They turned him over. Cut open his chest. Removed his heart. It was still beating! They handed the heart to the children who jostled one another to take bites from it.

"It will give them courage," Jonah explained.

"It will make them monsters, too," Malcolm said. He teetered and grabbed my shoulders for support.

"Are you alright?" I asked.

"Thanks be to God I baptized him," he said. "He's in the arms of the Lord now."

Adrienne approached and asked the assembled mass for quiet. She dropped to one knee before me.

"I should have done this yesterday," she said, "but I was distracted in the chaos." She bowed her head. "The king is dead," she announced. "Long live the king."

Others went down on one knee, facing me. Like dominoes the assembled crowd followed suit. Only Malcolm remained standing.

Hundreds of voices repeated Adrienne's words. "Long live the king."

Adrienne stood, faced the people, and raised her voice loud. "Long live the king!"

"Long live the king!"

Chapter 33

Malcolm declared it was time to go home. The situation had gotten out of hand. When we were alone in his cabin he performed an exaggerated curtsy and said, "That is, if you approve, my liege."

"Come on, Malcolm. You know I didn't ask for any of this."

"You married the girl."

"I love the girl."

"You knew you'd be king."

"I didn't know Berthold would die."

"Life consists of choices and consequences," he said. "Or so you and Jonah keep reminding me. Not all consequences are predictable, nevertheless you are responsible for them. So stop being a hypocrite and starting taking responsibility."

"Well, I'm happy to hear you've learned something in this place. Back home 'choices and consequences' would get you defrocked."

"We're going to find out." He was shuttling around the cabin, collecting and organizing. I realized he was packing.

"Right," I said. "Tell me more about this crazy idea of yours."

"We return to Kebek. Me as a kind of two-way ambassador. You as an envoy. You are, after all, King of Ellanoy."

"Oh, and they'll fall to their knees over that one."

"We'll put the two cultures in contact with each other. Kebek has much to learn from Ellanoy. Certainly Ellanoy can benefit from exposure to some traditional religion."

So that was it. Ever the missionary, Malcolm was bent on teaching scripture to the infidels and saving them from eternal damnation. Religionists ruled Kebek. Bounty Rock was a secular society. Any effort at homogenization was cultural assimilation in disguise. The natives learn about God. The missionary remains steadfast in his dogmatic beliefs.

It was necessary to test my theory. I asked, "How many missionaries do you think Bounty Rock needs?"

He reflected for a moment. "Oh, I'd say two or three would do, given the size of the population. Of course, there are other Ellanoy communities."

"Of course. How many Ellanoy missionaries will Kebek need?"

He looked at me quizzically. "Why would they need any at all?"

And there you have it, I thought. "They'll arrest us," I said.

"No they won't. Not after they've heard what I have to say. I'll convince the bishop. He'll listen."

"Malcolm, they'll burn us."

"Recall the Muslim contingent that visited from the Land of Flowers?"

"Yes, and I recall stoning them on the way out of town."

"They were welcomed like diplomats, that's the point. They were given latitude, the opportunity to explain themselves."

"We threw rocks at their heads!"

"God won't let me fail in this mission."

"Dammit, you keep changing the mission. You keep shifting the goal line."

"You have to trust me."

"I trust you. I'm not sure I trust your god."

He quit packing, stood to his full height, and put his face in mine.

"The situation has changed since we left Kebek, my young sovereign. We're now on a mission from God. These people know nothing of the Bible. It's our holy duty to teach the gospels to pagans and other miserable wretches. Even the Garhogs, if we get the opportunity. When the bishop learns of our mission he'll not only pardon any crimes we've allegedly committed, he'll give us keys to the city."

"What about the western passage? The Vermillion Sea? China?"

He was still for a moment, and I could tell the question caused him pain. "Those will have to wait."

"They're your passion."

"We found the legendary land of Ellanoy," he said. "That will have to do for now. We'll explore further when we return."

"Malcolm, the year is growing late. Winter will catch us. Can't this wait until spring?"

"We'll travel faster. We know the route. The currents will be with us most of the way."

"I'm not going to spend another miserable winter in the woods!"

"You won't. I promise. I've worked it out. If we average forty miles a day—and we can—we'll reach Kebek before the first freeze."

"*Forty?*" I turned to go. "I have to think about this."

"Well, don't take too long. We're leaving in two days."

"Why the rush? At forty miles a day we'll arrive in no time. Hell, let's accelerate to fifty!"

"Did you see what happened yesterday? Were you watching as they tortured the Garhog?"

"I saw what happened yesterday."

"And you still think this place is Utopia? We're leaving. We have a job to do. We're not going to waste any time going about it. As you point out, the season is already late. Two days is enough to prepare our departure. Get your life in order and plant your butt in the boat."

"You no longer have the authority to speak to me in that manner."

The arguing must have been too much for him, because he went into a coughing spasm. Bent at the waste, hands on his knees, he hacked and gasped until he regained control.

"Malcolm?"

"René, I have to go home. You have to come with me. I can't do it by myself."

"Malcolm, this is my home."

"I need you." He coughed some more and struggled to catch his breath. "I didn't want to tell you this, because I know how you like to worry. The bleeding is worse. Last night I dreamed of snakes again."

"Then maybe you should stay here. Delay the return until spring. Until you feel better."

He shook his head. "I don't know how much time I have left."

"What about Adrienne?" I said. "What about Eva?"

"Sacrifices," he answered. "The joys of life are but sacrifices waiting for an opportunity to be offered."

The joys of life. I thought of all the hours I'd spent in his classroom, in a kiddy desk in the front row, listening to him speak of integrity and morality and living the righteous life. He was a father to me when I lost my father, a mentor when I needed guidance, a partner in scientific pursuits, and a friend when all my other friends turned out to be acquaintances.

The joys of life. I missed my mother and sister. I was worried sick about them. If I never returned home, I'd never see them again. That was the tipping point.

So there would be one more canoe trip. Someday there would be one to investigate the mouth of the Father of Waters. There might even be one to visit the Vermillion Sea. At least there would be one to take Malcolm back to Kebek so he could share his discoveries with the people of the coast.

"Okay," I said. "I'll come with you."

"Good. We leave in two days."

"Right."

He began coughing again. "And that king thing?" he choked out.

"What about it?"

"Don't let it go to your head."

*

In Adrienne's arms that night, after the lovemaking, I said, "Malcolm is on a mission. To bring Utopia to Dystopia. Problem is, he's got the two mixed up. He can no longer differentiate between good and evil."

"He has learned a great lesson," Adrienne said. "For the boundary between the two is thin and permeable."

"I can't let him go back, not alone. And I don't think it's right to accompany him either. Even though I'm worried about my mother and sister, about how they've been treated during my absence. They'll lock us up if we show our faces in Kebek again. They'll tie us to a pole and barbeque us."

"Not if I come with you."

"What are you talking about?"

"You can't let Malcolm return alone. Fine. I can't allow you to leave without me. As an official and lawful representative of my people, as Princess—now Queen—of Ellanoy, they must accept me as a diplomat and treat me as visiting royalty."

"And me?"

"As King of Ellanoy, they must treat you likewise."

"What they must do, and will do, are conceivably different."

"My presence guarantees the safety of all of us. And besides," she hugged me, "I can't bear to spend another night without you."

"Spending another night without you is not an aspiration of mine, either."

"Then it's settled. The three of us travel to your home country as diplomats to arrange for peaceful exchanges between our two peoples. My father would approve. He often sent me on exactly just such missions, to the north and west. This time it's to the east. Now let's get some sleep."

"I can't sleep. I'm too wound up."

"You're always wound up."

"I don't suppose you have a cure for that."

"Two, as a matter of fact. One temporary, one permanent. The temporary one we just finished practicing." She stroked my cheek and kissed me.

"Hmm. And the permanent one?"

"The permanent cure requires that you find peace of mind."

"And where do I look for it?"

"Like everything else, it's a choice. You choose to accept things the way they are."

"You make it sound so easy."

"It's not. It wasn't easy for me. I didn't fully experience it until earlier this summer, because something essential was missing from my life."

"And that was?"

"You."

*

Malcolm wasn't hard to convince. I found him in the garden and said:

"Adrienne's coming with us."

"Is she?" He was harvesting radishes, working them individually with his fingers to remove the dirt.

"She's a diplomat, an emissary. It's her job."

"Is it?"

"She'll win over the bishop. She'll win over the council of bishops."

After a long sigh he said, "I hope so."

"She won *you* over, didn't she?"

He was still dressing in local garb instead of his traditional black robe. And he was avoiding Eva. She followed him around at first, watching him weed the garden, tend the cabin, and visit with others, her arms loose at her sides. Then she disappeared.

"Malcolm," I said, "we have to talk about Eva."

"No, in fact, we don't."

"If Adrienne accompanies me, Eva can accompany you. I'm sure it's what she wants."

"It's none of your business. Besides, I can't return to Kebek with a girlfriend, René. You know that."

"Your happiness is my business. The two of you are miserable."

"Sometimes misery is what it takes to serve God."

"Dammit, Malcolm, have you ever considered the possibility that God wants you to be happy? That kneeling and groveling and denying yourself pleasure, and scourging yourself when you have a 'weak' moment and act like a man—that all such self-debasing behavior might be the opposite of what God wants?"

"You need to shut up, and you need to do it now."

"You've been accusing me for months of losing faith. And you know something? You're right. The baptism you performed was the line in the sand. I have no faith in a god who considers his children to be incorrigible sinners. I have no faith in a god who would send a dying infant to Hell because of original sin. I have no interest in a religious sect obsessed with how to prepare a burnt offering, or about which animals 'cheweth not the cud.'"

He closed his eyes. He was kneeling among the radishes but had stopped pulling them. Now he collapsed into a sitting position, his legs splayed awkwardly before him. I had never seen him so weak, even after being tortured. He said, "Don't ever speak to me in this manner again."

"And what about Eva?" I asked.

"It's for the best."

*

We buried King Berthold and the others who had died in the battle. An Oak sapling was planted above the king, at Adrienne's request. It was already straight and proud. We predicted it would grow to be the tallest tree in the forest.

The feast that followed doubled as a celebration of Berthold's life and a farewell party for Malcolm and me. Ellanoyans threw parties for every event, happy or sad. Births, deaths, weddings, funerals. I thought if the sun failed to rise in the sky they'd throw a party to celebrate the stars. And if the sun returned and cast its bountiful light once more, they'd uncap the wine bottles and toast the end of night. I was going to miss Ellanoy.

During a final visit to the library I surveyed the work undone. The rest of the cataloguing would have to wait for my return, although I wasn't sure I could serve as both librarian and king.

Then again, why not? What better calling for a librarian? What better occupation for a king?

That night Tomas returned to me in a dream. A mere skeleton, wisps of remnant hair dangling from his skull, eye sockets dark and infinite. And snakes. They slithered around his neck and through his ribcage, flicking their forked tongues. His jaw clacked a warning, a vision of the future, of ordeals awaiting the disconsolate and the damned.

Part Three
The Light of the World

Chapter 34

On the morning of departure, as Malcolm and I were finishing preparations and rechecking checklists, Eli showed up, dressed in travel clothes and bearing provisions.

"What do you think you're doing?" Malcolm asked.

"Coming with you."

"Not this again, Eli. Someone has to run the show while we're gone."

"Jonah can do that. Someone has to look out for my sister."

"Oh?" I stood up from where I was working. "You don't think I'm up to the task?"

"As a matter of fact I do, but I need an excuse for coming along, and this one sounds better than a mere taste for adventure."

Jonah saw the party off. In fact most of the village was present riverside as we put the canoes in the water. Some brought presents of crystals and smoked meat. There were too many provisions in our canoe and they weighed us down. The crystals the Ellanoyans used as money wouldn't serve us any longer once we reached the Great Lakes, but we couldn't bring ourselves to refuse them.

"What have you got in this thing?" Malcolm asked mockingly. "It's displacing water like it's full of rocks."

"Rocks," I answered.

Malcolm's forehead was beaded with sweat, even though the day was cool. "Do you feel well?" I asked him.

"I feel fine."

"Fine enough to travel?"

"To Hell and back."

Eva appeared at the edge of the crowd. She and Malcolm made eye contact. She stepped into the river, a short distance from where the canoes were anchored in knee-deep water. Malcolm hesitated, looked up at the sky for a moment. Then stepped out of the canoe, trudged through the water to where she stood, and took her into his arms.

They held each other cheek-to-cheek. Malcolm spoke in Eva's ear, and she nodded. Tears ran down her face. He kept speaking. She nodded and cried. Finally he pulled away and she waded back to shore.

We were off. The villagers receded into the distance. Malcolm kept turning to look behind him, trying to locate Eva in the waving crowd. He settled into a stroking rhythm, his head lowered.

A small flotilla of canoes accompanied us, commanded by Eldon, a six-foot-six Ellanoy warrior. He and his companions would take us as far as the fourth Great Lake, where we'd left our own canoe.

We reached the inlet after two days of uneventful paddling, evenings spent on the river bank, smoking pipes next to the fire.

Eating our stock of smoked meat. Speculating on the nature and composition of stars.

The third morning Eldon's team beached and hid all but one of the canoes, which they portaged. We tramped the same well-beaten path Malcolm and I had taken when first captured by the Garhogs. Our Ellanoy friends were constantly on alert, their bows loaded and ready to draw. During our final evening together Malcolm quietly gave the crystals to Eldon for disbursement among his party, as a tip for escorting us.

We located Wilbur still tucked away and camouflaged where we'd left him.

"Hello, old friend," I said.

The next morning the Ellanoyans returned to Bounty Rock without fanfare, leaving their spare canoe with us. The four diplomats—Malcolm, Adrienne, Eli, and I—were on our way.

*

Adrienne and I took Wilbur. Malcolm and Eli boarded the other canoe. It was clear from the start that Malcolm wasn't feeling well. He paddled listlessly, and at first I thought he was grieving the separation from Eva or suffering from the stress of the last few hectic days. But late in the afternoon he slumped over in exhaustion. We halted on the bank for a break and I put my hand to his forehead. He had a fever.

We quit early and made camp. Eli and I hunted for fresh meat, thinking it would serve Malcolm better than yet another meal of smoked jerky. We brought home two squirrels and a pheasant. Malcolm ate little, after which he retired to the hut he shared with Eli.

Adrienne and I settled down in the second hut. I suggested we give Malcolm a rest from paddling for a few days, or until he recovered. And that we relieve Eli as necessary; he would be powering their canoe by himself.

Adrienne said, "I'm afraid it's worse than that."

"Why do you think so?"

"His temperature rose so quickly. He seemed fine just hours ago."

"Illness hits big men harder."

She nodded. "Let's just pray I'm wrong."

The next morning we were off again, paddling up the southeastern shore of the fourth Great Lake. The morning sun faced us, then gradually slid to our right each day as the shore curved northward.

Sand dunes dominated the bank. The wind had sculpted the terrain into smooth and pleasant shapes, parabolas and hillocks and parallel ripples, like a child playing in a sandbox. Hardy grasses and shrubs forced their way stubbornly upwards, freeing themselves from the sand.

Malcolm's strength ebbed with every stroke of the paddle. His fever rose and he shook with chills. He lost all appetite. Most of what he tried to force down came back up.

But the worst was the diarrhea. We had to stop frequently, and I had to help him stumble into the woods to squat. His condition became so distressing he took one of the huts for himself, after first insisting he sleep under the open sky. The other three of us crowded into the second hut.

As we progressed northward the landscape transitioned to woods and meadows. I scouted for a place to camp for a spell, to give Malcolm a chance to recover before continuing the strenuous journey home. The wind was against us and paddling became a frustrating effort in near-futility. Meanwhile Malcolm's diarrhea turned into a bloody flux. He grew so feeble, we had to carry him in and out of the canoe.

"I'm taking you back to Ellanoy," I told him. "They can help you better there."

"Don't bother. There isn't enough time. I'm not going to last much longer."

"Nonsense. Don't talk like that."

"Find a pleasant place for my journey to end."

"I'll find a pleasant place, but it will be for you to rest and recover."

"If you insist."

He never complained or lost his sense of humor. At one point, while lying in the bottom of the canoe he shared with Eli, he called over to me, "Wind defeating you, is it?"

"In the most humiliating way."

"Defeating the mosquitoes, too."

"Well, there is that."

"Always look on the bright side."

"You know," I said, "the wind could be at our backs and defeat the mosquitoes as well."

"Wind works in mysterious ways."

We passed a small stream emptying into the lake. Next to its bank was a gentle hill covered with short grass. Malcolm pointed at the hill. He said, "That's where I want my path to end."

Chapter 35

We no doubt could find a shadier place for Malcolm to rest, so I urged Adrienne and Eli to keep paddling. The wind rose against us, stronger than before. I took it as a sign and turned back. We canoed up the stream and beached the vessels. I ordered Eli to circle the area and look for evidence of mutants: paths, footprints, refuse, notched wood. It was a routine Malcolm and I had practiced almost since the day we left Kebek. Adrienne and I unloaded the vessels, carried gear and supplies up the grassy hill, and built a fire.

Eli returned shaking his head, and together we assembled the huts. We laid Malcolm down in his and arranged his hides as comfortably as possible.

His fever raged. Sweat covered his face and he shook violently with chills. Adrienne made a broth from leftover squirrel meat after sending Eli in search of orangeroot and carrots. She dispatched me to the stream bank to collect some clay to complete the potion.

The day passed and Malcolm only got worse. He begged me to read him his death meditation.

"Happy is the man who keeps the hour of death always in mind," I began, "and daily prepares for it."

At his request I brought him a bowl of water. He sprinkled some salt into it and said a blessing, making the sign of the cross. "Now it's holy water," he said in a shaky voice. "You'll need it in the hours to come."

His bloody flux had become intolerable, so he refused to take any food. He instructed me about his burial, which he assured me would take place within a day. He told me how to choose the location. The manner in which I was to position his hands and feet. At the moment of death I should ring the little bell he kept in his mass kit. I should ring it again as his body was lowered into the ground. He gave me these instructions calmly and stoically; we could have been discussing the burial of a stranger.

"Now go and get some rest, Grout. I'll call you when it's time."

A long time had passed since he called me that, and I smiled. "How will you know when it's time?" I asked.

It was his turn to smile. "You have to know these things when you're a priest."

His death was not something I could grasp. He was feverish, that was all. He was delusional. Too agitated to rest, I worked with Adrienne and Eli to prepare the camp for a long stay. We gathered firewood and cooked a meal. Eli had a notion to build a semi-permanent wooden structure for us all to live in, to which purpose he staked out a foundation and eyed the locale's trees and rocks.

Three hours after I'd left Malcolm I heard him call my name in a weak voice. I entered the hut and found him staring blankly at the roof.

"I'll hear your confession now," he said without looking at me.

Kneeling on the ground next to him, I said, "Bless me Father, for I have sinned." I confessed to straying from the church, from its doctrine. To entertaining competing philosophies. To doubting the wisdom and teachings of church doctors and leaders. To knowing the nakedness of a woman.

"Women," he corrected. "Are you sorry for your sins?"

After a moment's hesitation I said, "Yes, Father."

"As penance you'll immerse yourself up to your neck in the lake and say one hundred Hail Marys to the Blessed Virgin Immaculate."

"Yes, Father."

"You'll take my place on this mission. You'll bring the tranquility of Bounty Rock to Kebek and the faith of Kebek to Bounty Rock."

"Yes, Father." I wanted nothing more than to return to Bounty Rock and live out my days with Adrienne.

"Promise me. Without it, this adventure of ours is just that, an adventure. A sequence of escapades. Please give me this. It's my dying wish."

"Yes, Father."

"Swear to me."

"I swear it, Father."

"May God grant you pardon and peace. I absolve you of your sins. Now you'll hear my confession."

He confessed to being guilty of all the vices. Vanity, because he had worn his priesthood with undue pride. Envy and greed, because he had coveted the possessions of others. Wrath at common people who were guilty of nothing worse than ignorance and simplicity. Sloth. Gluttony.

"And lust," he said. He choked up and tears came to his eyes. "Eva."

"Any compassionate god would forgive you for Eva," I said.

"Compassion is not something man can demand of God, rather only God can demand of man." He pointed at the crucifix he always kept mounted on his wall. "Bring it to me, please." He caressed it, his fingers probing its familiar form. "It's time for extreme unction," he said.

With my fingertips wetted in the bowl of holy water I made the sign of the cross on his closed eyelids, his ears, lips, hands, and feet.

"Through this holy anointing," I said, "and by His most tender mercy, may the Lord pardon you what sins you have committed by sight, hearing, speech, and action."

He said, "*Credo quod redemptor meus vivit.*"

"Now's not the time to leave me, Father Malcolm."

"*Maria, mater gratiæ, mater dei, memento mei.*"

"You've always been there for me. As far back as I can remember."

"Fetch the others."

The three of us crowded around Malcolm, who was gazing at a faraway place.

"Hold the crucifix in front of my face," he said.

Eli removed it from his hands and held it up for him. He stared transfixed at the figure of Jesus on the cross.

"*De profundis clamavi ad te, Domine.*"

Adrienne dampened a cloth and dabbed his forehead.

"*Domine, exaudi vocem meam.*"

"Hold on, Malcolm," I said. "We need you. I need you."

He convulsed in tears. "It's because I had relations with the girl."

"No, no, not at all."

"God's punishing me."

"Don't do this to yourself."

He took control of his breathing. "It's time. I'm going to repeat the names of Jesus and Mary. If my voice falters, please pick up the chant for me." He began: "Jesus... Mary..." The chant went on for several minutes. Occasionally he opened his eyes and gazed at the crucifix, then closed them again and resumed his ritual.

"Jesus... Mary..."

When his voice failed him the rest of us joined in.

"Jesus. Mary."

He looked past the crucifix and studied an apparition visible only to him. He smiled hesitantly. His expression took on a warm glow. Recognition. Acquiescence.

Our voices rose in volume: "Jesus! Mary!"

The light went out in his eyes, the muscles in his arms and shoulders relaxed, and his chest heaved for the last time.

"Jesus!" I cried out. "Mary!"

Adrienne took the crucifix from Eli's hands and laid it on Malcolm's chest. She motioned for her brother to follow her out of the hut. I was alone with my mentor and friend. And yet it wasn't him anymore. It was his shell, a mere vessel for his spirit, an empty one.

He had survived a journey such as no man had ventured to attempt in a dozen generations. He had survived torture by the Garhogs, and then vicious battle with them. He had survived a Levitican education that nearly closed his mind to logic, to critical thinking, to hope and love.

Yet he had left Bounty Rock with hope, and at Bounty Rock he had found love.

The bell was in his mess kit. I fished it out and rang it. I left the hut and stumbled down the hill and into the woods. The air was still, the fabric of nature was static and calm. My footsteps crunched in the forest litter. The trees waited respectfully.

Of the breeze I made a request: tell Eva. Send word throughout the land. Father Malcolm Matthew Marchand, Order of Leviticans, has finished his journey.

The breeze responded. Tree crowns bent to the southwest, like brushes against the sky. Carrying a message from grove to grove, from the fourth Great Lake to Bounty Rock, from the end of his trail to the woman he loved.

*

We buried Malcolm's remains in the manner he had instructed. We didn't erect a cross, because mutants might find it and desecrate the grave. I smoothed the soil above him and covered it with leaves and twigs.

Except for the memories we, the living, carried with us, he might as well never have walked the Earth.

Round about midnight a storm rose to the west. It didn't touch us, nevertheless I stepped outside and watched bolts of lightning flicker and strike the horizon, and I listened to thunder rumble and drum from far away. Malcolm had at last arrived at the Vermillion Sea. I thanked God for granting my friend a final wish before calling him home.

Chapter 36

Adrienne, Eli, and I continued northward along the eastern shore of the fourth lake. For several days we hardly spoke to one another. "There," to indicate where to pitch the huts. "Ready," when the game was finished cooking. "Night," to Eli when Adrienne and I separated from him, retired to our shelter, and entwined ourselves in each other's arms.

The promise I made to Malcolm was to conclude the mission and bring the two cultures together. If not for Adrienne accompanying me, I would have lacked the confidence to do so. Once the Kebekians saw her, listened to her, got to know her, the rest would be easy. We would need only recruit a delegation to visit Bounty Rock. As soon as people had been exchanged, it was a matter of exchanging culture. And philosophy. The Ellanoyans would, hopefully, appreciate the steadfast faith of the Kebekians, even if they didn't understand it at first. And the latter could hardly resist the serene, pastoral ways of the former. Two civilizations that had been separated for a quarter of a millennium would live and work together once again. Father Malcolm Marchand had opened the door.

We rose at dawn to take advantage of the available light. The winds were against us, the currents were against us. Winds meant breakers, breakers meant swamped canoes. Bailing.

Paddling and bailing. Bailing and paddling and cursing the wind and swatting the bugs. We topped the fourth Great Lake and followed watercourses to the land of the rising sun.

When the water was too shallow we dragged the canoes upstream, ropes over our shoulders, leaning into headwinds, grunting in donkey language, slipping on rocks polished by eternally patient water. To preserve our shoes we often went barefoot, which added pain to the daily fatigue and frustration.

We towed our canoes up rapids that on the westward journey Malcolm and I had navigated in euphoric terror, battling impetuous cascades that toyed with our flimsy bark shell, provoking us to laugh and shout in mad delight. This time the rapids were mere chores. Sometimes they got the better of us and grabbed a canoe, flung it downstream into calamitous channels, or steered it merrily into boat-hungry rocks. We spent our breaks sealing leaks.

Portages sapped us. It was necessary to carry the canoes on our shoulders, and now there were only three of us, so we had to make two trips just for the canoes. The supplies required two more.

Unload the hulls. Turn them upside down and lift them above our heads. Haul them. Haul the supplies. Back and forth along the same path, often for miles each way. Drop stuff off. Return for more stuff. Reload the canoes. Launch. Back on water again. Smile. Exclaim "Finally!" And around the next bend, another portage. I counted portages until they numbered fifty, then didn't bother with the tally anymore. We fell well short of the forty miles per day Malcolm estimated we would make.

Evenings were spent before the fire, exhausted and listless, shifting weight to favor one aching muscle over another. We sheltered ourselves from lake storms, from furious skies attended by thunderclaps and torrential downpours, and from feverish waves pounding the shore.

And of course from mosquitoes. They luxuriated in one final meal before laying their last eggs of the year and expiring. A banquet of three slap-happy humans. Our huts buzzed with miniature flying dinosaurs until we smoked them out. And in doing so we smoked ourselves out too.

We were always on the lookout for mutants. I imagined them peering at us from the trees as we paddled silently past ominous groves. We had to enter those groves to hunt. Whenever the musket went off I pictured an army of mutants within earshot, salivating and shoving one another out of the way to chase down human snacks. When sufficiently unnerved we anchored the canoes offshore and slept in them. Of course the practice would only slow the mutants down, it wouldn't stop them if they too had canoes or were hungry enough to take to the water. Consequently I suffered nightmares of lumpy faces peering over the gunwales, and woke at regular intervals in a heart-thumping sweat.

We fished. We foraged. I shot a deer and we smoked the meat. As we approached Chartrain, and the passage between the third and second lakes, we slowed down and took extreme care paddling forward. When Malcolm and I had passed this point on our voyage west, hideously deformed men had chased us.

This time all was quiet. No one scrutinized us from the shoreline, although in my mind's eye all manner of mutants crouched behind the bushes, their twisted mouths slobbering, their stomachs growling for roasted man-on-a-stick.

The city on the horizon was an architectural cemetery. Jagged remnants of a grand civilization. Hollow dwellings, their broken windows the eyes of death, the tragic consequences of human avarice and aggression. With breathless relief we paddled it out of sight. The remainder of the journey should be clear sailing.

On the second Great Lake we once again hugged the north shore, to avoid dead cities to the south. They were untested legends we didn't care to test. The weather was turning cold. Before long it was biting cold. It would take a miracle to reach Kebek before winter, nevertheless we made the effort. I was eager to see my mother and sister again. Drained and worn at day's end, Adrienne and I collapsed into each other's arms, usually too tired for lovemaking or even conversation.

One night when I was collecting firewood I heard a Howler nearby. They'd kept their distance during our journey, but this one was close. I dropped my wood and followed the sound. As I approached, the whatever-it-was receded. Its mournful cries were gut wrenching. At one point they sounded so close, I lunged into the brush after them, only to come up empty-handed, to hear the cries grow yet louder, always out of arm's reach. Eventually I gave up and headed back to camp, the cries following me, filling me with despair.

"You think I don't hear you?" I called into the woods. "What are you trying to tell me? What lies ahead for me?"

The only answer I received was a low moan that rose to a heartbreaking wail. As I reached the cabins the howls receded again, until all was quiet in the woods.

That night over the campfire I mentioned a desire for something appealing to drink. The next day Eli constructed a still and fermented … something. After downing several shots I had few complaints about its rough heat. Nor any concern for Howlers. Nor fear of mutants, even. No cares under the far-flung stars or heartless sun. I sang "Twinkle, Twinkle, Little Star" to raucous applause and demands for an encore.

The concoction came in handy during the months that followed, for soon lake ice forced us to make camp for the winter.

Chapter 37

We lived in a sea of white powder. We hunkered down behind drifts contoured like deer licks that shielded us from the wind. Our lives alternated between suffering from the piercing cold while hunting and foraging and suffering from the smoke of inefficient fires while huddled in our shelter.

The rabbits had gone to finishing school and become insufferable. Or maybe they'd learned enough about humans during Malcolm's and my earlier passage and were now saying, "Fool me twice, shame on me." They dodged musket balls with agility and grace. Eli fashioned traps, however, and soon we were eating bunnies again.

He and I went ice fishing together almost daily. Once we had cut a hole in the surface we could use it repeatedly. We built short stools to sit on and made conversation as best we could through clattering teeth. The ice groaned under our weight. This detracted from our cheer and sense of security but we needed the fish to supplement our diets.

The sky was desaturated, the color and texture of indistinct dreams. We grew restless with cabin fever and the monotony of daily life.

Hunt. Check the snares. Gather firewood. Start a fire. Restart the fire. Melt snow for drinking, cooking, and bathing. Forage. Shovel snow. Make repairs to the hut. Fish. Daydream of an ethereal sun. Hunt. Check the snares.

The three of us occupied one hut for shared warmth and company. Adrienne and I slept in each other's arms, but our sexual liaison necessarily went on hiatus. I was content to hold her, to press my lips to her ear, whisper my love for her, and hear the same whispered in return.

Adrienne and Eli listened to tales of Kebek, my friends there, the seminary basement, my sister. And the authority figures we would have to persuade. Adrienne remained silent, and I knew she missed Bounty Rock. My secret fear was that she regretted making the trip. There was nothing we could do now but press forward.

Eli seemed to have a different opinion. "So," he asked, watching the snow fall in heavy flakes, "you think we should keep going?"

"You think we shouldn't?"

He shrugged. "The direction one chooses to travel depends on where the good things are."

The temperature improved, and our spirits with it. We watched the sky for the birds to return. Snow still blanketed the land, but now hope floated on stiff winter winds that abated more each passing day.

One morning as Eli and I walked onto the ice to fish we spoke of readying the canoes to continue our journey. I thought we still had plenty of time, but Eli was impatient and wanted to begin preparing. I agreed because it would give him something to do, it would scratch the intolerable itch he had to be on his way again.

We sat on our stools with our lines penetrating the icy water and planned the breakup of the camp. He spoke of how good it would feel to be paddling again. How satisfying it would be to put rested muscles to work.

From far away came a sharp noise, a cracking sound I couldn't place. At first I thought it was a distant gunshot. Or heavy branches splintering under the weight of ice and snow.

Eli stood up from his stool and said, "We need to get off the ice."

They were his final words. The ice opened beneath his feet and he plunged into the frigid water.

"Eli!" I lay down flat and crawled to the edge of the hole. I couldn't see him. The water was murky and bottomless. A current moved lethargically eastward. I crawled parallel to the current and tried to spot him under the ice. But the pane separating us was opaque and only reflected the gloomy sky above.

"Eli! Eli!"

An eerie silence gripped the lake. My friend was struggling somewhere in the numbingly cold and indifferent water beneath my feet. He had perhaps a minute of air left in his lungs, maybe less, and only needed an escape hole and a helping hand.

But I didn't know where to cut the hole. I tried nevertheless. I chose an arbitrary spot downstream and hacked at the ice with the hatchet until I could plunge my arm into the water. I reached around in vain, grasping at slippery swirls in the flow.

"Eli!"

Farther downstream I cut another hole. Minutes had passed since he went under.

"Eli!"

The silence was rent by more cracking noises, and by the viscerally nauseating sound of ice sheets grinding against one another, like tectonic plates exulting in their power and sovereignty, disdainful of anyone who dared tread upon them.

"Oh God, Eli, I'm so sorry. Eli! Eli!"

Chapter 38

Adrienne's face hardened when I gave her the news. She said "Excuse me" and went for a walk in the woods. Two hours later she returned and got busy about camp like nothing had happened.

"Talk to me," I said. She shook her head.

My journal was still taking shape. I'd been sketching waterways and asking myself what I should name them. As the region's only cartographer, naming features was a privilege I alone enjoyed. I elected to name the lake we were on Lake Eli. I told Adrienne.

"Then let's name the fourth lake Lake Malcolm," she said.

"Lake Marchand. He would prefer using his last name."

"Lake Marchand it is. And Lake Eli."

She was adding wood to the fire. She stopped, knelt before the fire, and began sobbing. I went to her side and put my arm around her. She buried her face in my neck and sobbed, "He was my brother. He was my little brother."

*

Spring arrived overnight in a breeze, dancing from tree to tree to the music of trickling meltwater. The lake ice broke into large restless pieces that jostled one another for room to maneuver. Buds dabbed the branches. Birds returned to the land in squawking reunion parties. The air smelled of promise.

We broke camp. I erected a cross to Eli on the shore, and we were on our way.

Down to one canoe now and it was my old friend Wilbur, who had served his masters so well. I took the front, which had been Malcolm's spot. We paddled and portaged from Lake Eli to the first Great Lake. This time it was all downstream. The waters were on their way to the Sea of Atlantis and we were along for the ride.

We hugged the south shore as before, to stay as far away from Turonado as possible. Malcolm and I had encountered no mutants here during our westward voyage, but Adrienne and I were taking no chances. Legends of mutant infestations in cities still glowing with radiation loomed fresh and vivid in our shared imagination.

We followed the shore silently, even dipping our paddles gently into the water, fearing that swirling and dripping water could be heard from across the lake's expanse. When I'd judged the city was behind us we made camp on the shore.

"No fire tonight," I said. "We'll wait another couple of days before we light one."

"What will we eat?"

"This." I removed some moldy old jerky from a hide pouch.

"Oh joy," she said.

After "dinner" I scouted the area for evidence of mutants, as usual, to prevent us being caught while sleeping and serving as someone else's hot meal. I was examining a raspberry bush, wondering when it would bear fruit, when I heard the sound of approaching footsteps. I crouched in the brush.

As the steps drew nearer it became clear they belonged to Adrienne. She was carrying my musket in one hand and an armful of gear in the other. I rose, and she saw me.

"What do Turonado mutants look like?" she asked. Her face was tense with deep concern.

"Ugly as all fuck," I said.

"They're here."

Leaving her there, I ran back toward the camp. As soon as it was within sight, four mutants landed in two canoes. I hid behind a tree and watched.

The mutants disembarked and dragged their canoes onto land, hopping over the mud and shale like frogs tramping on two legs. They peered into the woods, their eyes wide and their mouths slobbering. It felt like they were looking straight at me. I raced back to Adrienne and took the musket from her hands.

"I can make better use of this," I said. "You can have my machete." It was strapped to my belt.

"Too big."

"You have your knife, right?"

"Right." She patted its holster.

"Good. We have to split up. You run west, I'll run east."

"How will we find each other again?"

The mutants howled as they picked up our scent. We were out of time. I formed my hands into a ball and blew through a gap between my thumbs, making a soft bird call.

"When you hear that," I said, "it's me. Now run. Run for your life."

A quick kiss, and we took off in opposite directions. As I ran I made as much noise as possible, kicking brush, snapping branches, and grunting in exertion, to draw the mutants my way.

I knew Adrienne would slip so quietly through the woods, not even the mice and deer would know of her passage.

Crossing a stream gave me the opportunity to slow down and glance back. Three of the four mutants were following. Good, I thought. If they caught me I was confident Adrienne could find her way back to Bounty Rock.

The funny characteristic of these mutants was their bow-leggedness, making them awkward runners. They employed a stomping motion, back and forth from one foot to the other, like infants learning to walk. I almost laughed despite my situation.

An arrow whistled past my head and struck a tree in front of me. No time for laughing. I ran. I tried to keep large trees behind my back, to block arrows. I kept running even when my footsteps were the only ones audible in the forest. I shifted directions. I waded across a stream, and again across one of its branches, in case they were tracking by smell. I didn't know if their sense of smell was good enough, but now wasn't the time for the scientific method.

Finally I stopped to sit on a fallen trunk and rest. No sounds were out of the ordinary. The birds emerged from hiding and sang again, which indicated no monsters lurked in the area.

All I needed was one leafy tree with a branch within reach. I found one, climbed it, removed my shirt, pants, and belt, and used the articles to strap myself to the trunk.

Night fell. I dozed.

Dreams of childhood. Of climbing trees with other boys, boys whose names I couldn't remember, or possibly never knew. Their faces indistinct, their personalities mingled. Like a single cookie-cutter boy, playing multiple roles, incarnating as a circle of friends.

Climbing trees was fun then. Not for safety, not to escape wild animals or cannibalistic mutants. Merely for the sheer joy of being high in a tree, above the world. Of being as close to the moon as we'd ever get. Of calling down, "Look at me. Look how far up I've climbed."

Footsteps. Crunching back and forth in the thicket. Making no effort at concealment. Ghosts of man. Or premonitions of men.

Why did sounds carry so well in the darkness? What if the footsteps belonged to Adrienne? What if she was looking for me? But I was dreaming. I was dreaming of being a small boy again. When I was a small boy Adrienne hadn't yet been born.

Adrienne. I'd left her alone in the woods. Left the love of my life alone in the woods, armed only with a knife, hunted by cannibalistic mutants. Left the better half of my cleaved soul down there on the flat cartesian expanse with no company other than lines and curves and epsilons and deltas. I urged myself to wake up, so I could climb down and look for her. But the other boys didn't want to go home yet. They would make fun of me if I didn't stay longer, if I didn't try to climb even higher.

At dawn I woke stiff and numb and aching in all my muscles and joints. I stretched until some feeling returned, put my clothes back on, and climbed to the ground. If Adrienne had kept going she would be far away by now. But I suspected she had remained in the area to look for me, as I was now going to look for her.

Following a broad arc around the old campsite, to avoid mutants, would decrease the odds of running into her. It was a choice between risking meeting the mutants and risking not meeting Adrienne. I opted for the mutants. I crept back through the woods, pausing frequently and listening. Moving parallel to the shore, but staying far enough away from it to avoid visibility from the campsite. Occasionally I crouched in the brush and made the bird call I'd demonstrated to Adrienne. But it only met with silence.

Maybe she had indeed kept going. Maybe she was taking advantage of an opportunity to go home. I pictured her running westward, intent upon returning to Bounty Rock on foot, upon abandoning me and our mission. I should have been overcome with grief or anger, but it was disappointment that gripped me instead. Bottomless regret. Loneliness.

As I neared the camp I dropped to my hands and knees and crawled toward it. Mutants were talking and laughing. I crawled closer and peered through a bush. What I saw nearly made me cry out.

Adrienne was flat on her back, spread-eagle on the ground, naked. Her hands and feet were tied to stakes.

Jumping around and beating their chests were three mutants. They had flattened noses and foreheads, jaws bent strangely to one side, and tufts of hair sprouting from their cheeks. Even among mutants they were ugly. I made the bird call, low and mellow. Adrienne turned her head slightly in my direction; she'd heard. Only three mutants meant one was out and about. Maybe hunting, maybe looking for me. Maybe acting as lookout. If the latter, I had to find him before he found me.

A fire burned at Adrienne's feet. I assumed it was for torturing her. That's what fire was for. Cooking, keeping warm, and burning people.

One of the mutants, the largest and loudest, howled something unintelligible and dropped his pants. His huge penis hung down like an elephant's trunk. He frog-walked over to Adrienne and stood at her feet, peering at her openly spread legs. Torture wasn't the only thing these boys had in mind.

Adrienne closed her eyes. I raised the musket to my shoulder and readied to fire. The mutant wagged his dick at Adrienne and made thrusting motions with his hips. The other mutants laughed. A chuckle also came from the brush to my left.

The missing mutant.

He was invisible. I backed away from the camp, maneuvering behind the point where I'd heard the sound. As I crawled noise-lessly forward I kept my eyes open. But it was my nose that alerted me. The mutant smelled to high Heaven.

At first there was nothing but trees and shrubs. A form grad-ually took shape, a humanoid figure camouflaged with branches and leaves. He was on the lookout, all right; his job was to pre-vent me from ambushing the others. His performance review was about to take a hit.

The machete was still strapped to my belt. I unstrapped it, stepped behind him, and without giving him time to smell me or react, clamped my hand on his forehead, yanked his head back, and drew the blade across his throat.

He shuddered violently, kicking and flailing. Incredibly he rose to his feet and turned to face me.

Blood gushed from his neck. It spilled down his chest to the rhythm of his heartbeat. Any other creature would have gone unconscious from lack of blood within seconds. This one sized me up with hate filled eyes. I stepped back instinctively; an innate fear of the undead. He lurched forward, his arms outstretched, a scene straight out of my childhood nightmares. I struck the side of his neck with the machete and made another bleeding gash. He kept coming.

Holding the machete with both hands, I swung at his neck with all my strength. His head toppled off and thumped to the ground, where it rolled into the bushes, its eyes blinking at a furious pace.

His body remained standing. It took several tentative steps. Its legs picked up the pace and it scuttled into the woods, arms dangling, until it collided with a tree.

Never before had a thing so not wanted to die. I chased the thing down, thrust my machete into its back, aiming for the heart. The body teetered for a moment, then keeled over and hit the ground like a plank.

Back at the mutant's hiding place I surveyed the camp before me. Luckily none of the other mutants had noticed the ruckus. They'd had plenty to distract them. The big one was on his knees between Adrienne's legs, gearing up to rape her. She was her usual stoic self. No tension in her muscles. Her eyes open now, gazing at the sky. I raised the musket, aimed it at the mutant's head, and fired.

A loud blast, a plume of blue smoke, and the mutant rolled onto his back, his stiff dong swaying like a flagpole signaling surrender.

The other two mutants reached for their weapons. I picked up the bow at my feet, the one belonging to the headless monster, and fired an arrow at the closest of the remaining two.

It missed.

Two answering arrows whizzed past my head. I inserted another arrow and fired again. This time I hit one of the mutants in the leg.

He hopped about, howling in fury.

Again they fired back, and one of the arrows grazed my temple. Blood streamed down the side of my face. I fired once more, with the dead mutant's last arrow. This struck the chest of the howling mutant. He howled louder.

Meanwhile his companion ran to the water's edge and jumped into a canoe. I hurried into the clearing, reloading the musket as I went. As the mutant in the canoe paddled briskly away the injured one chased after him, but was too late. He ran knee-deep into the water and screamed for the other to return. I fired and hit him in the ass.

"Yeeowl!"

The now thrice-injured mutant braved the water. He would have stood a better chance against the musket, for as soon as his feet could no longer touch bottom he floundered, slapping at the water's surface, gulping and choking. I fired again and took off part of his skull cap.

He dog-paddled, blood spreading on the lake surface and drifting eastward with the current. I focused on the mutant escaping in the canoe. My first shot hit the canoe but did no damage. He crouched and paddled more energetically. My second shot missed altogether. I saw the ball splash in the water. I reloaded and aimed, but elected not to waste another shot. He was out of range. Meanwhile his less fortunate friend was now motionless, face-down in the water, drifting with the current.

Adrienne had waited with the patience of a sage for the battle to end. I untied her and retrieved her clothes from where they'd been strewn. We held each other for a few long minutes.

"Dramatic of you," she said, "waiting until the last second like that."

"It's how the hero always arrives at the scene."

She gasped at a movement behind me. I turned. The mutant I'd shot in the head had sat upright. His left eye was gory where the ball had entered. I snatched up the musket and fired at close range from my knees. The ball entered his right eye and scattered his brains behind him. He lay back down as though having reconsidered.

"Promise me something," Adrienne said.

"Anything."

"Next time we're fleeing from danger, let's not split up."

"I promise. And I'm sorry." I stood up. "We need to break camp and move on, without delay. The mutant who got away will alert others. A larger force will come. And obviously the last thing these fuckers want to do is practice good sportsmanship and die when they're supposed to."

Chapter 39

The days stretched as the year progressed. The sun delayed setting an additional couple of minutes each diurnal cycle. We rose accordingly earlier in the morning, and to spend our evenings in each other's company we quit earlier as well, foregoing an opportunity to paddle the watercourses further and rack up as many miles as possible.

The world woke with spring. Cormorants, geese, and loons chattered on the shore. Turkeys, woodpeckers, owls, and numerous other species swelled the woods with a jungle-like din. Nature's orchestra tuned up.

The landscape greened over and teemed with life. Cherry trees blossomed and buttercups bloomed. Ants and beetles emerged from underfoot, scorned our dominion, and relished the chlorophyll. We didn't mind them. We were alone together, sharing the verdant Earth and the glittering vault of night, as crickets sang love songs in the background. As lake water shimmered a full palette of blue, reflecting the sun framed in a regal sky. As crystal streams trickled into the lake, their murmurs, their cold fresh taste, their urgent odors appealing to all the senses.

Rain water percolated through the pines, weighing their drooping boughs with sparkling wetness. The air was heavy with moisture and scents of early morning dew. Breezes brought messages from faraway lands, of awakening, of energy and animation. Messages that were shared from tree to tree. A chorus of sighing, the hum of the woods, the language of the wild.

Our fires flickered and glowed on tree trunks surrounding the camp, illuminating them like stone columns from past civilizations. We stopped peering between them, into the blackness beyond the radius of light, searching for mutants. I had been this way before.

We ran the rapids. Shrieking in fear and delight as torrents of water lifted Wilbur and shook him left and right, as a crocodile might seize and throttle its prey before swallowing it whole. The rapids delivered us hurriedly from the first Great Lake into the Laurent River, gifting us with the sensation of flying before hurling us into the tumultuous, broad-shouldered currents of the region's largest artery.

"It's taking us home," I shouted back to Adrienne.

That's when Wilbur struck the rock.

The canoe threw me into the river. The river dashed me from boulder to boulder, knocking me nearly senseless. I came to rest against a weathered granite slab. After what seemed like hours but was probably only seconds I regained my senses and looked around. Adrienne and Wilbur were nowhere in sight.

Adrienne called to me, and I looked toward the bank. She had beached the canoe and was standing in ankle deep water, gesturing for me to swim over. I glanced downstream: rocks and rapids and a muscular, pulsing current; rippling energy, barely held in check by silt-soft, sinuous banks. An abiding hunger for hapless castaways, a longing to bash my head with fists of stone.

Adrienne was waiting. I looked back at her and shook my head. Following the tumble I had neither the strength nor clearness of mind to reach the bank. Yet I couldn't stay where I was. It was only a matter of time before I was pushed off the polished granite slab and washed downriver.

The water rushed over me. I felt the current's vitality. The living backbone of the river. Its life force. It had no mercy for woeful paddlers who sought preposterously to master it.

My fingers were slipping from the slick stone surface. I closed my eyes and conceded authority to the current, trusting it would recognize a kindred spirit and afford me some mercy. As my fingers lost their grip, as I relaxed, allowing the river to take me, a vessel crashed against the granite and a pair of arms encircled me.

Adrienne had launched Wilbur upstream and allowed him to carry her to the rock where I was pinned. She helped me over the gunwale and into the hull.

"From now on," she said, "stay inside the boat."

She pushed us away from the boulder with her paddle. We were immediately flung downstream. The river celebrated Adrienne's foolishness: two ill-fated boatniks rather than one. It whipped us from side to side, turned us sideways, flipped us backwards. It tossed us and battered us. Adrienne fought stubbornly, paddling demoniacally, pushing at jagged rocks with her paddle like she was spearing bears. The river growled back, wrestled with the canoe, splashed water into it, twisted its frame, punctured holes in its bark.

Eventually it gave up and calmed down. We settled into a wide and placid channel. I sat up from my sanctuary in the hull, looked around at the tranquil setting, at the innocuously passing timberland, and asked, "Need any help?"

Before she could whack me with her paddle I wrapped my arms around her, kissed her, and said, "Thank you."

"You're welcome."

"Maybe we should camp for a spell, so I can repair the tears in the bark and plug the leaks. Also, I would like an opportunity to properly express my gratitude."

She rested her head on my shoulder. "I have no objection to either."

*

It was the first warm night of the year. Adrienne and I knelt facing each other in the hut. Her skin glistened with sweat.

Several definitions of love were in circulation. I'd come up with a couple myself. But I'd never fully understood the concept until I met Adrienne. On the first level, the lowest level, love is about value, about the cost of replacing something if you lost it. About the tears you'd shed.

On the next level, love is about the discomfort of separation, the aching when apart. The yearning, the obsession. Apprehension over a slight. Fretting over a choice of gift. If love stagnates at this level, it fades. Because the intensity of a burgeoning relationship, the intoxicating desire, cannot last beyond the probation period, the phase of mutual forgiveness.

On the third and final level, love is about faith and commitment. Turns out, Malcolm was right. No matter what happens, you remain together. No matter the ravages of age, the death of civilization, the mortality of time. When the Earth turns to cinder, when the matter and energy of the universe coalesce once again in their infinite cycle, when no remnant of individuality any longer exists, your love smolders on, against the backdrop of barren space.

"I want to make you happy," I said to Adrienne.

"Making you happy makes me happy."

A scientist-philosopher from olden times, whose books were in the Bounty Rock library, once defined religion as a "feeling of being at home in the universe." It would have been hard to do better at a definition of love.

No one knew the extent of the cosmos. One of the raging scientific debates in Kebek was how far away the sun was. Eclipses had proven it was farther than the moon. But that's all anyone knew. Another debate was whether comets were meteorological phenomena, or whether they traveled through deep space. I believed in the latter. I believed they were messengers from the boundary of the universe, from the edge of time and dimension, glowing lanterns reminding us there was more to our world than the dirt beneath our feet.

When two souls in the vast celestial realm find each other, recognize each other, and connect in a way that can never be undone, it is love as true lovers experience it, and religion as it ought to be.

The universe contracted to the Euclidean three-space occupied by our little bark house. Nothing outside was of any consequence. Everything inside was a worldly treasure. The hides beneath us. The wooden bucket my foot kept hitting. Her soft, upturned lips. Our thighs rubbing against each other, like silken fire starters, like instruments coaxing a subtle tune. A pair of heartbeats, synchronized and accelerating. A coupling, an inseparability, a conjugation of two bodies, of symmetrical spirits, of blood and marrow.

Some indeterminable amount of time later I heard the crickets again. And hushed voices of nature, carried by the breeze. The world outside had returned. The bucket was just a bucket.

We rolled onto our sides and held each other against the backdrop of inquisitive nighttime sounds. The air scented with loam. And pine sap. And greenness.

*

Late in the night a familiar sound woke me. Footsteps. Careless, lumbering strides. A bear, I thought. Why tonight of all nights must I fend off a bear?

The musket was within arm's reach, as always. I wearily confirmed it was loaded, then dressed and stepped out of the hut and into the starlight. Surrounding the camp was a squad of armed men.

Martinets!

At least they weren't mutants. I was going to have to face justice sometime. It might as well be now. I dropped the musket. It was useless against the odds.

The men closed in. One of them, a bald, pear-shaped fellow who looked distantly familiar, approached and squinted at me.

"You're not René Jordan," he said. It was a question.

"Would it serve me better to be someone else?"

The men exchanged startled glances. I felt a presence behind me, and turned to see Adrienne had also dressed and emerged from the hut.

"Who else is in there?" the bald man asked.

"No one."

"Where is Father Malcolm Marchand?"

"Dead. Of the bloody flux. We buried him on the shore of the fourth Great Lake."

Again the men exchanged glances. The bald one said, "You've been to the fourth lake?"

"And beyond. Shouldn't you arrest me before you interrogate me?"

There was a long silence. The men stared at me blankly. The bald one snickered. The others followed suit, and soon they were all laughing. At a joke that went over my head.

"Master Jordan, don't you recognize me?"

Then it came to me. Bennett. Elijah Bennett. *Bishop* Elijah Bennett. A Jesuit sympathizer. "They sent a member of the Council of Bishops to capture me?"

Again the men laughed.

"My dear René," Bennett said. "You may not know it, but you and Malcolm are legends. In Kebek and up and down the coast. Your escape inspired a revolt. We're exiles. There's a whole community of exiles a couple of miles from here. And more are joining the cause each day."

Chapter 40

It was a ragtag community of men, women, and children. The men busied themselves whittling arrows and spears, or cleaning firearms if they had them. Otherwise they stood in small clutches, smoking hand-carved pipes, waiting as men wait when a battle is on the horizon.

The women hurried to and fro, sometimes carrying babies or other loads of domestic obligation. Children chased one another barefoot and often naked on the muddy paths, squealing in playful terror.

Most of the structures were fabric, and the few made of wood and bark were at the mercy of the wind. A signpost welcomed visitors with a crudely painted "New Kebek." More of a camp than a town, cloistered in the shade of a virgin pine forest, and indeed consistent with Bishop Bennett's description of its purpose. The residents didn't intend to stay long. As soon as their numbers and armament were sufficient they resolved to capture (Old) Kebek and govern it themselves.

"We don't have enough resources to take on the martinets," Bennett told us. "Not yet. The manpower is growing, almost daily, but we're critically short of firearms."

So they were making up the deficiency with spears and arrows. And catapults. They showed us horse-drawn wagons loaded with classic trebuchets straight out of antiquity. The counterweights were massive boulders elevated to position with winches. In theory the trebuchets could fire anything, but Bennett favored an oversized Molotov cocktail made of various breakable or porous vessels filled or infused with a concoction of pine tar and other ingredients.

"Kebek is made of wood," he said. "Wood welcomes any opportunity to burn."

Adrienne said, "If you burn the town down you'll have no town to occupy."

"If we burn the town down," he responded, "the autocrats who run it, led by Father Caleb Mitchell, will have no town to occupy. We'll rebuild the town and establish a democracy."

"A democracy based on faith?" I asked.

"A democracy envisioned by this country's founding fathers."

He must have seen my confusion because he said, "You're wondering how I know of their vision. Someone had to decide which books people could and could not read. The only way to do so was to read them all. That's the privilege of bishops. I intend to make it the privilege of all the people."

Families from other communities were also in the camp. They came from as far as Manhattan City to the south. Bennett's followers had learned that the entire island of New Scotland had defected from Levitican rule and all able bodied men had been conscripted into a militia loyal to the Society of Jesus. A revolt indeed.

"All inspired by you and Malcolm," Bennett said. "The two of you are household names up and down the coast."

We were fed and assigned a place to sleep. We made the rounds. The tents and cabins were interspersed among the chapped, sturdy trunks of mature pines. Needles from the previous fall, rusty with age, still littered the dappled ground, lending a cushioned feeling to the landscape.

The people were friendly but guarded, always on alert. Their eyes darted regularly to the thin columns of light leaking through the pines, keyholes that would turn to shadow with the approach of unwelcome men. They treated Adrienne and me with reverence, deferring to my alleged wisdom. I had to be careful what I said because they took everything as gospel. Malcolm would have been in his element. We didn't have to lift a finger, and if we lifted one anyway, camp residents scrambled to relieve us of our exertions.

Wherever we went, clusters parted and heads bowed. Some were so moved by my presence their lips quivered and they choked back tears. I could have been a king and wouldn't have received better treatment. In fact I was a king and felt no compulsion to mention it.

On our third evening in the camp Bennett said it was time to talk. He escorted Adrienne and me to a clearing where camp residents were gathering. Bennett, Adrienne, and I perched on an elevated platform while the audience sat cross-legged in the grass.

"When we start, speak loudly," Bennett said, "so all may hear."

It was the way they governed, he told me. A gathering, a vote, a majority decision. As pure a democracy as a community could practice. If communities remained small enough they could vote on every issue that came before them, and government officials acted as administrators rather than lawmakers.

"And if the communities are big?" I asked.

"Then they should break up into smaller communities."

285

"But the various communities can disagree among themselves about common interests, and even if they attempt direct democracy, at some point the gatherings become too large to manage. You need a central government of some kind, a representative democracy."

"A benevolent monarchy," he corrected.

"A monarchy? Really?"

"Someone predisposed to justice. Someone enlightened enough to question, to even doubt, the virtue of his own power."

The people had finished gathering and were sitting in the grass, patiently waiting for the meeting to start. Bennett rose and greeted them.

"You all know our special guests," he began. "I hope you make an effort to greet them personally, to speak to them, if you haven't already. You'll probably never again have an opportunity to meet such legends in the flesh."

He went on to remind them of their mission, of their imperative devotion to it, similar to how he and the other bishops and priests reminded their congregations on Sunday of their devotion to God. But his message wasn't religious, it was political, it was economic. The mission was to complete the revolution they'd started, to transfer power from the Leviticans to the people. To establish a capitalist democracy shepherded by a leader committed to fairness and compassion.

The term "shepherd" struck me as telling. It was a euphemism for dictator. The benevolent shepherd was Plato's philosopher king.

Adrienne, who had been witnessing the event in stoic silence, whispered in my ear: "It sounds like Bishop Bennett is lobbying for a job."

And there you had it. The prophet advocating the establishment of a supreme leader wants to be that leader, even if during his prophecy he demurs. Had Plato seen his political visions become reality, he would have ruled the Earth.

A gentleman raised his hand. "Will René Jordan lead the revolution?"

The question took me aback. Everyone, including Bishop Bennett, waited for me to respond. But how? With yes? Yes, I'll march at the head of your ragtag army, my sword raised high? Or no: even though my actions, my very existence, inspired this insurgency, I'll observe from a safe distance, snacking on walnuts, and wish y'all Godspeed. I thought, how would Malcolm answer?

"I intend to seek a peaceful solution," I said. "Adrienne and I will visit Kebek as emissaries, not only of Ellanoy but also of the coastal provinces in rebellion. Our mission will be to convince the Levitican leadership of the need to compromise, to avoid chaos and bloodshed."

My speech met with silence. They were waiting for me to continue.

"The relationship between Kebek and other Christian enclaves with the Jewish and Muslim colonies must improve. The wars must end. We don't have to agree with each other, but we do have to get along."

Bennett smiled broadly. A woman stood up from her seat in the grass and said, "They'll arrest the both of you. You realize that, don't you? Have you looked in the mirror lately, Adrienne?"

"We're the King and Queen of Ellanoy," I said. "We're serving as ambassadors. Even in Kebek, even in the jurisdiction of the Council of Levitican Bishops, we're afforded diplomatic immunity. It's the law."

"He's right," Bennett said. "They can't legally be touched."

"I'll argue for a compromise," I continued, "a separation of church and state. The two entities independent from each other and functioning side by side. It's better than war, better than either of the entities crushing the other. In conflicts like the one now brewing, no one wins. Even the victor is crippled."

There followed a stillness, mottled only by the trills and warbles of thrushes high above in the pines. An old man in the audience stood and said, "Hail to the king! Hail to the queen!"

The rest of the audience rose and repeated him. They lifted their right fists straight above their heads.

"Hail to the king and queen!"

*

Bishop Bennett provided instructions on how to contact him while inside the city. He had planted informants there, he said, but couldn't reveal their identities. If we wanted to send a message, one of us should go to the well at the center of the market square and gaze into it for a few minutes. Then proceed to Bellarmine Church, when mass was not in session, and sit in the second to last pew.

"Then wait," he said. "Someone will occupy the pew behind you. Do not turn around and look at him. Relay your message. Give him time to leave both the church and its vicinity before rising from your seat."

Most of the community followed us to our canoe and stood in awe as we cast off. I felt like a gladiator, a David. And a fraud, because I was neither. But there was no turning back. What had started as an escape from justice, or rather injustice, and had evolved into a diplomatic mission, had now become nothing less than a quest to save what remained of the civilized world.

"You were a footnote in history," Adrienne said as we paddled away. "Now you're an entire chapter."

"Let's hope it's not the last chapter in the book."

Chapter 41

During our final leg we dined on trout and venison and the ubiquitous wild strawberries. We camped for days on end. We made love in our bark shelter, on a bed of pine boughs and wool blankets, the latter a gift of the exile army.

We sat shoulder to shoulder before the fire, engrossed in its agile dance moves, the blaze merely a third member of our party. We spoke fondly of the two members we had lost. And after doing so we always observed a respectful silence, gazing into the flames, remembering.

On my daily hunting jaunts I kept an eye open for wildflowers and usually returned with a bouquet for Adrienne. She loved poppies and forget-me-nots and anything yellow. I found no evidence of human occupation. We passed Saint Maurice and Mount Royal without incident. Adrienne remarked how strange it was that a city could still be smoldering after so many years.

"It's ash," I said. "Raised by the wind."

"If I didn't know better I'd swear it was smoke."

The current pulled us toward the ocean with hushed and scarcely visible power. The watercourses between Ellanoy and Kebek had dashed us and bashed us, capsized us and dunked us, frolicked and clowned with us, exhibiting a catalogue of moods that spoke to the many gods of nature and their various temperaments. The god on watch over the Saint Laurent during our homeward stretch was modest and humble. Maybe a little bashful. Or else incompletely aware of its authority and conspicuous brawn.

As we glided closer to the coast I thought I detected the ocean in my nose, but of course we were on the water most days, so my nose was easily tricked. Probably my imagination was at work, hyperactive now that I was close to home. Probably too my senses succumbed to wishful thinking. I missed my mother. My sister too, despite her act of disloyalty. I worried about both.

Gulls and terns appeared overhead and squawked their welcome. I imagined they were delivering greetings from loved ones.

The landscape transformed into a vibrant green fairyland. The higher latitudes were always grateful for what the lower latitudes took for granted: abundant sunlight, consequent warmth, copious rainwater. Birds singing in happiness or horniness, it didn't matter, and insect kingdoms arising from hibernation to power the cycle of life. The high latitudes were so grateful for these, they swooned over them, celebrated their arrival, decorated themselves in regal fruits and flowers. They rolled out a delicate green carpet for appreciative visitors, even for audacious travelers passing through in flimsy arks.

My habit while hunting was to take a break after bagging something, to sit on a fallen trunk and open my senses. Nature was a canvas no artist could replicate. The complexity alone. The depth of view, from nearby shrubs to distant hills, the latter dressed in desaturated hues, yet no less awake or vibrant than the former. The fall of light, the dappled ground, the cathedral effect when tree crowns met and touched. The apex of pines spearing the low fog, like Christmas trees emerging from the snow.

Contrasts. The craggy branches of a shagbark hickory and the delicate, upturned branch tips of a black spruce. Emerald green moss on dull weathered boulders. Mushrooms on stumps, saplings forcing their way out of glacial till, demanding access to the light. The dead and the living. The moribund, the acquiescent, side by side with the vigorous, the enterprising.

Summer had settled in and nestled itself in the hollows and pockets of the land. Perspiration by day turned to goosebumps by night as the sun grew tired of scorching our part of the world and slipped away to find other sandboxes to play in. Some nights were so cool we could see our breath. We held each other for shared warmth, under the wool blankets, and whispered the endearing things inappropriate to daytime sweat and labor.

On rainy days the soil released its signature odor, the earthy smell of humus. The substrate of all plant life was all the life that had preceded it. The aroma of pine sap permeated evergreen forests. Deciduous groves offered the musty scents of fallen leaves, of mushrooms and mosses, and the pungent, lemony perfume of honeysuckle blossoms.

Cricket music at night. The trickle of spring water, the song of mallards, the call of a lone and distant wolf. The friction of one leaf caressing another in the breeze, multiplied a hundred thousand times to produce a lingering sibilant sigh, a carrier wave for the delivery of news, rumors, and prattle from neighboring forests to the south.

And indeed the woods spoke to me. They tried to hold me back, to keep me from returning to civilization, from leaving my rightful place at the hearth of nature. If not for running out of gunpowder, or for my promise to Father Malcolm, I might have stayed in the northern forests the remainder of my life and relished their hospitality, their fertility. Each day paddling, or hunting and foraging, each night in Adrienne's arms, I was severing an umbilical connection with my native land.

The trees especially called to me. Like distant cousins, like descendants from mutual ancestors. I recognized them, understood their language.

Stay with us, they said. We'll give you a roof, a meal. We'll feed your fire.

Yet Adrienne and I traveled onward. Bobwhites and whippoorwills sang their pleas to us. Cicadas hypnotized us and droned us to sleep. The rich, loamy soil reminded us, with its ancient aromas, of that from which we had come, and to which we were ultimately going. The breeze warned us the paradise we were leaving behind was the one true Utopia, authenticated by comparison with what lay ahead.

The forest was my home. But I had business to attend to. My mother and sister were calling to me as well. I ignored the messages on the breeze and dipped my paddle resolutely into the ocean-bound water of the Saint Laurent.

During my days away from Kebek I had grown strong and wiry. Adrienne had become even more alluring during our journey together. Her complexion was as smooth as a school girl's. Her hair shined in the sunlight like translucent obsidian strands. It radiated a full spectrum of reflected light when she sat before the fire, like moonlight refracting through crystals.

It felt insufficient to say I loved her, employing the same word one used to describe a fondness for apples. Yet there was no stronger word. I had never needed a stronger one before. I hadn't known such love was possible. I hadn't known love could so consume a man.

Wilbur, tired and beaten, reached the outskirts of Kebek. People tilling the fields stopped and stared at us. We continue past the outer farms and through the river industry suburbs to the main landing on the north bank, upriver from the ancient ruins. Where, apparently, word had reached we were coming. A delegation awaited us on the dock, led by Father Mitchell himself.

As we stepped out of the canoe he said, "René Jordan, seminarian, you are under arrest for treason against the state."

Chapter 42

After asserting my rights under the *Constitution Modifié* I demanded to see the bishop.

"All in good time," Father Mitchell said.

"You are addressing the King and Queen of Ellanoy," I declared.

Father Mitchell and his men stood bug-eyed for a moment before bursting spontaneously into laughter.

"Well well," Mitchell said. "We'll just have to treat you like royalty, won't we?" Then to his men: "Shackle them."

The crimes were mine alone. But Adrienne was charged as well, as an "accomplice." Martinets escorted us to the prison on Nicolet Street where we shared a cell. A concrete block with a bare earthen floor and no windows. Like Bounty Rock's prison, this one seldom housed prisoners, because the ordeal was so nasty that all rational and most irrational citizens opted instead to obey the letter of the law. It's disturbing how much Utopia and Dystopia are alike when you scratch deeply enough.

They locked us up for three days in near total darkness, feeding us bread and water once a day. Our toilet was a bucket emptied with unpredictable frequency.

Adrienne and I held each other in the chilly shadows. "We'll get out of this," I assured her. "Once I get a chance to speak to the Council of Bishops."

"I trust you," she said.

"They'll listen. They have to. Even in the Levitican world, justice requires all sides be heard."

"I believe in you."

On the fourth day the rusted metal door opened and a young woman entered the cell, carrying a thin burning candle. At first I didn't recognize her.

"Danielle?"

"René…"

"Good God," I said, "they haven't put you in here too, have they?"

"Don't be silly. They're allowing me to visit."

We hugged and held each other. I overcame my embarrassment at being filthy. She was taller than I remembered, and her baby face had hardened into a kind of severe elegance. She'd grown into a woman during my absence but clearly had not had an easy or happy time doing it.

"Why are they allowing it?" I asked. "Surely not out of compassion."

"No, they are not a compassionate lot. They think I might be able to extract some information from you."

"Specifically?"

"Specifically, what Ellanoy's military weaknesses are."

"How little they know me."

She introduced herself to Adrienne. The two women shook hands and studied each other's faces as best they could in the semi-darkness. We took seats on the dirt floor.

"René, it's best you cooperate," Danielle said. "For two reasons."

"I'm listening."

"First, they won't let me continue to visit if my visits don't benefit them."

"I see."

"Second, there's going to be a trial. If you're found guilty of treason, the penalty is death."

"When do I get to speak to the bishop?"

She was silent. I couldn't read her expression in the flickering candlelight.

"Danielle?"

"You don't," she said. "A council of clergymen will serve as judge and jury. That's how famous you've become. They're bending all the rules to the breaking point. Father Caleb Mitchell will act as prosecutor."

"And our defense attorney?"

"You won't have one. Turns out there's a loophole in the constitution that allows them to rescind due process in cases of treason."

"What about our status as ambassadors? When do we get to argue our case?"

"You'll be allowed to make a statement at your trial." Danielle took my hand in hers. She said, "You've yet to ask the most important question on your mind."

She was right. I was afraid to ask it. I was afraid that since she hadn't yet made any mention of the subject, the news must be bad.

"How is she?" I managed to say.

"Mother was taken into custody when you and Father Malcolm deserted. I mean departed."

"I understood as much. And?"

"And she was to occupy a cell like this one until you returned."

"Well, I've returned. So where is she?"

"René, you've been gone two years."

"And?"

"I'm sorry, René, but while she was in custody…"

"What? Tell me."

"They didn't feed her, René. Not once. She was buried anonymously outside the city walls."

"As heretics are buried."

"I'm sorry."

The glow from our candle didn't quite reach the walls. I stood up and approached one of them. In the dim light I was able to discern an odd texture. A pattern of parallel streaks, of gouges in the concrete surface. They were finger scratches. I looked at Adrienne. She sat on her haunches, watching me.

"René," Danielle said, "you have to give me something to give to them. So I can come back."

"I'll give you something. A demand. I demand candles. I'm not going to cooperate if I have to live in the dark."

"René, please."

"And food. Real food. A proper toilet. Tell them we'll share what we know about the west and the legendary empire of Ellanoy. That should arouse them."

"René…"

"Tell them we'll confess to everything they accuse us of having done. Because we did them."

Chapter 43

Danielle brought candles. The light allowed me to work in my journal, as well as gaze upon my wife. She also brought blankets. Our diet improved to include mutton and garden vegetables.

"Told you," I said to Adrienne. "It's going to take baby steps, but we'll get through to these people."

Nevertheless the days passed with no new information about our case. I doctored my journal, improving passages with recalled memories and with the perspective of hindsight. Scenes of torture I'd softened or glossed over got a rewrite. It was best to tell the story as it happened and not hold back on account of delicate or squeamish readers.

The sex scenes were a different matter. It had been hard enough just mentioning the subject. I raised the issue with Adrienne.

She asked, "Do you enjoy having sex with me?"

"Enjoy is not the word to describe it. Sex with you is a drug that induces ecstasy, and to which I am hopelessly addicted."

"Then you aren't ashamed of doing it."

"Not in the least."

"Then there's no reason to be ashamed of writing about it."

Danielle brought soap and buckets of water. She brought toothpaste and toothbrushes. Fresh clothing, combs, razors. She helped cut and style Adrienne's hair.

"Everyone's talking about you two," she said. "The whole town, the whole countryside. As far as I can tell, the whole world."

"What are they saying?" I asked.

"Some are saying you deserve to burn."

"Great."

"But when they say it, their voices falter. More and more each time. People keep disappearing. We think they're joining the exiles."

"We?"

"A handful of us who think alike and get together to compare notes."

"Be careful. One of you might be an informant."

Adrienne asked, "What do you know about the exiles?"

"Not much. They exist, we're sure of that. They're run by Bishop Elijah Bennett. He disappeared, and if his disappearance were haphazard or meaningless the other council members wouldn't have defrocked him, wouldn't be touting his Jesuit sympathies, wouldn't be vilifying him and scaring children with stories of his evil cannibalism. Word is, they live in a camp some distance from the city. That's all we know."

Adrienne and I exchanged glances. We'd been to that camp. There was silent understanding between us that we should say nothing of it.

Danielle got what she needed to keep visiting and supplying us with food and candles. I told her at length about my adventure. I shared advice on how to snare game, locate roots and berries, and generally how to stay alive in the wild. About fending off bears, mosquitoes, and even mice that hankered after food stores. About staying warm in cold weather. How to ride rapids and how to fix canoes afterwards. About the superior intelligence of rabbits.

And about the weaknesses of Bounty Rock. I drew a map of the area. Ellanoy could best be conquered, I confided dishonestly, if the attacking army appeared in force before the palisade wall and demanded unconditional surrender. The Ellanoyans, who infrequently fought off attackers one or two at a time and had no experience facing armies, would see what they were up against and wave a white flag. The kingdom would be Kebek's to own and govern without shedding a drop of blood.

"Is that true?" Danielle asked.

"No. A militia from Kebek, with no experience laying siege, would be slaughtered attacking Ellanoy's palisades. That's the point. That's why you share the plan with Mitchell."

"Understood, but couldn't the militia starve the Ellanoyans out?"

"Doubtful. Their food stores are vast, and besides, they grow gardens and keep livestock within the palisades."

"Then they're unconquerable," Danielle said.

"Effectively."

Except they weren't, not quite. They had one vulnerability. One apparatus that without ready access to water would bring them down: fire.

*

One morning it wasn't Danielle who came to visit us, nor the man who emptied our bucket, rather a martinet in full dress uniform who said, "Your trial has begun."

"It started without us?"

"Opening arguments against you have been read. I'm here to escort you to the courthouse to participate in the rest."

Adrienne and I were shackled once more. The martinet and two flanking colleagues escorted us to the courthouse on Borgia Street. Still in shackles, we were led before a council of three judges consisting of Fathers Adler and Faye and Bishop Hennessey.

Behind us, the courtroom overflowed with spectators. More spilled out the doors and into the street. I could imagine, from my own experience attending trials, the people who couldn't fit inside pestering those closest to the door for news and updates.

Everyone stared at us. I winked at Adrienne to reassure her. I knew Bishop Hennessey to be a fair man. Father Adler had been a good friend to Father Malcolm. Only Faye would be predisposed against us, because he was tight with Father Caleb Mitchell, who was prosecuting us. I was counting on Father Faye being outnumbered and outvoted.

Father Mitchell approached the bench and waited for the buzz to die down. Of all the priests in Kebek, he looked the least ordained, chiefly because he sported long hair, like the martyrs illustrated in our catechisms. His detractors nicknamed him Saint Caleb.

Mitchell called the city's chief quartermaster to the stand. The quartermaster testified that bags of corn had gone missing from the community stores at the same time Malcolm and I disappeared. Mitchell stood in front of me and asked, "Do you deny taking them?"

"I do not."

He paused as if surprised, his mouth open and ready to challenge my denial, but quickly recovered and said, "Let the record show, the witness admits to theft of food stores, and thus to placing his fellow townspeople at risk of starvation."

He called other witnesses in sequence who testified to stolen knives, ropes, and other articles. In each case he queried me, "Do you deny the theft of this article?"

"I do not."

The owner of the canoe we borrowed testified to his inability to fish as a result. The owner of the flintlock musket was called forward to identify it. He testified he'd been unable to hunt. It seemed Malcolm and I had damn near brought civilization to its knees when we escaped with our spare provisions.

Danielle was visible in the gallery. Her eyes communicated fear and anguish. She raised a pair of crossed fingers for me to see.

Survivors of the posse sent after us were questioned one by one. Each of the men identified me as the outlaw who murdered Karl Rasmussen, even though none of them had been within a country mile of the killing. One of the men described how I allegedly hacked Rasmussen's head and limbs off with a machete, all the while cackling in delight. Spectators in the gallery drew breaths sharply in response to a vivid description of blood gushing from Rasmussen's neck.

"Do you deny this murder?" Father Mitchell asked.

"It was in self defense."

"You decapitated and dismembered a law enforcement officer in self defense?"

"I neither decapitated nor dismembered him. The testimony is a lie. I shot him as he was trying to shoot me."

"Do you have a witness to corroborate that?"

"No, of course not."

"But my dear Monsieur Jordan, we have a witness, sitting right here in the witness box, who swears to seeing you decapitate, dismember, and laugh. This witness is lying under oath?"

"Yes. One of us must be lying. We're both under oath."

"Let's make sure we're on the same page." Mitchell handed the witness a Bible. "Place your hand on this," he said. The man did. "Do you swear, on pain of an eternity in Hell, your testimony is honest and accurate?"

"I do, and it is."

The gallery buzzed, and Bishop Hennessey ordered silence. My guess was that Mitchell had promised the man absolution in advance. I looked to see how Danielle was taking it. Her eyes were closed.

Mitchell called Rasmussen's wife to the stand. She testified, through unabashed tears, to her profound loss, to the hardships she had endured without a husband. She never made eye contact with either Adrienne or me. Afterwards she had to be helped off the stand.

No one could blame Mitchell for what he was doing. I'd been raised in the same environment, even if one more liberal, and I knew what his education had been like, what he'd gone through to enter the clergy. The power of teachers to wash the brains of their pupils was extraordinary. If they taught you as a child to believe in an omnipotent creator and to regard every object and affair, whether good or evil, as a manifestation of the creator's indecipherable machinations, they stripped you of objectivity, rationality, and decent common sense.

Once I'd stumbled upon Father Mitchell struggling to suppress tears over a dead cat, so I knew there was a gentle soul somewhere deep inside. But his soul had been caged by an upbringing that stressed reverence for cryptic fables scratched on parchment eons ago, loyalty to Yahweh over compassion for human suffering, and blind obedience to more senior clergymen who professed direct communication with the spirit world.

Mitchell's next questions were for Adrienne.

"State your name for the record," he ordered.

"My name is Adrienne."

"What is your last name?"

"I don't have one. None of my people do."

"Ah, your people. You lead me right to the point. Tell us, you have a title, don't you?"

"I am Queen of Ellanoy."

"And this man next to you, your husband?"

"He is King."

There was tittering in the gallery. Bishop Hennessey banged his gavel.

"King of Ellanoy," Mitchell said. He moved over and faced me. "How did you become king?"

"By virtue of marrying Adrienne."

"And she is queen by virtue of…?"

"Being married to the king."

"Well isn't that convenient for the both of you! What happened to the previous king? Did you depose him?"

"He died in battle."

"Again, how convenient. Enlighten me here, Monsieur Jordan. As King of Ellanoy you're naturally loyal to the people of Ellanoy, is this not so?"

I knew where this was going, but I had no interest in trying to squirm out of it. I said, "It is naturally so."

"Then what has become of your loyalty to Kebek, your majesty?"

Laughter broke out. Hennessey said, "Silence, or I'll clear the courtroom."

"Well?" Mitchell said.

"Despite my title, despite my marriage to a foreigner, I remain steadfastly loyal to the people of Kebek."

"The people."

"Yes, the people."

"But not the government."

"Not the present government. To a democratic government, yes. To democratically elected representatives of the people, yes. To dictators, no."

The gallery sat in stunned silence. Even the judges stared vacantly. Bishop Hennessey leaned forward and studied me as he would an indecipherable puzzle.

"Clarify," Mitchell said. "Are we dictators?"

"With all due respect, Monsignor, are you democratically elected representatives of the people?"

Mitchell faced the judges. "The accused has acknowledged the crime of theft, which is punishable by death. He has confessed to murder, which is punishable by death. He has admitted not only to treason, but to sedition as well. Both are, of course, punishable by death."

He confronted Adrienne once more.

"Tell me, my dear queen, what race are you?"

"I am human."

"How funny. You know what I mean."

"I am of mixed race."

"Mixed as in one kind of European ancestry with another?"

"Yes, and mixed as in white Europeans blended with all the colors of the rainbow."

"Including black?"

"Especially black. Lots of black."

Mitchell redirected his attention to the judges. He nodded at Fathers Adler and Faye and bowed his head to Bishop Hennessey.

"The prosecution rests."

Chapter 44

Bishop Hennessey called a recess. As he stepped away from the bench he threw a glance at Adrienne and me that said, How can you be so stupid? We spent our break in the dock, standing in shackles. Danielle and a handful of curious townspeople gathered round, the latter no doubt to enjoy a closer look at the zoo specimens, the transgressors, the infidels. Danielle wasted no time admonishing us.

"How can you be so stupid?" she said.

There was no need to ask what she meant. I said, "Sweetie, there's no point denying the charges. It's better if we confess them and get to the point of all this."

"Which is?"

"Which is not whether we're guilty of breaking the law, rather of whether breaking the law was justified."

"Good luck with that. And what about Adrienne's testimony?"

"What about it?" Adrienne said.

"You don't stand up in a Kebek courtroom and brag about how black you are. Didn't René tell you? In this part of the world, people with dark skin share the same social stratum as goats and pigs."

"He told me. I cannot change who I am. And besides, any society in which skin color dictates social stratum is one in need of an emancipator."

"You mean a martyr."

By this time a small throng crowded the dock. Some of the townspeople viewed us with scorn, but an encouraging number wore expressions of interest, even of budding enlightenment. I put my hand on Danielle's shoulder. "Our arguments are yet to come. We have a pulpit and we intend to make use of it."

*

Bishop Hennessey banged his gavel for silence and told us it was our turn to speak. He warned us to be brief. I opened with confessions.

"It's true Malcolm and I took the corn and other supplies. We needed them for our survival. If we hadn't taken them, if we hadn't run when we did, we would have been tried and almost certainly convicted of the crime of reading books."

Mitchell sprang up from his chair. "Reading books is not a crime."

"Reading unapproved books is against the law. It is also against the law to own them, to hoard them. Father Malcolm and I did both. We did not—I do not—believe these activities should violate any law. They are neither wicked nor repugnant. I believe people have fundamental rights, one of which is the pursuit of knowledge."

Mitchell addressed Bishop Hennessey. "Your Eminence, please. The people of Kebek have more books at their disposal than any one person can read in an entire year. The pursuit of knowledge is by no means a crime, otherwise we'd have to arrest all the teachers and students, up and down the coast. Monsieur

Jordan has no business challenging the law in these proceedings. The only relevant question is whether he broke it."

"I did," I said. "I broke the law. I broke many laws. Examining illicit materials is a trivial violation, one every person present has committed at one time or another, when he or she has stumbled upon printed matter from olden times. I'll repay the corn. And the canoe, and the musket. I ask the esteemed judges to weigh the guilt of these crimes against the extraordinary value of having contacted a new civilization, one previously thought to be mere legend."

"And murder?" Mitchell asked.

"I killed Karl Rasmussen for the same reason I killed mutants: in self defense. There's nothing more I can say about it except I'm sorry for his widow's loss and suffering. I've not committed treason or sedition. I love my homeland, I love my people. I want for them what will best serve their health, happiness, and prosperity."

Mitchell interjected again. "What about that which will best serve their God?"

"Their health," I said. "Their happiness. Their prosperity."

"Now we see you for what you truthfully are. You wandered among pagans, you bedded with pagans. You spurned your God and became a pagan."

The gallery buzzed restlessly. I detected a sea change. It was no longer a lynch mob. Some people still shook their heads disapprovingly, but others whispered to one another, their hands cupped about their mouths for privacy.

Mitchell raised his voice. "Answer the charge!"

"Reverend Fathers," I said to the judges, "I thought this was my opportunity to speak."

Hennessey rapped his gavel. "Let the accused have his say."

Mitchell sat down. I continued.

"Although I began my journey to escape what I believed was unjust punishment, I finished it as an emissary of Bounty Rock. As a diplomat from Ellanoy. As such, under Kebek law, I am to be afforded diplomatic immunity. I could have remained in Ellanoy and avoided all this. I choose instead to return and face the charges, to bring the two peoples together, for the benefit of both. Regardless what you think I did, or even what in fact I did—regardless of the crimes I indisputably committed—you cannot legally detain me, punish me, or harm me in any way. As for my wife Adrienne, she has violated nothing. She merely accompanied me here as an official ambassador from a sovereign state."

"Which state?" Mitchell scoffed. "Sodom ... or Gomorrah?"

"She was a princess when I met her. She's now a queen. She ought to be treated accordingly, not locked in a cell with a dirt floor. If you must punish someone, punish me. But let her go."

*

It was Adrienne's turn. Rather than address the judges she faced the gallery. Her message was for the people of Kebek.

She spoke of her own people, the Ellanoyans. Of Bounty Rock, of her heritage. She spoke of two populations, hers and the gallery's, coming together, working together to make a better life for everyone. She spoke of learning from each other, of sharing. Of Ellanoyans giving Kebekians anything they needed or wanted: food, building materials, books. Even gemstones.

At the mention of the latter, the three clergymen judges glanced at one another.

Our two cultures had a common threat, she argued. Mutants, who were reproducing exponentially. It was only a matter of time before they swelled to numbers sufficient to seize the cities

311

from the living. She used the word "living" as though the mutants were dead.

"We are one people," she told the overfilled room. "Separated by geography, by some trivial aspects of culture, and by our disagreement about the existence of supernatural beings. Surely we can overcome these differences."

At the mention of "supernatural beings" Father Mitchell leapt out of his chair. "If you cannot call God by His given name, confess here and now to witchcraft, and let's not keep the stake waiting."

"God," she said without hesitation. "Who sent his only son to die here on Earth after having shared messages of tolerance and forgiveness and love. I've listened carefully to all my husband has told me about your religion. Particularly striking is the Sermon on the Mount, beginning in Matthew, chapter five. Blessed are the merciful: for they shall obtain mercy. Blessed are the peacemakers: for they shall be called the children of God. My husband and I ask for your mercy and for the opportunity to pursue a peaceful bond between our two cultures."

"Very pretty," Mitchell said. "But let's move a little farther along in the Good Book, to Matthew 19:17. If thou wilt enter into life, keep the commandments. Tell me, your majesty, how many of the commandments have you disobeyed?"

"Tell me, Father Mitchell, how many would Jesus refuse to forgive?"

Mitchell positioned himself directly in front of her. "Leviticus," he said, glaring into her eyes. "Chapter 19, verse 34. And he that blasphemeth the name of the Lord, he shall surely be put to death, and all the congregation shall certainly stone him."

"Leviticus," Adrienne responded calmly. "Chapter 24, verse 16. But the stranger that dwelleth with you shall be unto you as one born among you, and thou shalt love him as thyself."

The gallery buzzed, and it was hard to tell which way it was leaning. Mitchell's face turned red. He addressed Bishop Hennessey: "It's pointless to argue with an infidel. I urge the court to proceed to judgment without further delay."

"Is the prisoner finished with her statement?" Hennessey asked.

"Just one more point, your honor," Adrienne said.

"Well, get on with it."

"It's merely this. Kebek and other Christian enclaves are intermittently at war with Jewish and Muslim enclaves, for no other reason than religious differences. Yet all three religions trace their lineages back to the prophet Abraham. The people of Ellanoy—the Pagans of Ellanoy, if you insist—will embrace Abraham as a prophet as well. My people will eagerly work with yours to reunite the children of Abraham and bring peace to the world."

"Is that all?"

"I love my husband. Where you send him, send me as well."

Adrienne turned to me. Her eyes radiated affection. If she was confident we'd go free, I was already resigned to a long prison term.

Bishop Hennessey and Fathers Adler and Faye consulted quietly among themselves for a few minutes. Adler appeared to argue with the other two. My hopes rose; maybe Adrienne was right. Maybe she'd talked us out of our mess. There was no dismissing her confidence and eloquence.

If only Malcolm were present. He'd known these people better than anyone. He'd known where their buttons were and how to push them. When something got under his skin he could turn another person's argument into pretzels of self-contradicting fallacy. He would have felt at home in this courtroom. He would have relished the challenge.

The three judges stood, as did everyone in the gallery. As did Father Mitchell, who had been sitting in the prosecutor's chair, his hands clasped. Surely he hoped for an outcome that was the polar opposite of one for which I silently prayed: *Dear Invisible Sky Wizard...*

Bishop Hennessey looked straight at me. Father Adler avoided eye contact. Father Faye suppressed a smile.

Hennessey said, "René Jordan and Adrienne, you are guilty of all charges. You are sentenced to burn at the stake as soon as preparations can be made. May God have mercy on your souls."

Chapter 45

We returned to our cell. It wasn't long before we had a visitor. Father Mitchell.

"Here to gloat?" I asked.

"Not at all." He leaned against the door frame, his hands in his pockets. "I came to thank you for the information you've given us about Ellanoy."

"Most welcome. Now keep up your end of the bargain and let us live."

"Oh, but you didn't keep up your end. Nice try on the full frontal assault, by the way. Your sister finally broke down and gave us the truth about Bounty Rock's defenses."

Adrienne and I glanced at each other. "Now why would she do that?" I asked.

"She had, shall we say, a wistful notion doing so would assist your cause, that you'd go free in exchange for the information."

"She was lying."

"I think not."

"Well, what of it? You're not going to make use of any information about a remote colony of pagans."

"Oh, but we are, my treasonous young seminarian. The Kebek militia and many of the city's martinets are preparing, as we speak, to march on the Ellanoyans and exterminate them."

Adrienne raised her head and glared at him.

"Call it a crusade," Mitchell added nonchalantly.

"Father Mitchell, have mercy on your enemies," I implored. "The Ellanoyans mean you no harm."

"They're infidels."

"They're people, just like you and me."

"They're godless scum."

"They're just trying to live their lives in peace. Isn't that enough to satisfy your god?"

"Deuteronomy 13: Certain men have withdrawn the inhabitants of their city, saying, Let us go and serve other gods. Thou shalt surely smite the inhabitants of that city with the edge of the sword, destroying it utterly, and all that is therein, and the cattle thereof, with the edge of the sword."

Blushing, I recalled having quoted the same passage to Malcolm, having rubbed it in his face. I replied, "I'm surprised a different verse doesn't occur to you first. Mark 12:31, Thou shalt love thy neighbor as thyself."

"You never had an appreciation for the Old Testament," Mitchell said. "It shows."

"The problem with Kebek today is that it's run by Leviticans who have slipped back into an Old Testament way of thinking. It shows."

Mitchell smiled. "Soon you'll have a chance to find out exactly what God thinks of you." He looked at Adrienne. "Both of you. But I'll give you one thing, Master Jordan. You were right: I did come here to gloat. And I've had a capital good time doing so."

He left, closing and locking the door behind him.

"Adrienne," I said.

"Don't worry about me. I'm ready to die."

"I'm not."

"You haven't learned to accept things the way they are. You haven't found peace of mind."

"The world is a frightful mess. I won't accept it."

"The world is what it is."

*

Danielle visited in a panic. "I'm so sorry. I was just trying to get you out. I've made everything worse."

"Don't worry about it," I said. "There's something we need you to do for us."

"Anything."

"Go to the well in the center of the market square. Stare into the well for a few minutes. Pretend you're lost in thought. Then go to Bellarmine Church, sit in the second to last pew, and wait."

"For what?"

"Someone will sit behind you. Don't turn and look at him. Tell him the Kebek militia and some of the martinets will soon leave for the Ellanoy country, to do battle with Adrienne's people. They can't be stopped, but the Ellanoyans can be warned."

"What about you? They're going to burn you."

"That's the other thing. Remind the man in the pew behind you that Kebek's defenses will be weak. Fatally weak." I allowed myself a smile. "There are two ways to overcome your enemy. One is to amass a larger army. The other is to wait until your enemy's army leaves on a crusade."

Chapter 46

Danielle delivered the message to the exiles. We waited. She continued to bring food and sundries, but soon the guards decided it was too generous for convicted traitors on death row, and confiscated it. They restricted us once again to a diet of bread and water.

We still received candles, however, and I kept working on my journal. And gazing at my wife, who looked more bedraggled each passing day.

Adrienne had been losing weight since the beginning of our incarceration. Weight she didn't have to spare. Her hair was greasy and matted, her eyes were sunken. She grew listless and slept twenty hours a day, which was a sure sign of depression. Like a flower plucked from its natural habitat, she needed to return home to Bounty Rock, the only place she could flourish. And if there was where she belonged, it was where I belonged as well.

Nevertheless she didn't complain. She spoke little except in response to my questions. "I'm fine," she repeated. "I'm ready to die."

Danielle slipped contraband under her skirt before visiting us in the cell. Strips of cooked meat. Stalks of raw vegetables.

Even a flask of something fermented. She didn't know what. "It could be wine," she said, "if it had any color."

After tasting it, I coughed. "It's not wine."

Danielle brought baked goods too, which were still warm, or rather had been warmed again from being strapped to her inner thighs.

"I hope you don't mind," she said to Adrienne.

"I don't mind, honey. I love you for what you're doing for us."

Danielle blushed and squirmed. Love wasn't a word tossed around much in Kebekian society. Given a glimpse of a chance, we would have changed that.

*

There was nothing for Adrienne and I to do but wait. I asked her whether she believed in an afterlife. Before she could respond I told her what I thought about the subject. I'd been raised Levitican, or more accurately brainwashed Levitican, so for most of my life I believed in Heaven and Hell, in an eternal judicial system that demanded the life you live on Earth be a kind one. But during my travels, seeing the dead cities, the mutants, and what they did or yearned to do, I'd come to believe no legitimate god would allow such ugliness to exist, such suffering to occur.

If he in fact existed, what I'd witnessed was proof he couldn't be what the Leviticans said he was, omnipotent and benevolent at the same time. It was the same conclusion I'd drawn during an argument with Malcolm soon after we escaped Kebek together. The Epicurean paradox. Since the Levitican definition of God included both omnipotence and benevolence, Levitican dogma stood on shaky ground. Concepts like Heaven and Hell were pared down, at best, to mere abstractions.

There was no afterlife. We die. We rot in the ground. Our remains disperse in nature. The day comes when the Earth, little troubled by our presence to begin with, shrugs us off as the echoes of our footsteps fade and dissipate. We might as well never have been.

"Maybe that's what happened to God," I conjectured. "He died and his ashes were scattered at some undisclosed location. Ugliness and suffering bloomed in his absence. He might as well never have been."

She was silent for a while. She licked her dry lips and said, "We die. We rot in the ground. Our remains disperse in nature. But the time never comes when no trace of us remains. The Earth never shrugs us off. We live on in the memories of those who knew us, and indirectly in those who knew them. We live on in the new forms of life we nourish when we're buried."

"That isn't much in the way of immortality to look forward to," I said. "Feeding a worm, inhabiting a shrub."

"It is if you think about it, if you consider the alternative. But there's something else. I believe some part of me, my essence, survives the transformation. It's like our lives are tapestries left unfinished when we die. We keep reincarnating into new life forms, and each time we return we add to the tapestry, we make it more complete. A patch here, a thread there. None is complete or perfect, and we should concentrate on the intricate threads and patterns rather than the gaps, tears, or frayed ends."

"So the purpose of life is to weave a rug."

"Metaphorically speaking, yes. And to make it as exquisite as possible. At home, atop Bounty Rock, I always had the feeling the ghosts of my ancestors still walked the streets, still carried on like they hadn't died. Still weaved their tapestries."

We stared at the sole burning candle, its flame struggling to cast light into the corners of the cell. I digested what Adrienne had said. It sounded grand and appealing. There was just one more question.

"What if all of life is a dream," I asked, "or taking place on a stage, as some people think?"

"Would you know the difference?" she said. "Would you care? Would it diminish your purpose? Your values? Your reverence for truth and beauty?"

"Passionate words from someone so ready to die."

"Who, me? That was yesterday. Today is different."

"What has changed?"

She reached for my hand and placed it over her lower abdomen. "It's too early to feel anything yet. But we're going to have a baby."

*

Danielle brought news from the Bellarmine contact. The exiles had dispatched a small party to Bounty Rock, to warn the Ellanoyans of an imminent attack.

A tear rolled down Adrienne's cheek. It was the first time she'd smiled since our capture.

"The rest of them are preparing to attack Kebek," Danielle said, "now that it's about to become relatively unguarded. And something else: the townspeople, many of them, are preparing to rise against the priests and bishops. A similar movement has spread down the coast, to Jewish and Muslim cities too. The two of you have given birth to a Reformation, only this time it's a secular one."

"You're sure of all this? The attack on Kebek?"

"Absolutely."

She was more at ease than I'd ever seen her. I leaned closer to her and spoke in a whisper. We normally lowered our voices when discussing sensitive subjects, but this time I didn't want to risk a guard overhearing. I asked, "When is the attack?"

She whispered as well. "On the Sabbath. At the stroke of noon."

"What day is today?"

She blinked. "You don't know? It's Friday."

"So, the day after tomorrow."

"You only have to endure this for two more days, René and Adrienne. We're going to get the two of you out of here. Bishop Bennett knows exactly where you are. Once you're under his protection he'll burn this godforsaken city to the ground."

Chapter 47

Early Saturday morning a squad of martinets woke us. The leader, an imposing man who had to bend at the waist to get through the doorway, held a lantern. He lifted it to Adrienne's face, then to mine.

"We're here for the girl," he said.

His face wore a smirk. I rose and confronted him. "Why?"

"It's her time."

"No!" I pushed Adrienne into a corner and stood in front of her.

"Don't make this harder than it needs to be, Mr. Jordan."

"You're not taking her."

The leader nodded to his subordinates, who pressed in on us. I swung my fist and caught one on the jaw. He went down. I kicked another between the legs and he doubled over, croaking.

The remaining martinets surrounded me. I pleaded with them, "Someone please find my sister. Tell her what's happening."

They clubbed me. I heard the thud, thud, thud of blows raining on me even after I became numb to them, and in the background Adrienne screaming for them to stop.

*

When I came to, I was strapped to a chair, facing a low pyre in the Place de le Lévitique. Adrienne was on the pyre, tied to a stake. A pile of kindling lay at her feet. Father Mitchell gradually came into focus as I regained consciousness. He stood next to Adrienne with a burning torch in his hand.

"Young Jordan has decided to join us," he said. "It's fitting. We couldn't conduct these proceedings without him. They would lack a certain poetry."

"Father Mitchell," I implored, "she's with child."

His eyebrows went up. "One more soul for Heaven."

Behind me were people, hundreds of spectators. Jostling for position. Pressing forward to improve their view. It felt like the entire population of Kebek was present.

A guard bent over me and said, "If you look away, I'm under orders to gouge your eyes out." He held a rusty screwdriver in his right hand. "Please don't make it come to that."

Mitchell ordered the spectators to hush. He waited until the noise died down, then announced:

"Adrienne, Queen of Ellanoy, you have been sentenced to death for complicity in treason and sedition, for blaspheme, and for the sin of being mixed race."

"Burn the sable!" someone shouted from the crowd.

A cheer went up. But there was something odd about it. I knew what Kebekian mobs sounded like, and this one sounded like only half the people were participating. I struggled to rise but my arms and legs were bound to the chair. So I leaned forward and rose to my feet, taking the chair with me.

Guards roughly forced the chair back down.

"Do that again," the lead guard said, "and you lose an eye."

Adrienne watched me from the pyre. She appeared sadder for my impending loss, for my own suffering, than for hers, about to begin. I kept my eyes fixed on her but they were already flooding with tears. I prayed quietly to myself: *Dear God, right now would be the perfect moment for Bishop Bennett and his exiles to attack.* But I knew the attack wasn't scheduled until the next day. We hold dear the most desperate of hopes when such hopes are all we have left to hold.

Mitchell continued. "Your sentence will now be carried out." He removed a bottle from his robe and sprinkled its contents on Adrienne's head. "I baptize you in the name of the Father, and of the Son, and of the Holy Spirit."

Adrienne shook her head vigorously in an attempt to flick the water off.

Mitchell said, "You may now enter the hereafter with a cleansed soul."

Adrienne smiled at him. "I forgive you."

Mitchell's expression soured. He stuck his torch into the kindling at Adrienne's feet and held it there. At first nothing happened. Then gradually the kindling ignited.

As flames lapped at Adrienne's feet she called out to me. "How beautiful the sun is, that I have you to love for the rest of time."

Mitchell piled more wood on the fire. "You should be grateful to us, girl. We're sending you to God."

Adrienne's clothes caught fire. The flames climbed through the thin fabric like it was paper. She sang my favorite lullaby, the one I taught her in Bounty Rock. She'd chosen it as her death song.

Sleep, sleep my beloved one
Close your eyes, your day is done

Her hair caught fire. I lost consciousness and a bucket of water was thrown in my face. "Throw the water at *her!*" I screamed.

Morning comes, we'll play again
Cuddle again, be gay again

Her flesh turned red. It charred and peeled.

Fill the day with joy and fun

Her flesh melted away. I lost consciousness again. And woke again, this time to the searing pain of my left eye being gouged out. The lead guard held me by the hair with one hand while twisting the screwdriver into my eye socket with the other, making circular motions, scraping the cavity clean. The goo of my ruptured eyeball spilled down my cheek.

The air filled with the acrid aroma of burning flesh. Adrienne's eyes popped out of their sockets, leaving blackened holes staring vacuously. Mitchell added more wood to the fire. It roared and consumed my wife, until all I could see of her was a trembling shimmer behind a wall of flame and soot.

Some of the spectators chanted, "Burn, sable, burn!"

Adrienne's bowels spilled from her disintegrating frame. A glistening, goopy mess that hissed and sputtered as it landed in the coals. Her figure reduced to a charred skeleton, held intact by stubborn tendons and the roasted remnants of other tissues.

The fire subsided. Her jaw rested on her ribs. Brittle tufts of carbonized hair fluttered away from her skull like ash from a scorched bush.

Chapter 48

Father Mitchell brought a doctor to my cell who patched my eye. I sat in rigid silence as the doctor worked, my legs sprawled out before me on the earthen floor. When the doctor had finished and departed, Mitchell said, "As you can see, Mr. Jordan, and as I've been trying to tell you, we're a compassionate people."

With my one remaining eye, I scrutinized him. I wasn't sure I'd ever experienced true hate before. I'd disliked certain people, and I'd fought with some, but I'd never wished anyone pain. Pain so excruciating he'd crave death as much as a castaway stranded on a desert island craved water.

"You look like a man with something on his mind," I said. "Although I can't be sure of such observations anymore, not without stereoscopic vision."

He squatted in front of me. "I wanted the pleasure of telling you. You're going to be executed tomorrow."

"Tomorrow? The Sabbath?"

"The Sabbath seems appropriate to punish heresy, don't you think? Also, everyone's off work and can come to the show."

"Seems appropriate for inquisitorial executions too. If you move it to Monday I'll have the Sabbath to spend in prayer before I die."

"I'm afraid what is already underway cannot be reversed. But I can offer you an out. If you're interested."

My wife was dead. I wasn't the least bit interested. Tomas was dead. Malcolm was dead. Eli was dead. My mother was dead. The love of my life was dead. I wasn't interested in anything Mitchell had to offer. But I wanted to live a while longer. Long enough to take revenge upon him, to thrust a blade into his gut, to wrench it upwards, to twist it. To yank it out and thrust it in again.

"I'm all ears," I said.

"You traveled successfully to Ellanoy and back, through some of the most dangerous country known to man. Our army is preparing to depart. Tell me how you did it, how you avoided the mutants, or defeated them, and I'll arrange for your sentence to be commuted to life in prison."

"To spend the rest of my days here, on this dirt floor?"

"Better on the dirt floor than beneath it."

"Won't your throngs be disappointed over the show's cancellation?"

He shrugged. "There's always a miscreant or two we can string up and burn. Mobs are easy to please."

"Fair enough," I said. "There's nothing to it. Tell your people to stick to the north shore of the first Great Lake. That's the secret of making it through safely."

"The north shore? And pass directly by Turonado?"

"The Turonado mutants are friendly. They gave us food and directions."

"You're pulling my leg."

"If they hadn't been friendly, I wouldn't be here today. They're physically disfigured, it's true, and frightful in appearance, but they mean no harm. They'll help your men. They'll share their knowledge of the lakes."

"How do I know whether to believe you?"

"You don't. You have to take my word for it." I looked him in the eye with my one eye until I won the stare-down contest. "Stick to the cities. It's the best way to encounter mutants, who are friendly and helpful. They just want us to accept them back into normal society, to treat them as human. The most effective strategy to survive the voyage to Ellanoy and complete the mission is to befriend as many mutants as possible."

"Your wife spoke of them as evil."

"They are, in her part of the world. The lake mutants belong to a different world order."

He stood up. "I hope you're telling the truth. The army leaves within the hour."

"And now, the commutation?"

"I have no authority to commute your sentence."

"But you said—"

"What I said is what you needed to hear. As I told you, what is already underway cannot be reversed."

Mitchell turned to leave. My execution was scheduled for the following day. The exiles were coming for me then as well, commencing an attack on the city at the stroke of noon. They constituted my only remaining hope for an opportunity to grab Mitchell by the throat, to choke him until he turned purple, until his eyes bulged in terror and his tongue dangled from his mouth.

"Can I ask you a question?" I said.

He hesitated at the door. "Well?"

"What time is my execution tomorrow?"

"It takes place at the stroke of noon. And by the way, your stake will have a crossbeam, one that fits your arms. Make of it what you will. We're having a barbeque afterwards. No need to decline the invitation. We know you'll be tied up."

Chapter 49

Sunday morning Danielle showed up for what she'd been told would be her final visit. She was allowed to bring food this one last time; she didn't need to hide it under her skirt. And food she brought. Including blueberry pie, my favorite, made just like she'd learned from our mother. And a jug of apple cider.

"I'm so sorry about Adrienne," she said. "How are you handling it?"

"I'm not handling it. I just don't want them to see what they've done to me."

We got tipsy sitting on the floor of the cell, taking swigs from the jug, talking without saying anything. I asked, "How does my eye look?"

"Fine. All you can see is bandage anyway."

"Be honest. You saw it before it was bandaged."

She looked away. "Bad. It looks bad."

"Have the militia left for Bounty Rock?"

"Yesterday afternoon, with most of the martinets and with volunteers from cities all around. They made quite an army. But don't worry, the warning party is ahead of the army."

"And the army will move more slowly."

"Because it's bigger."

"And … for other reasons."

She stood and paced. "I tried to contact the man in the church pew at Bellarmine, but he didn't show up. I guess this is a busy time for him. The attack on Kebek takes place today and no doubt he has more important matters to attend to."

"You've done all you can."

"Surely they know," she said, "about your…"

"About my appointment at precisely the same hour."

"They have to know. People are talking about it. Spectators are arriving from miles around. Thanks to the departure of the army the visitors in this city now outnumber the residents. Surely the exiles will change their plans and attack earlier. They have to."

"Military plans are notoriously hard to change at the last minute," I said. "There are elements in motion that can't be stopped, people on missions who can no longer be reached."

"I'm sure Bishop Bennett will do the best he can."

"If the best he can do is noon, I'll be watching the attack through a cloud of smoke of my own making."

"Hang on, René. Don't lose faith."

Truth was, I hadn't had any faith to begin with. Therefore I didn't have any to lose. No one was in control of my destiny, least of all me. That was the great truth it took all of my years to learn.

Flip a coin. My life depended on whether Bennett attacked early or late. On whether Mitchell's plans were delayed, even by minutes. Or not. Maybe even by seconds.

My thoughts returned to my little brother Tomas, and how his curiosity had cost him his life. More accurately *my* curiosity. All he did was show up at school, looking for me, inquiring after a piece of chalk. If he'd gone somewhere to play instead, my life wouldn't be boiling down to relative punctuality. To ticks on a clock.

The exiles would take the city. Clambering over the gate like an insect horde. Sprinting down the streets. Their catapults close behind, hurling fiery cannonballs like comets, the missiles crashing through roofs, dousing neighborhoods with all-consuming flames, engulfing the city in a ravenous inferno. Hell on Earth. Residents scattering, screaming, their hair and clothing ablaze.

There would be scuffling outside my cell door. A pair of gunshots. The door forced open. And then Bennett's patronizing mug, saying, "Told you so."

"I'll look for you at the exile camp after the battle," Danielle said.

"There's something you mentioned earlier," I said. "The visitors in this city now outnumber the residents."

"That's right. Or so it seems."

"The visitors outnumber the residents…"

"What are you thinking?"

"I'm thinking, we don't know what Bennett's battle plans are. We're just assuming he's planning a frontal assault on the city gates."

"Oh my God, you mean some of those visitors might be—"

"Shh! Footsteps." Boots were clumping down the hall, approaching the door.

"But René," Danielle whispered, "that would mean they've already taken the city. Effectively speaking. It would mean your rescue is all but guaranteed."

"Yeah, but something else has occurred to me as well. If Bennett wants to rule Kebek, as I suspect he does, then I'm in his way. Delaying the assault until after the execution serves his ultimate purpose."

A key turned in the lock and the door opened. Guards, not exiles, entered the cell.

"We're here to take you to the pyre," one of them said. He extended a hood for me to put over my head. When I glanced at it curiously he explained, "To spare your sister the … sight."

"I just need a few more minutes," I pleaded, "to complete my journal entry."

"Make it fast."

＊

The journal is going to Danielle for safe keeping. She'll hide it somewhere until I have an opportunity to continue making entries. Assuming there's anything more to say. I've also asked her to take care of Wilbur for me if I'm unable to myself. There's a leak somewhere along the keel I was never able to find. And one of the thwarts is loose.

It's almost noon. The guards are shifting weight from foot to foot, sighing audibly. Time to wrap things up.

As I write this, Father Mitchell is building a fire.

Epilogue
by Danielle Jordan

The exiles launched their attack, initially catapulting a solitary projectile over the city wall. A blazing fireball that floated, sputtering, in a graceful parabolic arc over the larder district until it struck Dubois Boulevard, where it rolled with a hollow whistling sound and crashed into a rickety wooden bakery.

The bakery went up. Fzzt! Whoosh! And the battle was on.

Fireballs vaulted across the sky. They found the wood, the trees and gardens, the silos of winter corn. Women ran through the streets, children clutched to their breasts, embers scurrying about their ankles.

The city's remaining martinets lined up in formation to meet the invading army. But they were picked off from behind before the invaders breached the gate. Bishop Bennett had planted soldiers inside Kebek beforehand, behind-the-lines volunteers who'd comported themselves as loyal citizens and waited for the first catapult volley to signal the attack.

A battering ram took down the main gate. The exiles charged in, firing arrows as well as muskets. Bennett himself led them, waving a yellow flag on a long pole. The martinets were caught between two forces. All the martinets, even those with their hands raised high in surrender, were callously shot, and the wounded dispatched with hasty machete slashes to the throat.

A pall of smoke covered the city. As fires were extinguished, columns of steam rose above the smoke and drifting ash. It felt like the inside of a crematorium. Bennett arrested Father Mitchell, charged him with treason against the people, and claimed Kebek in the name of the Society of Jesus.

*

René made it back to Bounty Rock. As he and Wilbur drew near, oaks and maples reached out with their branches to embrace them. Robins and wood thrushes sang greetings in chorus. Even the wild cows were happy. This is hyperbole, of course, but it's fun to imagine it really happened that way.

The breeze that had so reliably communicated nature's messages to my brother during his long journeys welcomed him to the Ellanoy country and spread the news to all life for miles around: "René has returned. René is home again." That much, at least, is no exaggeration.

He found Malcolm in the garden as usual, battling weeds, and joined him. After a few minutes of pulling and yanking in silence René said, "You beat me here."

"Hello, Grout. I waited all my life to reach this place."

"How did you know it would be so peaceful? How any place could be so serene, so tranquil?"

"You have to know these things—"

"—when you're a priest," René finished for him.

That first night back, in Adrienne's arms, under hide blankets, under a roof of bark, under a sky dense with stars, he only wanted to hold her, share his warmth with her, feel her skin against his. He'd been to the mountains and seen the lakes. The malachite and turquoise water. Reflections of the sun on vitreous surfaces, disturbed by translucent purple stones released one by one from his hand. He tried telling Adrienne about it but his voice broke.

"Your eyes…"

"I know," she said. "Yours too."

The breeze, its work finished, hurried back across the plains to attend to other urgent business.

From the Author

The Plains of Abraham presumes a dystopian future in which technology has retrogressed to resemble a colonial past. History buffs will recognize similarities between the character of Malcolm Marchand and the 17th century explorer Jacques Marquette. Malcolm was modeled loosely on the Jesuit missionary, who with Louis Joliet was the first European to explore the upper Mississippi valley. In a later voyage he ministered to the Illinois nation adjacent to Starved Rock State Park—"Bounty Rock" in the novel—near Ottawa, Illinois, where I grew up. Like Malcolm, Father Marquette died of the bloody flux on the eastern shore of Lake Michigan, with traveling companions chanting "Jesus, Mary!" after his own voice became too feeble.

Starved Rock earned its name a century later when, according to much disputed legend, remnants of the Illinois nation took refuge atop the 125 foot sandstone butte and were besieged by Ottawa and Potawatomi warriors avenging the assassination of Chief Pontiac. Pontiac was the catalyst of what became known as Pontiac's War, an uprising on the heels of the French and Indian War. The Illinois captives attempted to draw water from the Illinois River by lowering buckets on ropes from the butte. As in the novel, the ropes were cut by besieging forces.

For the sake of story I've taken liberties with the geography of the Great Lakes region, and have thinly disguised its cities with names corrupted by generations of oral tradition. Turonado, for example, is Toronto. I've also increased the inhabitable area on top of Starved Rock to suit my needs. Finally, although the Ellanoyans I've invented little resemble the native Americans who occupied the rock, I hope I've honored the latter by depicting a culture that does justice to their virtues.

Several good biographies of Jacques Marquette have been written, though none remain in print. The most accessible is *Jacques Marquette*, by Joseph P. Donnelly, Loyola University Press, 1968.

The torture described in *The Plains of Abraham* is not exaggerated when compared to the 17th century accounts that inspire it. Breathtaking first hand narratives are documented in *The Jesuit Relations and Allied Documents: Travels and Explorations of the Jesuit Missionaries in New France, 1610—1791* (73 volumes), edited by Reuben Gold Thwaites, published by Burrows Brothers, 1896-1901. The collection has been scanned and posted by Project Gutenberg and other organizations.

I only touched on the subject of birchbark canoes, whereas I happily would have bogged the story down with fascinating details. *The Survival of the Bark Canoe*, by John McPhee, published by Farrar, Straus and Giroux in 1975, is filled with lore. For a concise guide to building your own birchbark canoe, see Judy Kavanagh's excellent site: jumaka.com/birchbarkcanoe.

*

I'm grateful to Sarah Specht for critting and for benevolent brutality. They say it takes a village; actually it takes a daughter. To Wendy Russ for critting, for help with the storyline, and for everything. To Kevin Aicher for critting and for supplying numerous valuable resources. To Camille Griep, Sarah Hina, Dieter and Heike Imbsweiler, and Shannon Morley for reading and enduring the early drafts. To Jack DeWees for the tapestries. To Valerie Gray Beguin, who was there when it all started.